The Talent Thief

Mike Thayer

FEIWEL AND FRIENDS

NEW YORK

To my mother.

Lover of music, literature, and science.
Fellow late-night toiler. You've spent a
lifetime dedicating all your many talents
to make others look far more talented than
they are . . . including me. Thank you.

A Feiwel and Friends Book
An imprint of Macmillan Publishing Group, LLC
120 Broadway, New York, NY 10271 • mackids.com

Our books may be purchased in bulk for promotional, educational, or
business use. Please contact your local bookseller or the Macmillan
Corporate and Premium Sales Department at (800) 221-7945
ext. 5442 or by email at MacmillanSpecialMarkets@macmillan.com.

Library of Congress Cataloging-in-Publication Data is available.

First edition, 2023
Book design by Mallory Grigg
Feiwel and Friends logo designed by Filomena Tuosto
Printed in the United States of America by Lakeside Book Company,
Harrisonburg, Virginia

ISBN 978-1-250-77102-5 (hardcover)
10 9 8 7 6 5 4 3 2 1

Cursed

*W*ith her dying breath, my loving, sweet grandma left me with something I never expected: a curse.

"Tiffany," Mimi whispered, her soft, wrinkled palm cupping my cheek. "Be brave. Let the world see my Shining Star." Her last words were hardly audible as she relaxed back into her bed, her hand slipping from my face. She was gone.

That was two years ago today. And look, I get it. I know it doesn't *sound* like much of a curse, and I'm like 65 percent sure legit curses aren't actually real, but I don't know how else to explain my sudden turn in bad luck over the last seven hundred and thirty days. I haven't even hit puberty yet, like a handful of other twelve-year-old girls, so I can't blame it on that. I'll prove it to you (that it's a curse, not that I haven't hit puberty—that would be weird). Let's just go straight to the dictionary and see if what my grandma said at least fits the definition of a curse. Was it a solemn utterance? Check. Has it inflicted harm and punishment upon its intended victim? Double check. Did it invoke a supernatural power? Okay, maybe not *literally*, but I will let my track record speak for itself here.

I know my grandma was only trying to get me to come out of my shell a little bit, telling me to be bold, to let the world see the real Tiffany Tudwell. As some kind of motivational poster or meme, that all sounds dandy. In practice, however, things have played out . . . what's the opposite of dandy? Un-dandy? Anti-dandy? They've played out poorly, let's just say that. Over and over again. Don't believe me? Well, I've got three journals full of this stuff, so buckle up.

November 17 of last year, I was a bit under the weather and had a couple of sneezing fits. The first time, I blew straight through my tissue and covered my hands in snot. The second time, I somehow missed the tissue and shot a giant wad of mucusy goo on Ellie Bird's leg. Then, fearing another snot rocket, I tried to hold *back* my sneeze but ended up pushing out a fart right as Barry Deluka, the *cutest* boy in class, was bending down to pick up a pencil. Yeah, that's right. I farted directly into the face of the cutest boy in class. Can anyone else claim that one? And that was just *one* day.

Thumbing through the rest, we got other classics. On September 5, I tripped over a backpack and fell face-first into the trash can. March 23, I was too nervous to ask to use the restroom and peed my pants. I've gone into the wrong bathroom, been pantsed in front of a hundred students, had pink eye on picture day. And this isn't even mentioning the granddaddy of them all, the one that kicked this whole thing off: the time I became an internet sensation for all the wrong reasons, thanks to our evil popularity overlord, Candace Palmer. But we do not speak of the Candace Palmer incident.

When Mimi died, a counselor told me about the five stages of grief: denial, anger, bargaining, depression, and acceptance. I miss my grandma so much that it hurts, but

I've accepted it, so I guess I'm at stage five there. With the curse, I seem to just spin around in circles on stages one through four. At any given time, I'm confused, frustrated, trying to find meaning, and helpless. But I absolutely *refuse* to move to stage five. I just cannot accept that Mimi would do that to me, not without some grand reason behind it all.

For now, I've learned to avoid putting myself in situations where I'm exposed. No volunteering for stuff, no speaking up in public, limited eye contact with people. Since the Candace incident, I've even changed my hair and let my cool green color fade back to its natural brown. I've toned down the way I dress, put away my collection of funky earrings, and generally tried to blend into the background of life . . . which, I realize, is kind of the exact *opposite* of what Mimi wanted me to do. Look, what do you want from me? There's no need to keep trying to climb over the electric fence once you know it's got ten thousand volts of social embarrassment on it. There's nothing wrong with keeping my distance and trying to find the off switch. Luckily, Tudwells were built for punishment. Not the greatest talent in the world, but one that certainly comes in handy when you're cursed.

CHAPTER 1

Curtain Call

I stood alone, tucked away in the shadows where no eyes would see me, where the curse couldn't harm me. In front of me, a spotlight painted a bright circle in the middle of the stage floor. All it would take was thirteen steps. I'd measured it, paced it out a dozen different times when no one else was around. Just thirteen steps forward and I would be bathed in light, ready for the world to see me.

A rhythmic thumping drummed from the auditorium speakers as the music started. I swallowed back a rising nervousness, but my feet didn't move. No matter how much I wanted to know what that light would feel like, how much it would warm my soul, my curse *fed* on the light. And so, I didn't perform in spotlights; I *pointed* the spotlights. Actually, that's not exactly true. I didn't even do that. Still too much exposure. I was a curtain jockey, pulling curtains open and closed from the cover of darkness. I was tech crew. Good for avoiding curses, bad for trying to break them. Those thirteen steps toward center stage might as well have been thirteen million.

I watched as Candace Palmer, wireless mic in hand, strode forward and paused, the bright stage lights casting silvery glints on her shiny black hair. Her high-rise jeans, chunky sneakers, and crop-top hoodie were the epitome of Wyoming middle school fashion. Her outfit would be different during the actual performance of *Peter Pan*, of course, but whatever she wore I was sure she'd look amazing.

She lifted the mic to her lips, closed her eyes, and started to sing, sinking into the lyrics and notes. Even with how much I despised her, I couldn't stop the chills from prickling every square inch of my skin. If her voice had come out the business end of Dumbledore's Elder Wand, it couldn't have cast a more powerful spell over people. Last year, Kenny Bowser's dad had *wept* during one of her performances. Like full-on streaming tears. *My* attempts at singing (with or without the curse) sounded like a stray cat getting slowly backed over by a pickup truck. What must it be like to have such a talent, to wield such a power? To have expression and mastery over something like Candace had? To be seen and adored for what you could do?

I absently rubbed one of my earlobes, pressing my fingers on a piercing hole. I used to get compliments on my earrings. Toilet bowls, Captain America shields, dangling snakes. I tried not to think about it, just like I tried not to think about how it would be to have what Candace had. Lingering on big dreams was a good way for a cursed girl to accidentally draw attention and get in trouble, *doubly* so with Candace nearby.

My pocket buzzed, snapping me from my thoughts. I slipped out my phone, careful to cover the glow of the screen as I read the new message from my gamer group chat.

I rolled my eyes. We had an online raid tonight in *Warcraft of Empires*, a popular online role-playing game. The group was divided on strategies: Half wanted to send the rogues out ahead to scout, while the others thought we wouldn't have time and needed the barbarians and paladins to push immediately into Skullgrinder's Keep. I wasn't even close to being the strongest or most experienced character in our group, but somehow it always fell to me to keep the peace and come up with a workable strategy before the whole thing imploded, which it threatened to do before almost every big raid.

I typed my response, suggesting they send the rangers and elves out in front with the rogues while our slower-moving characters methodically pushed in with the wizards. The solution seemed obvious, but it often took an outsider's perspective to see these kinds of things. I wasn't exactly a lifelong gamer like most of the group. Video games had been more of a recent find, a way to operate from the "digital shadows." The curse, for whatever reason, seemed not to have made the jump online. Must have been an analog curse. Made sense coming from my grandma. Old-school curse for an old-school lady.

I watched the chat and stared at the three jumping dots that indicated someone was already typing a response. I held my breath and crossed my fingers. The raid *had* to go through. For someone whose social life revolved around actively avoiding all social situations, these video game events were basically all I had.

"*Tiffany*, open traveler curtain one," a voice came over my headset.

"What?" I said, looking up from my phone.

"Traveler one, Tiffany. Open it *now*." It was Marco, the tech crew team lead. From his tone, I could tell he'd said it more than twice.

I fumbled my phone back into my pocket and snatched a nearby rope, pulling down as fast as I could like some pirate working the sails during a hurricane. Pulleys squeaked as Marco barked into the headset.

"Tiffany!"

"I'm going as fast as I can," I hissed back, not wanting to raise my voice and draw too much attention. I kept my head down and pulled harder, faster.

"You're pulling the *front curtain*!"

I looked up to see a confused Candace trapped behind the now closed main curtain.

"Oh no." I gasped, grabbing an adjacent rope and yanking down even faster than before to reopen the main curtain. I dashed to another rope and tugged open a second set of curtains, revealing a group of three backup dancers at the rear of the stage. I took deep breaths, as much from the stress as from the exertion, and placed my rope-burned palms on my knees.

"Yeah . . . I think we already missed our mark," one of the dancers sneered while the others laughed. While her pixie-cut, strawberry-blond hair and freckles made her look nothing like Candace, she was every bit as beautiful and intimidating.

The music stopped abruptly, and my pounding heart seemed to hold for its next beat. Even concealed in the backstage darkness, I felt like all the spotlights in the world were blazing down on me.

Please don't let Candace know it's me. Please don't let Candace know it's me. I chanted the words in my brain like some incantation to ward off the curse.

"From the top," Mrs. Willard intoned, sitting alone down in the auditorium seats. She clapped her hands three times, her large turquoise bracelets clattering like dice in a cup. Her black-rimmed glasses, shock of white hair, and hippie-style outfits made her an icon as the drama teacher at Peak View Middle School. She'd made a name for herself by implanting her own random musical numbers into every one of her plays, and this version of *Peter Pan* was no exception. "We haven't time to waste, my dears. The play is in two weeks and this musical number will be the crowning jewel. We do not practice until we get it right, we practice until we cannot get it wrong."

Candace furrowed her perfect eyebrows and made a show of glancing around backstage. "Well, I think we might be in trouble, then, because *apparently* there's a lot of ways for someone to get the curtains wrong."

I gulped and took a step backward, retreating deeper into the darkness. I could feel the curse searching for me like Sauron's eye trying to find Sam and Frodo on their way to Mount Doom. I tensed, bracing for someone to yell my name, to identify the culprit. But nothing happened. Candace had said "someone," *not* "Tiffany." My armor of darkness had done its job against the curse.

After running through Candace's special "Lost Boys" musical number a few more times, Mrs. Willard finally stood. "That's a wrap, my beauties. Same time tomorrow."

I whipped out my phone like some cowboy unslinging his revolver on a quick draw. One hundred and forty-six unread messages. That meant the team was either arguing or excitedly strategizing. I held my breath and scanned the conversation, a smile creeping across my face. They'd liked my strategy and been busy working through tactics. The raid was still on.

"Let's go," I said, pumping my fist.

"Tiffany." I jumped as Marco yapped in my earpiece. "I need to get a commitment from you to do better on the curtains."

I said nothing. It was one thing to get chewed out by a teacher, but Marco was just a student on a power trip.

"Tiffany?" he repeated.

"What's that, Quinn?" I said to no one as I held down my talk button and pretended not to hear Marco. "Oh, sure thing. No, the math test is *tomorrow*, not Friday. Okay. I'm just gonna put my mic back and then I gotta run. Peace."

"Tiffany? Tiffany!" I could hear Marco even without my earpiece.

I retreated into the curtains and waited. Thirty seconds later, I saw Marco come onto the stage from the direction of the radio-equipment storage cabinet, spinning around in circles with his hands on his hips like he was trying to find a bike that had just been stolen.

I smiled as he quickly gave up and stormed off. That was one thing about bumbling into countless embarrassments over the last two years: I'd leveled up a bit. If the curse was looking to use Marco Benavidez to catch me off guard, it was fooling itself. Maybe two years ago, but not now.

I waited until the auditorium had cleared out before slipping from the curtains. I glanced around to make sure I was alone and tentatively walked forward to where Candace's spotlight had been. With eyes closed tight, I imagined being someone else, someone who didn't have to slink around in the shadows, someone who could sing or dance or play the guitar in front of a crowd of adoring students. Maybe even just the old me but leveled up a bit. Green hair back, new set of trippy earrings. I could almost *feel* the—

"Oh my gosh, please tell me you saw that boy working the spotlights."

I jumped at the voice and skittered to the shadows like a scared mouse. I reached up and felt my headset. I'd forgotten I was still wearing it. Someone must have left their mic on when they turned theirs back in, and it was picking up a nearby conversation. Against my better judgment, I reached down to the receiver clipped on my belt and turned up the volume.

"You mean did I *smell* him?" It was Candace's voice, laughing. "I thought someone had brought in spicy Taco Bell from a hot car."

"At least he could do his job," someone else said. "What about whoever was doing the curtains?"

"Like, does she even go to school here or does she just live under the stage?"

"She totally lives under the stage. Oh my gosh, she's like our very own Phantom of the Opera!" The group erupted in laughter.

"Except the Phantom was good for something, right?"

"Yeah, and he covered his face with a mask." It was Candace again. "We're center stage doing a legit three-minute song and dance routine and she, like, can't even get the *curtains* right."

More laughing.

"Candace, you know who that was, right?"

My eyes went wide. *No, no, no.*

"It's the poem girl. It's totally Ugly Cry Girl."

"No way," Candace said. "I thought she'd transferred away or something years ago."

"Facts. She's on the tech crew web page. Here."

There was a pause. This *wasn't* happening. This *couldn't* be happening.

"Oh my gosh," Candace said, vicious delight dripping

from every word. "Look at those bangs! It looks like she cut them with a weed whacker."

"They're to cover that forehead!"

"Forehead? That's more like an *eight* head. What's her name again?"

"Tiffany Tud—"

I clicked off my receiver and slowly removed my headset. I was frozen, my whole body numb. Why had this happened? *How* had this happened? I had kept to the shadows. I hadn't tempted the curse. I hadn't stepped out of line. I could handle it being anyone but Candace. Two years ago, she had used one of my most vulnerable moments to make me into a laughingstock. I had sacrificed so much of myself to make sure it wouldn't happen again. And yet here I was.

My view of the stage blurred with tears as I wrapped my arms around my chest, bracing against an imploding tightness.

"Be brave, Tiffany. Let the world see my Shining Star." The phrase was an unrelenting mock. Let the *world* see? The world had seen, and it had laughed. I didn't know how I could ever even face four girls at my school, let alone the world. My grandma was wrong. I was the *opposite* of anyone's shining star. I was a black hole.

CHAPTER 2

Planetarium

my legs and lungs burned as I pulled my bike to a stop at the top of Galaxy Hill. Behind me, the sun was setting on a commanding view of the steep switchback road that ran down the hillside and back toward town. In the winter, the descent made for a fantastic sledding hill and a terrifying bike ride. In front of me sat an octagonal brick building that could have been mistaken for some castle fort if not for the large slate-shingled dome sprouting from its center. At the bottom of the stairs leading up to the double-door main entrance was a sign that read MYERS PLANETARIUM AND SCIENCE CENTER, or at least that's what it was *supposed* to read. Over the years, vandals and graffiti artists had slowly morphed it into the MEGA BORE-ROOM AND SCIENCE CENTER.

I continued along a walkway to the back of the planetarium before turning off onto a well-worn dirt path that wound around for a few hundred feet. At the far side of the hill, deposited between two dead trees, sat a double-wide mobile home, its pukish-yellow paint chipped and peeling.

"Home sweet home," I said as I put my bike down next to my dad's old, boxy Oldsmobile sedan. I walked up the front steps (skipping the collapsed one in the middle) and paused before I opened the door. I undid my helmet and took a moment to wipe my eyes with the back of my sleeve, although the sheets of sweat pouring down from under my helmet probably already did a good enough job at masking my tears. There was a life lesson in there somewhere.

"Dad, I'm home," I announced as I opened the door and hung up my backpack on my way to the kitchen for a glass of water. "Dad?"

"Out back, kiddo."

I gave a soft grunt. I knew what that meant. I opened the cupboard to find three mismatched plastic bowls and a Kennedy Space Center collectible shot glass. On top of a sink full of dirty dishes were two white plates blotched with a red and brown crust, the remnants of yesterday evening's microwave lasagna.

"Is the dishwasher clean?" I called back to my dad.

There was a pause. "Uh, I don't know."

I also knew what *that* meant. With the dishes in the sink, there wasn't room to duck my head under the faucet, so I just pulled out the side sprayer and drank from it like a dog from a garden hose. Not my proudest moment, but my life was short on those in general, so I wasn't too picky. I wiped my mouth on the dish towel and inspected the pile of mail unceremoniously littered on our small IKEA dining table along with this month's copies of *Astronomy* and *Sky & Telescope*. An Amazon box lay discarded on the floor, the cardboard ripped open with all the grace of a rabid badger.

I checked the time. It was already almost 6:30 p.m.

Opting for a Tudwell family classic, I plopped four hot dogs down on a paper plate and took out a box of macaroni and cheese. I boiled the water, did the dishes, and soon held two bowls of gloppy orange noodles accented with chunks of pink, microwaved hot dogs.

I pushed open the screen door with my foot and walked across my backyard of yellowed grass and hardened dirt to find my dad fiddling with a camera attached to a tripod, a giant lens pointing skyward.

"Hey there, Tiffy." My dad turned around and used his fingers to squeegee the sweat from his bald head and flick it to the side. His blue Best Buy polo still bore his gold nametag and was accented with dark armpit stains. He glanced up at the evening sky. "Won't be long now. How was your day, sweetie?"

I bit my bottom lip. A part of me wanted to unload, wanted to tell my dad everything about school, my mistake with the curtains, the bullying from Candace and her friends . . . the curse. But what good would it accomplish? It wasn't like my dad was in a position to solve any of it. It would only spread the worry to him like some kind of disease. Getting other people sick didn't help you get better any quicker. My dad had his own problems. He was a single parent working two part-time jobs to make ends meet, or at least make ends almost meet. The ends were within shouting distance, let's say that.

"Another day in paradise," I said, forcing an unconvincing smile as I handed him a bowl.

"Oooh." My dad finally looked down from the sky, his eyes growing wide. "Dogs and mac. Thanks, Sparkles."

Even though the nickname sounded like something a five-year-old would name her cat, I didn't mind it. My dad loved the stars and he loved me. Heavens knew I'd probably be called much worse than Sparkles tomorrow at school thanks to Candace and her friends.

"Sorry I didn't do dinner. Must have lost track of time," my dad said between mouthfuls. "Got back from Best Buy and went straight to the planetarium with all the new touchscreens for the interactive exhibits. Earl showed up, so we tried to figure out how we're gonna set up the moon-walker rig. That one's a head-scratcher. Didn't even *think* I'd get my new wide-angle lens in before tonight's meteor shower, but then I saw the UPS truck and *boom*. There it was. Pretty wild, right?"

"Pretty wild, Dad." I puffed out a short laugh. However much it was probably the source of a lot of our problems, my dad's childlike enthusiasm for upgrading the planetarium was a sight to behold. He was a bit of a paradox like that. The things that made it easy to get mad at him also made it hard to actually stay mad. "Don't you already have a wide-angle lens?"

"I have an f/1.8, Tiffy. Not an f/1.2."

"Ah." I gave a slow nod.

"Gonna really take my astrophotography game to the next level. Could start holding classes at the planetarium once I get it all figured out. Everyone thinks they're a professional photographer these days. Could be *real* popular. Been busy trying to get it all squared away. Just in the nick of time, too. You can already see Venus and Jupiter. Meteors won't be far behind. This should be a once-in-a-generation type event, Tiffy. Should be a dandy."

"Shouldn't you have something going on at the planetarium for this?" My question came out more critical than I had intended.

My dad stopped short of shoveling another spoonful of mac into his mouth and let out a brief sigh before covering it with a forced cough. "Got, uh, one later on tonight."

"Oh, that's good," I said unconvincingly. Any frustration I had toward my dad mutated to guilt. There was something he wasn't telling me. His work at the planetarium meant everything to him, especially after my mom bailed on us seven years ago. The planetarium was pretty run-down when the owner, Mr. Myers, all but turned the keys over to my dad to run tours, put on shows, build exhibits, and perform general maintenance. Mimi had said it was good for my dad to have something he could focus on, something he could work on and fix. Not that my dad got paid much, but the planetarium was what got him out of bed in the morning and often what kept him from *going* to bed at night. Maybe even more than all that, it was the only place we had to call home.

My dad must have read the look on my face, because he immediately conjured up his best smile. "I'm thinking I can get some pretty spectacular footage tonight with my new lens. Maybe we can use it in a promo video or something. Post it on FaceTok or TikBook or whatever."

I gave a playful roll of the eyes. He knew full well what they were called. "FaceTok is *so* for old people, Dad. It's all about the SnapGram now."

He nodded appreciatively. "You know, we also got the annual fundraiser coming up in a month or so. Maybe a viral video would drum up some interest there."

I winced internally. I had been the subject of a viral video once, thanks to Candace. They could definitely "drum up some interest." Both the kind you wanted and the kind you didn't want. "Yeah, that'll be good," I said, checking the time. "I'm gonna go get ready for a raid now, okay, Dad?"

He suddenly reached for his pocket, pulling out a buzzing phone. "Oh, gotta take this one, Sparkles. Go do your raid, but don't be too late. You won't wanna miss this shower. You know, it just so happens to commemorate two years since Mimi passed."

"I know, Dad," I sighed.

He flashed a weak smile and walked into the mobile home with his phone to his ear. "Hello, Mr. Myers. To what do I owe the pleasure?"

Mr. Myers? My dad didn't get too many phone calls from the planetarium owner. I went back into the kitchen and quietly put my macaroni and cheese bowl into the dishwasher, all the while straining to pick out any words from my dad's muffled voice. He was in his bedroom. I knew I probably shouldn't eavesdrop, but maybe I wanted to go use the bathroom right now, which just so happened to share a wall with my dad's room, and just so happened to have a vent that kind of maybe let you hear almost perfectly on the other side of the wall. Nothing wrong with that.

I tiptoed to the bathroom and sat on the closed toilet lid.

"Yes, one tonight, actually," my dad said. "The other two? They, um, well . . . they both canceled earlier today. No one is more disappointed than me, trust me, sir. But look, reservations for shows are bound to pick up when . . . The exhibits? Well, we're making lots of progress every week. We're a bit, uh, shorthanded, as you know, so it's just taking a bit of time, but Earl and I are figuring it out. You are going to be *blown away* by the lunar . . . How long? Well, if Earl and I keep making steady progress, then I'm pretty confident we can have everything done and dusted in a year. Ready for schoolkids, the community, the whole darn galaxy . . . What? . . . Well, how long *do* we have, then? . . . That's it? . . . I'm doing everything I can, Mr. Myers. I'm spending every night there. I'm gonna get some great footage of tonight. Maybe do a promo of some sort. Look, I've even been dumping what little personal money I have into these exhibits so they can . . . I see . . . No, I understand. I'd probably do the same thing in your shoes. It's just, I've got my kid with me, Mr. Myers. Please remember that . . . Of course. I understand. Well, I appreciate it, Mr. Myers . . . You too. Bye."

I felt myself go white as I took shallow, silent breaths. I couldn't hear Mr. Myers's half of the conversation, but I didn't need to. The planetarium was in deep trouble, which meant *we* were in deep trouble. Flashes of old memories burst into my mind like the undead thrusting their hands out from dirt meant to bury them forever: the vacant expression on my dad's face as he read the goodbye note from my mom, the edge in his voice as he pleaded for our landlord to let us stay just one more month, the hospital-like smell of the disinfectant they used to clean the floors at the homeless shelter, the watery taste of the mass-produced spaghetti at the soup kitchen.

Those memories were swamped with shame, guilt, and confusion. My dad promised we'd never go back, that he'd make sure of it. I was beginning to think I wasn't the only one in my family to carry a curse.

CHAPTER 3

Twinkle, Twinkle

"Merlin?" I called out in a pleasant singsong as I entered my room. "Merlin, where are you? I need you, buddy." I checked his favorite hiding spots—behind my bookshelf, in my dirty clothes hamper, and on top of the AC vent—before ducking under my bed and coming face-to-face with the twitching nose of a fat, white rabbit. "There you are, Merly."

I reached down and picked up the rabbit, cradling him like a baby and nuzzling his impossibly soft fur. I held him tight and took slow, deep breaths. He wasn't medically classified as an emotional support animal or anything, but I was pretty sure he was largely responsible for my continued sanity most days. I focused on my breath and allowed my heartbeat to slow before setting Merlin down on my lap. "Thanks, buddy. Now it's time for my emotional support video game." I turned on my PC, logged on to *Warcraft of Empires*, and donned my headset as I joined my party's private lobby.

"Hello, fellow Teton Raiders," I said as my character materialized on screen. She was a blue-skinned battle sorceress, decked out with steel-plated armor, an embroidered cape, a long staff of twisted metal with a blue crystal shard, and a golden-crowned helmet. Oh, and green hair, of course.

Someone came off mute. "Queen Astrid, master strategist, commander of the cosmic elements, graces us with her presence on the dawn of yet another epic quest. One that will surely test our party's mettle and push us to the very brink!"

"Hey, Simon," I replied.

"Hey, Tiffany." Simon's voice cracked as he turned off his narrator accent. His burly barbarian character walked up to Queen Astrid and emoted with a dramatic bow.

"You ready for this?" I did a quick head count and could tell most of the rest of the team was already logged on as well.

"I was born ready," Simon said. "Which is probably weird since that would mean I was born ready to infiltrate a subterranean stronghold to slay an undead dragon and claim an enchanted chalice that bestows magical talents to those that drink water from its cup." There was a pause. "But here we are."

I laughed. "I have little doubt." Simon by far had the strongest character on the team, and from my calculations he must have put in at least three hours a day, *every* day, for the past three years to get where he was. He was also the president of the school Video Game Club and had recruited me a little over a year ago, although I'd never shown up to any meetings in person. A few more people said hello, either directly or through a character emote.

"Everyone ready?" Simon asked the group. "Then game on."

A chorus of "game on" resounded over my headset and we were underway. For a few hours I lost myself in the game, the objective, coordinating the teamwork, and operating in a world where the curse appeared not to touch me, where Candace never was, and where my worries about my dad and the planetarium didn't belong. It was like pulling a plastic bag off my head and breathing clean, free-flowing air. My plan from earlier in the day worked brilliantly, and we only lost three of the fifteen people in our party before we were standing atop the vanquished bones of an undead dragon and staring at the brilliant light of the enchanted chalice.

"We have claimed the chalice from the foulest of foes!" Simon said in his orator's voice.

"Huzzah!" the group responded. However much time I spent playing with this group, I still couldn't get myself to join the victory huzzah. Even isolated in my room behind a planetarium atop Galaxy Hill, I felt like someone might be filming me from the window or something and I'd see it in a post tomorrow. It was entirely irrational, but there was a name for having thoughts like that. What was it? Oh yes, being cripplingly insecure. That was it. A nice little emotional souvenir you take away when so many seemingly innocent situations explode in your face.

"Let us honor our three fallen brothers and sisters, Liz, Zeke, and Cole," Simon intoned. "May their hit points be restored and their experience points be made whole."

"Huzzah!"

"Cheers to High Paladin Grant, for striking the final blow," Simon intoned.

"Huzzah!"

"With cunning and strategy, we obtained victory. A last huzzah for master strategist Queen Astrid!"

"Huzzah!" I smiled to myself as the group gave one final cheer before we all teleported back to our custom-built communal tavern for some post-game banter.

> I don't know how you do it, but you did it again, Queen Astrid.

The direct message from Simon popped up in my chat box.

> Thanks, Simon. These raids are the highlight of my week. Like honestly. You don't even know.

> Which is why you NEED to show up IN PERSON to our next meeting. Do you want me to beg? Because I'll beg. If you think begging is beneath me, you're WAY wrong.

> Haha. Trust me. Me not coming is for your own good. We've been over this before.

> Look, even if you do have some "supernatural bad luck," it's not like it's contagious.

> A grenade isn't contagious, either, but I'm pretty sure you don't wanna be near it when it goes off.

> Oh come on. Do you honestly expect me to believe that you've been cursed?

> It doesn't require your belief, Simon. It's kind of like gravity. Whether you believe in it or not, it won't change the outcome if you fall off your roof.

> Man, you've really thought through these analogies, haven't you?

"Sparkles, you gotta come out and see this," my dad called from outside.

> Hey, my dad's calling me. I gotta go.
> Good gaming tonight, Simon.

> As always, it is an honor to serve with you, my queen.

I logged off and stared at my blank computer screen. I was amazed Simon still put up with me. I acted like his best friend online and yet I wouldn't even make eye contact with the kid at school, or anyone else from the club. I picked Merlin up from my lap and gave him a kiss on his tiny, twitching nose before setting him on the ground and going out into the backyard.

It was nighttime. My dad was lying back on a foldable lounge chair and sipping a thermos-size Monster energy drink. "It's more amazing than I imagined."

I sat down beside him and tilted my head back. The cloudless night sky was awash with an ocean of brilliant, twinkling specks. We were even far enough away from the city lights to see the galactic haze of the Milky Way. Living in a remote mobile home did have one or two perks.

"There's one," my dad exclaimed as if he'd just spotted a unicorn darting away into the bushes. "Did you see it?"

"Dad, I've seen plenty of shooting—" Before I could finish, another shooting star zipped across the sky, then a third that stretched nearly halfway across the horizon. "Whoa."

"Who knows how far that meteor traveled to get here?" my dad mused. "If it was in our solar system, it would be hundreds of *millions* of miles. If it was from a nearby system, it could be *trillions*, maybe even *hundreds* of trillions of miles for billions of years before burning back down to basic elements right above our heads, showering us in cosmic, alien dust. How impossibly lucky are we that these things find their way here?"

"Tell that to the dinosaurs."

My dad snorted. "You got me there." We sat in silence for several minutes watching the celestial spectacle.

"Grandma would have loved this." The thought escaped my lips before I even knew I had it.

"No doubt." My dad paused. "She would have come up with some mystical meaning to it all. The universe sheds tears of shooting stars."

"Seems so." I gave a weak sigh. "Dad?"

"Yeah, kiddo?"

"If you weren't into all of Mimi's mystical astrology stuff, why are you still so fascinated with stars?"

I guess the answer to my question was important, because my dad sat up and turned to look at me. "You know, Sparkles, I think it's because these small blinking lights, millions and billions of light-years away, have somehow always contained the answers to mankind's biggest problems."

I raised an eyebrow. "Now you're starting to sound like Mimi."

"I'm serious," my dad defended. "Look, thousands of years ago, we were just big ol' Neanderthals clubbing animals for meat and gathering nuts and berries and whatever. And then we looked upward." He glanced dramatically toward the sky like he was caretaker of the stars themselves. I could tell he was giving me a bit of his well-practiced planetarium presentation. "We tracked the movement of the stars and developed calendars, which helped us predict the seasons and start agriculture. From there we used the stars for navigation to explore the world. It changed everything. If there's answers up there for mankind, then maybe there's something up there for me ..." My dad trailed off, speaking more quietly as he continued. "So I guess Mimi and I *both* look to the stars for guidance, just in our own ways."

"Maybe so, Dad," I said, knowing full well that my dad and I were going to have to do a lot more than stare at twinkling lights a bajillion miles away to fix our current problems.

My dad checked his watch and stood up. "Well, Sparkles, I gotta make my way up to the planetarium to get ready for tonight. Don't stay up too late and don't—"

"Touch the camera," I interrupted, finishing his sentence. "I know the drill, Dad."

He smiled and patted me on the head before going back inside. While I usually spent my nights alone either playing video games or watching movies I wasn't supposed to, I opted for leaning back and gazing upward. There certainly was something undeniably hypnotic about a meteor-streaked sky accompanied by the endless refrain of chirping crickets.

Time slipped away and after a while I struggled to keep my eyes open. "Mimi," I whispered, holding my breath as if half expecting her voice to echo down from the heavens in reply. "You always told me that you'd be in the stars watching over me. Are you still there?" I drifted in and out of sleep, visions of video game dragons, my grandma smiling, Candace laughing, and a star-streaked sky swirling in my mind. When I spoke, I wasn't sure if I was mumbling the words or just thinking them. "We could really, really use some help."

I awoke to the softly glowing horizon of pre-dawn. Dang it, I'd spent the entire night outside? I'd need to get ready for school soon. I grabbed my phone and checked the time. It was only 2:22 a.m. "What the heck?" I rubbed my face, blinking hard as I stared at the lightening sky. It grew brighter and brighter before my eyes. Was I dreaming? Where was the sun? What was going on?

A distant rumble rose to a roar and I winced as the sky flashed to noonday brightness. I watched in amazement as twin meteors streaked overhead like low-flying missiles.

"Holy guacamol—!"

The meteors smashed into each other at an angle, exploding into a brilliant cosmic firework. A split second later, a deafening boom hit me like an invisible punch, knocking me back onto my chair. I lay there frozen, my body in shock as the sky quickly faded back to black. It was gone as quickly as it had come, the only difference now the distant chorus of car alarms and howling dogs echoing up from the city.

I must have been frozen for a while, because it was my dad's voice that finally broke me from my stupor.

"Tiffy? Are you okay? What was that?" My dad was breathing heavily, his voice a mixture of concern and genuine excitement.

I turned to my dad, a blank look written across my face. "Two meteors collided right above me."

"They *what*?" my dad said, shaking his head in disbelief. "That's impossible, sweetie."

"They crashed into each other *right there*, Dad." I jabbed a finger to the sky. "How could you not have seen that?"

"We—we were looking east," my dad stammered like he was trying to explain an alibi to a police detective. "We saw the light and heard the boom."

"Maybe your new lens picked something up."

"Of course!" My dad ran to check his camera. "No, no, no, no. You gotta be kidding me!"

"What?" I said, still struggling to get my bearings.

He hung his head like he'd just missed the game-winning field goal in the Super Bowl. "SD card ran out of room thirty-five minutes ago. I must have screwed up the settings somehow when I was getting it adjusted for the new lens."

Typically, I would have been right there to complain with my dad, to tack this onto the long list of ways the Tudwells had rotten luck. Something stopped me, however. Despite the impossible odds of what I had just seen, there was an unmistakable feeling that it had *nothing* to do with chance. Something had happened. Something had changed. I just wasn't sure what.

CHAPTER 4

Angels and Ravens

The meteor shower was the talk of the school. Not that I was participating *in* any of those conversations, but the topic was inescapable. I even heard two girls in neighboring stalls talk about it in the restroom. My science teacher, Mr. Bangerter, skipped his entire lesson just to take an hour-long tangent on asteroids, black holes, and whether or not we'd been visited yet by aliens, which he was certain we had.

At lunchtime, I got my food and slowly wove around the cafeteria tables, eavesdropping on as many people as I could on my way to my usual spot against the far wall by the garbage cans.

"No way you slept through it! Half my Funko Pop collection shook off my shelf and landed straight on my face . . ."

". . . woke up and thought my brother was playing Xbox in the theater room with the volume cranked up . . ."

". . . scared my grandma so bad that she almost had a heart attack. But she's better now . . ."

". . . my buddy's uncle's in the military and said that it

wasn't even meteors. It was actually two enemy drones that we shot from the sky with missiles . . ."

With all this meteor talk, I couldn't help but breathe a bit easier, like someone had loosened a collar around my neck. I hadn't heard a single mention all day of "Tiffany Tudwell, the Phantom of the Auditorium." It was a minor miracle, but I'd also long since structured my day to keep maximum distance from Candace, so I knew I couldn't claim victory quite yet.

I pulled out my phone and shot Simon a text.

> I have a scouting job for you.

His response came back so fast it was almost like he'd pretyped the message and was just waiting to hit send.

> Ooooh, you know I can't ever turn down a good side quest. I stand at the ready, Queen Astrid! What do you require of me?

> Can you hang around Candace's table for a couple mins and see if they happen to mention anything about me and the Phantom of the Opera?

> I knew you were going to say that.

> You DID?

> Absolutely not. That is an incredibly random
> request. Consider it done, however.

As I waited for Simon to work his magic, I thought through everything I'd heard people say or claim about the meteor. It seemed like folks had seen the flash, been woken up by the bang, and even saw the two meteors streak across the sky, but *no one* had witnessed the moment of impact, except for me. I didn't want to get my hopes up, but I couldn't help but think that it had to mean something.

Just as lunch was ending, I got another text from Simon. No mention of the Phantom. I gave a small sigh of relief but still couldn't shake a sour pang in my stomach. I knew the coast wouldn't be completely clear until I made it through play rehearsals.

When I finally showed up to the auditorium after school, I tried busying myself the best I could. I grabbed a nearby curtain and made a quick "pod," which amounted to folding it, twisting it, and tucking the bottom end inside itself to lift the curtain off the ground and get it out of the way. I stared at the wrapped, torqued, and tucked fabric. It kind of looked the way I felt, to be honest. Balled up, trying to disappear within itself and not doing a very a good job of it. I gave a pathetic little laugh despite myself.

After everyone arrived, we ran through most of the play without incident, but the moment I saw Candace walk to center stage, my heartbeat jumped up to my skull. I wiped my palms against my pants and prayed she wouldn't look over in my direction. *Nothing to see here. No Phantom of the Auditorium lurking in the shadows and I certainly wasn't Ugly Cry Girl from two years back.* I focused on the task. That was my best chance. Just do my part. If I hadn't screwed up yesterday, then everything would have gone smoothly.

The music kicked on, Candace started singing, and I pulled the curtains to reveal the backup dancers. I'd never felt so relieved to have done such a simple thing . . . until Candace's microphone went dead.

"New microphone to center stage, please." Marco's voice came over my headset. I stared at Candace holding out her microphone like she would a dead rat by the tail. When I didn't move, he repeated the order. "Tiffany, swap out the mics, please."

Go out there? He might as well have ordered me to come out of a World War I trench and storm across No Man's Land in my underwear. Without me making a foolish mistake, the curse couldn't come into the darkness, so it was drawing me out.

"Tiffany!"

"Okay," I hissed, straightening my shirt for some reason. I walked over to our audio cart, picked up a spare mic, held my breath like I was plunging into the deep end to pick something up off the pool floor, and walked out from cover.

Should I make eye contact? Should I look away? What looks the most casual? Can she tell I'm holding my breath? Am

I swinging my arms too much? Maybe she won't even recognize me. My mind tumbled around like loose change in a clothes dryer as I closed in on Candace. I held out the mic, averted my gaze, and prayed to whatever entity would hear me that she would just take it and let me slink back to my velvet curtains.

She didn't.

After I took her mic, she refused to take mine, stepping back and folding her arms. The awkward standoff forced me to look up and address her.

"Here—here's your new mic," I stammered, holding it out.

A devilish grin split her perfect features. "Test it to make sure it works."

I gulped awkwardly as I turned it on and tapped the top, sending muffled thumps from the speakers.

"You sure you don't want to test it some more? Maybe read a poem or something . . . Phantom."

That was it. She knew who I was. She knew I was the same girl from her English class two years ago. She also knew I was the girl who had screwed up the curtains.

"What's the matter?" Mrs. Willard called up from her spot in the third row.

"Oh," Candace said, pointing to me. "Tiffany just wanted to read a few lines from a poem she wrote. Give the microphone a real good test to make sure it doesn't cut out again. As long as that's okay with you? I've actually heard she's got quite the hidden talent."

The world slowed to a stop. I might as well have *been* a phantom for all the warmth that was left in my body.

"That's a bit irregular, but far be it from me to deny an artist an opportunity to share their art. Go on then, dear, but make it quick," Mrs. Willard said, motioning me onward with her hands.

My head swam. How did I even get into this situation? No matter what I did, I'd look like a fool now. Candace was just too many steps ahead of me, in *everything*. She was more beautiful, popular, talented, wealthy, and, apparently, clever. Why didn't all that satisfy her? What pleasure could she possibly get from being cruel to some poor, outcast, talentless, cursed mobile-home dweller? Bullying me should have been as satisfying as stepping on an ant.

"Dearie," Mrs. Willard said. "May we proceed?"

Candace stood back, arms folded, smirking like she'd just moved her final chess piece in for checkmate. But checkmate or not, I wasn't going to utter a single word into that microphone. I muscled down the urge to cry and turned to leave, but something made me stop. Some stirring of emotions in my chest. I wasn't nervous; that wasn't it. It was a longing, a *yearning* to perform, to bring the microphone to my lips and to . . . *sing*? Never in my entire life had I been so confused by an emotion and yet so confident in what I wanted. Confident that I could not only do it, but do it well.

Without even thinking, I cleared my throat, brought the microphone in front of my face, and started to sing Candace's song. Inexplicably, the noise that sounded over the auditorium speakers wasn't a noise at all. It was a rich, smooth, and beautiful tone. A surprised smile blossomed across my face. I wasn't just singing like an angel; I was ascending to heaven. I opened my soul, not knowing how this was happening or how long it would last, and poured every ounce of my emotion, my anxiety, my frustration into the words, and *still* my voice was equal to the task. Chills raced up my spine as I broke off into an improvised harmony to finish the first verse. I closed my eyes as my last perfect note faded away and was met with stunned silence.

"Thank you . . . uh . . . tech crew," Mrs. Willard stammered.

I opened my eyes and held out the microphone to Candace. She couldn't have looked more bewildered had the song come from a second head freshly sprouted from my shoulder. Stunned, she took the mic and I hardly even remembered walking back to my spot behind the curtains. What . . . on . . . earth . . . just . . . happened? *How* did that happen? And why didn't I say a snippy one-liner to Candace when I gave her the microphone? *How's that for a hidden talent? That mic gonna work for ya?* Dang it! Either of those would have been epic, but I was kind of preoccupied with whatever the *heck* that was! What did this mean? What did this—

An earsplitting caw sounded over the auditorium

speakers. It was like a dozen cats were in a battle-royale death match with a raven. I looked back to the stage. It was ... Candace? Her magical, flawless voice had been replaced by the vocal equivalent of closing your eyes and randomly poking at keys on an out-of-tune piano. My brain couldn't piece together what I was seeing, couldn't square the image of Candace with the sound from her mouth.

She stopped, as confused as everyone else, and faked a few coughs. She started again, but stopped after the first note. Her eyes went wide and she cleared her throat like she was hacking up a fur ball.

"Can someone get her some water?" Mrs. Willard said to no one in particular. "She's probably parched, poor thing." A few seconds later another techie came from the other side of the stage with a bottled water.

Candace took a swig, gargled it, then swallowed. She looked up and bobbed her head and I could hear her trying to hum the tune.

"Is everything all right, dear?" Mrs. Willard said, adjusting her thick-framed glasses.

Candace's face twisted with panic, a look I liked even better than bewilderment. "I—I think I need to take a little break," she stammered as she rushed off the stage, leaving a wake of murmurs.

My brain felt like it was going to explode. Was I dreaming? This was a dream. It had to be. Any moment now I'd start flying or aliens would show up or something and I'd pop out of bed back at home. I pressed my eyes shut and opened them. I tapped my cheek with my hand, then harder, then harder.

"Ow!" If I wasn't dreaming, then I was going to need to talk to someone about this, and there were only a few people on the planet I could trust with something so unbelievable: my three oldest friends. If visiting hours weren't already over, of course.

CHAPTER 5

Old Friends

My tires squealed as I skidded to a stop on the circular driveway of Sunny Vistas Assisted Living. The large five-story building, with its covered entryway, towering cottonwoods, and array of dozens of identical balconies, looked more like a three-star hotel than an old-folks home.

I propped my bike against a metal bench and looped my lock over an armrest before passing through the double automatic doors.

"Hola, Tiffany." A middle-aged Hispanic woman smiled from behind the front desk. "I saw Eleanor head to the rec room about twenty minutes ago. They should all be there."

"Thanks, Gabriela," I said, grabbing a pen with a fake flower taped to the end and scribbling my information down on the visitors' log.

"You look happy, muchacha," Gabriela said, with a bit too much surprise.

Do I usually just look sad? "Just a good day at school is all," I said.

"Oh, is it a *boy*?" Gabriela flashed her wide, bright smile again as she handed me a visitor's badge clipped to a neon yellow lanyard.

Gonna need five friggin' meteors smashing together for that to be the case. "No, just some things going my way for once."

"Okay, then." Gabriela shot me a look like she didn't believe it wasn't about a boy.

I thanked her and headed toward the west wing of the facility, catching the familiar fresh scent of chlorinated water as I passed the two-tiered fountain in the center of the lobby. I walked to the end of a long hallway and passed through a pair of open French doors. To my left, an audience of four people on leather recliners watched an old John Wayne cowboy movie on a large flat-screen TV. To my right, two men played billiards, the pool cues doubling for canes as they hobbled around the table for their next shot. I didn't even need to scan the room to know where my friends would be: sitting straight ahead in the back of the room at the card table.

"Well, bless my soul," a diminutive lady said in an adorable British accent. She wore a collared green sweater over a floral dress and had large gold-frame glasses that magnified her already large round eyes. She put down both her tea and her hand of playing cards, throwing her arms wide as I approached. "If it isn't the lovely Ms. Tudwell."

"Hello, Eleanor." I said, giving the old lady a hug. The usual mix of hair spray and vintage perfume filled my nostrils.

"Buongiorno, fragolina." The man to Eleanor's right stood and gave a slight bow. His thinning, slicked-back hair was dyed jet-black. "So good to see you."

"Stefano." Instead of receiving a hug, the man leaned forward and touched his stubbled cheek to either side of my face, making a kissing noise each time. The first time he'd given me the traditional Italian greeting, I was left a bit confused, but now it would be weird if he *didn't* do it.

I turned to see the last person at the table. A skinny man in a tweed suit and tie with a matching flat cap. In all my years visiting Sunny Vistas, I had never seen Frank *not* in a suit and a flat cap.

"I take it by your silence, Frank, that you're losing at cards." I placed a comforting hand on the old man's surprisingly bony shoulder, his suit coat concealing a wiry frame.

"If I had half this woman's infernal luck playing cards back in the war, I could have swindled every soldier in my platoon out of half their food rations and owned every last cigarette in Korea." Despite his gruff demeanor, he reached up and tenderly patted my hand with his own, which shook with a constant tremor.

"Frank, you eat like a bird and you've never smoked so much as a bubble-gum cigar in your whole life," Eleanor countered. "The keen mind of a card shark would have been wasted on you. The good Lord only blesses people with talents if they can make something of them."

"Bah," Frank grunted and waved Eleanor off.

"Speaking of talents." I took a seat at the table and leaned in conspiratorially. "I need to tell you guys something."

"Is it about a boy?" Stefano quickly scooted his chair in closer.

"Wha . . . no. It's not about a *boy*," I said. "What is it with people here?"

The old Italian took out a little comb and ran it carefully over his slicked-back hair. "You have a glow about you today, principessa."

I knew that Stefano meant the comment as a compliment, but I couldn't help but think what it implied about all the *other* times I came. I didn't *normally* have a glow?

"Look, it's not a boy, but something *did* happen." I cast a meaningful glance around the table. However wild it would sound about the meteors, me suddenly being able to sing, and Candace suddenly *not* being able to sing, I needed to tell *someone*. No one had known my grandma better than these three, no one cared about me more (except my dad), and I was 100 percent sure they wouldn't violate my trust and blab about it online. Mainly because they didn't know how to get online and their phones still had cords running to the wall. Having your best friends all be north of ninety years old might be a bit out of the norm for a seventh grader, but it did have its advantages.

"Well, out with it," Frank said, gathering up the cards from the table and deftly shuffling them like he worked at a casino poker table, despite his shaky hands. "You wait too long and you risk one of us keeling over dead before you get to your point."

"Frank, patience is a virtue, my dear," Eleanor said, taking a refined sip from her teacup.

"Not when you're a few days short of ninety-four years old, it's not," Frank grumbled. "Proceed."

"Are you sure?" I asked. "I don't want to bore you with my problems." The statement was a bit of a tease, since I knew they always loved hearing my stories, whatever the topic.

"Don't you worry," Frank said, pointing to his ear. "We can always just turn down our hearing aids. It's what we do every time Stefano starts droning on about how his grandma used to handmake pasta."

"If you had tasted my nonna's pasta you would not make such a joke," Stefano said, pressing his fingertips together and shaking his hand in the air.

I couldn't help but laugh. The banter between these three was one of my favorite things in life. "Okay, I'll tell you, but keep your hearing aids on full blast." I gently nudged Frank with an elbow, which accidentally threw off his shuffle and caused a few cards to spray across the table. I leaned over the table and returned the cards to Frank before launching into an explanation of everything that had happened since Mimi's death. While I had mostly listened to *their* stories over the years, I shared plenty of my life with these three. The curse, however, had remained a secret, until today. I told them about Mimi's final last words, how the curse (starting with Candace) had kept causing me problems, the things I'd changed in my life to stay off everyone's radar, and finally my theory that the colliding meteors was a direct answer to me.

"I know you guys probably think I'm being a bit over-dramatic," I said, putting my hands up in defense. "But I swear to you that I've been fighting this curse ever since Mimi left."

Stefano brought his finger to his forehead and did the sign of the cross on his chest, mumbling something in Italian.

"I quite liked your earrings," Eleanor said, taking a sip of her tea.

"Your grandmother was a unique lady, Tiffany, I'll give you that," Frank said, quickly dealing a hand of cards to all four of us. "But it seems like an awfully strange thing for her to do, to leave you with a curse."

"Now is not the time for rummy, Frank," Eleanor said, sliding her cards back across the table. "This is important."

I shrugged my shoulders and slid my cards back as well. Frank rolled his eyes and grumbled.

"Look," I said, pausing briefly as I glanced down at the cards. I suddenly had to fight the urge to take the deck from Frank and shuffle them myself.

"Look at what?" Frank said, bending down to intercept my gaze.

"Sorry." I shook my head. "I was saying that something weird happened after the meteor crash." I cleared my throat in anticipation of singing, a bit nervous to unveil my unexplainable newfound talent.

"It sure did," Frank said, gathering the cards together. "When I heard the boom, I rolled off my bed and hit the deck. I was half convinced I was back in the war getting bombed by the—"

The cards erupted out of Frank's hands mid-shuffle, sending them flying all over the table and floor.

"What was that all about?" Stefano asked, rubbing his nose where one of the errant cards had struck him.

"I don't know. They got away from me. Must be slippery from your greasy hands."

I bent down and picked up all the cards off the floor, handing them to Frank.

"As I was saying," Frank said, splitting the cards into two piles to shuffle, "when those blasted meteors exploded, I thought we were—"

The cards sprang from his hands again, even worse than before.

"Frank, are you feeling all right?" Eleanor asked, genuine concern in her voice.

"I feel fine," he shot back. "I ain't having a stroke or nothing. I just can't seem to shuffle these dadgum cards."

I helped gather all the cards *again* to give Frank another try, but the result was the same. It was like he'd never handled a deck of cards in his life. I could see Frank's frustration slowly turn to mild panic, and my mind flashed to Candace.

"Wait a second," I said, covering my mouth with my hands. "It's the curse."

"It's the what?" Frank said.

"The curse," I whispered, standing up and scooting back away from my friends. "This is exactly what happened to

Candace. It wasn't until after I . . . touched her microphone. It didn't happen until I touched the cards."

"Dio mio," Stefano said, making the sign of the cross again.

I continued to back up, glancing over my shoulders so I wouldn't bump into anybody. I didn't want to pass it along to anyone else. I thought I'd handed the curse over to Candace, but maybe it was less like a hot potato and more like a sickness that could infect others.

"Tiffany, darling," Eleanor said. "Where are you going?"

I didn't actually know. I just knew that I couldn't stay here. Not when something was so very, very wrong, and I still didn't have a clue as to what in Saturn's seven rings was happening.

CHAPTER 6

Serenade

*D*ad?" I called out as I entered the front door of our double-wide mobile home. I wanted to know where he was so I could keep my distance more than anything. The last thing my dad needed was even *more* bad luck than he already had. "Dad, are you there?"

I walked to the kitchen and found a message written on a paper towel: "Out hunting for meteorite fragments with Earl, then to the Planetarium to troubleshoot the remote-control lunar rovers. Be back late. Dinner's in the fridge. Love you." Curious more than hungry (although I *was* hungry), I opened the fridge to find a white Styrofoam container half-full of Chinese takeout. I grabbed the food, a quart of ice cream, and a pack of Oreos, and did what any right-minded twelve-year-old girl would do in my situation: I ate my feelings. I'd seen it in a bunch of movies. I think the idea was that a little physical pleasure would improve your emotions. I found it just gave me a stomachache. So basically, it just brought down how I felt physically until it matched how I felt emotionally. Friggin' movies.

I waddled my way to my bedroom for phase two of my sulking. I took off my shoes, plucked Merlin off the ground, switched off all the lights, turned on Billie Eilish, and collapsed onto my bed. I stared at my ceiling, awash with constellations of glow-in-the-dark star stickers.

"Hopefully I can't pass this thing on to lazy ol' rabbits," I told Merlin as he shuffled over to my face and licked my cheek with his small, dry tongue.

It had gotten worse. My situation, my curse, my life had actually gotten *worse*! I mean, maybe there were certain advantages to being able to infect other people with a curse, but the enjoyment would be pretty short-lived if I couldn't control *who* I affected. Being cursed was one thing, but being able to curse other people basically just made me a witch. No doubt I would check the mirror tomorrow morning and be greeted with a bulbous wart on the tip of my nose. As if my physical appearance needed any more challenges. The responsible thing to do would be to wander off and take up residence in some abandoned cave or at the center of a forest or swamp. I'd be sure to start scouting for locations on Google Maps later.

But something still didn't add up. If I had just infected Candace, then why could I suddenly sing? Wait a second. I . . . could . . . sing! I had been so worried about the curse becoming contagious that it had completely overshadowed the fact that a full-blown miracle had occurred in the auditorium.

I started humming along to the music, then softly singing before opening up and letting it all out. My voice rang from Galaxy Hill in perfect pitch as I sang along to the song, improvising a perfect duet. I had never felt more alive and free in my entire life. It wasn't just that it felt like my soul could finally breathe; it now had a language to express itself. How did I even *live* before I could do this?

The song ended and I sat there on my bed, chest heaving like I'd hiked a mountain. "How is this possible?" I mumbled, staring down at my hands as if they held the answer. "Wait a second!" Merlin sprang from my lap. "Merlin. Do you realize what this *means*? Of course you don't, you're just a rabbit. Actually, *I'm* not even sure what this means, but if I can suddenly sing and Candace can't, then I wonder . . ." I trailed off. "Merlin, please tell me we have a deck of cards somewhere."

"Morning, Dad," I said, skipping over to the kitchen table and giving him a big hug.

"Well, hello to you," my dad said, almost choking on his bacon in surprise. He was already dressed in his blue Best Buy polo. He no doubt had the first shift or there was no way he would have been up this early after staying out so late. He looked tired. "Sorry I missed you last night. The surface of the moon exhibit will be fantastic once it's done, but getting those darn little lunar rovers to sync with the touchscreen controls will be the death of me. YouTube tutorials will only take you so far, you know. Earl was working on the wood framing for the solar system exhibit, but I swear the guy's more likely to cut his fingers off than cut a board the correct length. I think we actually somehow ended up further behind than we started. Anyway." My dad waved off his troubles. "Enough about my woes. You gonna tell me why you're so bubbly this morning, or am I supposed to guess?"

"I mean, you *could* guess, but I guarantee you'll never get it." I stood there expectantly, fighting down the smile that tugged at both sides of my face.

My dad put his hands in his lap and squared up to me. "All right, you got my attention. Now what in Jupiter's moons is going on?"

"How about I *sing* it to you?" I swept my hand out wide in a grand, operatic gesture, except what came out of my mouth sounded more like when my dad was choking on his bacon than an opera singer.

My dad crinkled his forehead with a look like he didn't know whether to burst out laughing or call me an ambulance. I quickly cleared my throat and tried again, but it didn't help. My face flushed red, and I managed an uneasy laugh.

"You okay there, Tiffy?"

I shook my head, unsure of what was happening, questioning for a split second that last night even happened before taking out my phone and pulling up a video. "Dad, look at this." I pressed play and showed him a video of me nailing every note to Bon Jovi's "Livin' on a Prayer."

My dad squinted and leaned in for a closer look before bursting out in laughter. "Is there *anything* these apps can't do these days? This is almost better than that one that turned my profile picture into a supermodel. Great stuff, kiddo. I bet you and your friends had a blast with this stuff."

I opened my mouth to protest but stopped. What was the point? Why would anyone believe I had miraculously gained supernatural singing abilities for an evening when the video could be explained away by some advanced auto-tune? And it wasn't like a clip of me shuffling cards was viral video material, either. "Yeah, that's it."

I sat down and grabbed a piece of toast, chewing it absently. What was happening? Yesterday I could sing like a rock star, and Candace couldn't carry a tune to save her life. The same thing happened to Frank with shuffling cards. It was like I'd been handed some wild new enchanted item in *Warcraft of Empires*, one that could do a lot of good to me and a lot of damage to my enemies, if I just figured out how it worked.

"You and I both better get going, kiddo," my dad said, checking his watch as he wiped his mouth with a dish towel and stood up from the table.

This was usually the time in the morning where a bit of dread would start bubbling up in the bottom of my stomach, but not today. Today, I was going to school with a superpower, an uncontrolled and mysterious superpower. What could possibly go wrong?

CHAPTER 7

Prison Break

Caution. That was the name of the game today. Since I still didn't understand this thing, I was at its mercy. It was like I was playing a game without knowing the rules. Things had worked out *wonderfully* with Candace, but that had been pure luck. And I was probably just as lucky to have escaped Sunny Vistas without doing anything worse than throwing off Frank's ability to shuffle cards. I needed caution until I figured out what exactly was going on.

I usually felt pretty exposed to the curse when I walked the hallways, so I'd long since strategized all the best routes between classes to avoid all the bullying hotspots. With a bit of effort, I had even transferred out of all the classes I originally had with Candace and her friends. Queen Astrid had learned how to navigate this dungeon.

My first three periods were uneventful—no strange new talents, no sudden ability to ace my German test during second period, no matter how hard I strained my brain. I set out for fourth-period PE, taking my standard Thursday route: left at the library, down the stairs to wind around past the orchestra room, and doubling back after I passed the commons.

I got to the locker room and quickly changed before

making my way to the gym. The chaotic drumming of bouncing balls and squeaking shoes greeted me as I pushed open the double doors and slunk over to my favorite spot next to the wooden roll-out bleachers.

I scanned the crowd, noticing that there were way more kids than normal. That typically just meant we were teaming up with the other PE class to do some kind of tournament or to . . . oh no.

A dreaded cackle rose above the clamor and I turned to see Candace and two of her friends (normally *not* in my class) laughing and pointing at Wendy Cochran, a heavyset girl who now sported a very unpleasant nickname written in permanent marker on the back of her shirt. I wanted to help, but what was I going to do except join her in front of the social firing squad?

Our PE teacher, Mr. Gilroy, eventually blew his whistle and gathered everyone together.

"All right," Mr. Gilroy said, his bristly mustache twitching as he spoke. "We'll split up into two teams. Standard dodgeball rules. You can't cross the half-court line. You get hit, you're out. You catch someone's ball, they're out, and someone on your team gets to come back in. At any time you want, you can try to shoot the dodgeball to make a half-court shot. If you make it, then your whole team gets to come back in, but it's risky because the other team will probably just stand there and catch it. Got it?"

Everyone nodded and Mr. Gilroy designated two team captains to pick teams: Candace Palmer and none other than Brady Northrup. The envy of all the boys, the object of affection for all the girls, Brady had matured early and (unlike many middle school students) matured well. No awkward stage, no zits, no braces. Just broad shoulders, an easy smile, and shoulder-length hair that was even fuller, silkier, and smoother than mine. With almost thirty thousand followers on TikTok, it seemed like everyone on the planet liked him. The only part I couldn't quite square was the fact that he'd just spent six months at Thunderbird Intermediate, the school where they sent all the troublemakers. That and the fact that he used to go out with Candace.

Knowing I'd probably get picked last, I took a seat on the bleachers. Avoiding physical contact during PE was usually pretty easy. I hardly ever got picked and no one ever passed me the ball, unless it was a day like today and they were throwing it at my face, of course. Then they were *actively* seeking me out. I hated dodgeball. With other sports, like basketball, I could just stand there and be useless. With dodgeball, I had to stand there and get pummeled.

"Wendy Cochran," Brady said with his first pick, drawing an eruption of gasps and laughter. I sprang up from my seat to see a very confused Wendy make her way to Brady, who gave her a high five and patted her on the shoulder while shooting Candace a challenging stare.

The pool of unselected students was quickly whittled down to just one. I stood alone, head down, silently pleading Candace wouldn't recognize me.

"I guess that means we have to take Phantom," Candace said.

I didn't even look up as I trudged over to Candace's team.

"Don't cry 'cause you're last pick," Candace said, leaning in close although I still refused to meet her eyes. "We both know it's not a good look for you. And please don't pick up or throw any balls. The other team will just catch it and get one of their people back in. Easy as pulling curtains? Good."

I said nothing, choosing only to set my jaw and walk away to the far corner. She was a vampire. An emotional vampire, sucking the feelings and happiness out of others so she could maintain her untouchable social status. Queen Astrid knew how to deal with vampires, and if I had a crossbow with garlic-infused wooden-stake bolts, I might have tried something drastic. As it was, however, I decided to spend my energy fighting back tears.

The whistle blew and the game began. Students rushed to the center and kicked off a chaotic war of rubber balls. Kids laughed, called out shots and game plans, argued over whether they were hit, and yelped in pain. A ball rolled my way, so I just nudged it to the side with my foot. I'd rather get hit with a hundred dodgeballs than take the emotional shots Candace would give me if I disobeyed her orders.

Brady Northrup was on a tear. He moved more gracefully than any of Candace's backup dancers, ducking, sliding, and jumping out of the way of any incoming balls. He caught dodgeballs one-handed, instantly zipping them back across half-court to ricochet off heads, shoulders, and hands. The whole time, he stayed by Wendy, using his ball to deflect any thrown her way like some kind of PE bodyguard. With his team well in the lead, Brady pulled up at half-court and drained a shot, just to show that he could do it. The first game was a massacre.

The second game was far more competitive, not that it had anything to do with me. My strategy of standing in the corner was working out pretty well . . . until I suddenly noticed that it was just me and Candace versus Brady, Wendy, and a boy with blond permed hair.

"Toss me those balls, Phantom!" Candace yelled, darting her eyes between me and the other team.

I panicked and kicked three balls over toward Candace, accidentally sending one of them wide and straight back to the other team. "Sorry."

"Oh my gosh, you're worthless." Candace picked up a ball just in time to use it to deflect one of Brady's throws.

Both our teams cheered from the sidelines for us to do something. Throw the ball, catch a ball, dodge a ball, shoot a basket. Unfortunately, it looked like most of our hopes and dreams were with Candace.

Brady zipped a ball in my direction. It whizzed by my head so fast, it rebounded off the back wall and bounced straight back to him. He dodged one of Candace's throws and tossed the same ball again in my direction. It bounced back again. He was a lion just playing with his food. On the third throw, it bounced off the wall and glanced off another ball on the ground before rolling to a stop at my feet. I reflexively bent down and picked it up.

"Don't you dare throw that ball," Candace barked as she tossed a ball wide of Wendy.

Normally, I would have done exactly as Candace demanded. I didn't even want to try and throw it . . . except I kind of did. I couldn't explain it, but my nervousness about looking goofy or not knowing how to throw a ball just wasn't there. I held the ball in one hand and took a couple steps forward.

"Are you deaf?" Candace spat.

I ignored her and confidently strode forward. The perm-haired boy chucked two balls in my direction. I ran forward, deflected the first throw with my own ball, ducked under the second, and slid on my knees across the hard gym floor. Before I even came to a stop, I flung my ball at the boy and tagged him square in the stomach. The crowd gasped at the sudden display of athleticism.

Oh my gosh.

It had happened again.

I was a friggin' dodgeball ninja!

I sprang to my feet and whirled, coming face-to-face with Brady, dodgeball in hand. I was ready, though. I could take on whatever he dished out. I knew I could. I could dodge, deflect, dive, or—

Brady's throw slipped out of his hand and rolled harmlessly toward the opposite wall. The crowd burst into laughter, no doubt thinking he was still just toying with me. But I knew better. I saw the flash of confusion on Brady's face before he covered it up with a smile and a playful shrug. I picked up another ball and stood defiantly at the half-court line, waiting for Brady to take another shot.

"What are you doing?" Candace yelled. "Get back."

Brady grabbed another ball and ran toward me. This time his throw lofted toward me in an uncoordinated two-handed shot put. I casually batted it to the side with my ball.

"Quit clowning around, man!" someone said from the sidelines. "Finish them off!"

I could have hit Brady right there, but something else caught my attention. The basketball hoop on the other end of the gym. *I could totally make that shot.* I knew the arc the ball would have to take, the power required, the proper amount of backspin to put on it. I bent my knees and in one fluid motion brought the ball up, extended my arm, and flicked my wrist.

"Phantom, don't you dare!" Candace screamed.

It was too late. The whole gym watched in amazement as the ball sailed through the air and passed perfectly through the net with a swishy snap. The breath left the room as if sucked out of a space-station air lock.

"Prison break!" my entire team yelled as they stormed back onto the court. In a few more seconds, the round was over. We had won—because of me. I couldn't even remember the last time something like that had happened, outside of video games, at least.

A few kids came up to give me props, but from the way a lot of kids were looking at me and snickering with their friends, it looked like most just chalked it up to some fluke. I caught Candace's eyes boring into me with a deep scowl. She wasn't one to share the spotlight, especially not with someone like me. Well, too bad, because we had a third round to play, and I was just getting warmed up.

When the whistle blew for the next round, I had never been more ready for anything in my entire life. I was a Jedi Knight among mere mortals. I snatched balls out of the air with one hand and lasered them back with the accuracy of a Navy SEAL sniper. As the round progressed, people started handing their dodgeballs to me. One down, two down, four down, six. It was like a human carnival game. It wasn't until we'd almost won that I noticed Brady chilling in the back corner. To his credit, his face betrayed no sign of worry or confusion. And it was because of that that no one dared throw one in his direction, for fear it was some kind of trick.

"Here," a girl said, handing me her ball. "You do it."

Instead of throwing the ball at Brady, I pulled up and took another half-court shot. After soaring in a perfect, smooth arc, it bounced squarely off the backboard and straight through the net.

The whole gym exploded as if I'd just hit a buzzer beater in the playoffs. Even the other team was cheering despite themselves.

"Prison break! Prison break!" my team started chanting as they mopped up the extra dodgeballs. Just as we loaded up to fire a barrage at Brady and his few remaining teammates, a long, shrill whistle echoed off the gym walls.

"All right, class," Mr. Gilroy bellowed. "Gotta end it there. Go get changed or you'll be late to your next class."

The students poured out of the gym, stopping on their way to the locker rooms to put their dodgeballs back in the bin. Brady lagged behind, numbly hefting a ball in one hand and repeatedly hitting the side of his head with the palm of his other.

It was impossible to pay attention in any of my remaining classes, and not just because of the lingering thrill of being a dodgeball ninja. Over the last two days, the curse had dragged me out on stage with Candace and pitted me against Brady Northrup in dodgeball, but I'd been able to flip the script this time. I'd been able to fight back.

I still didn't know exactly how my ability worked, just that I seemed to be borrowing people's talents by touching an object they had recently used: Candace's microphone, Frank's cards, and Brady's dodgeball. It made me look at the world differently. A boy in science class deftly twirled his pencil around his fingers. A shy girl in English doodled expressive Pokémon characters. The soccer team out on the neighboring field passed, kicked, and dribbled with impossible levels of coordination. Normally, I wouldn't have given any of these a passing thought. Not now, though. Not now that I could be the one with the talent. Anything I'd ever wanted to do was currently on the menu, and after a two-year curse, I had built up one heck of an appetite.

CHAPTER 8

Sketches

That evening, I sat in my bedroom, twisting the tip of my pencil into a dollar-store sharpener after finishing my fourth page of handwritten notes. Was I prepping for a test? Uh, no. I probably *should* have been, but that didn't seem nearly as important as writing down all the things I had always wanted to do, listing all the talents I wanted to try, and mapping out where and how I might go about getting them. If the curse was still lurking out there, I was preparing to come locked and loaded—after I iced my right shoulder, though. It felt like someone had slugged me with a baseball bat. Yesterday I could throw dodgeballs like a machine, but that didn't mean I was conditioned for it. I was beyond excited to try new things, but I apparently had to be careful not to overextend myself. I also couldn't forget to return to Sunny Vistas and explain to Frank that he *hadn't* been losing his mind the other day, but I was going to have to come up with an explanation that didn't make it look like *I* was losing my mind.

I went to the fridge to see if I could sneak one of my dad's energy drinks only to find a note from my dad. He'd be out late again. When I woke the next morning, there was *another* note. It was one thing to be obsessed with the planetarium, but this was different. My dad wasn't famous for taking care of his health in the first place, and these hours couldn't be helping. That last call from Mr. Myers obviously had him anxious, which made *me* anxious.

Despite the worry about my dad gnawing at my stomach, I couldn't help but head into school feeling different than I had in a long time. Something was happening. Something magical. Something both terrifying and exciting. And I was going to hit it head-on.

"Yo, Prison Break!" someone shouted as I passed through the commons.

I turned in a circle and braced myself, instinctively expecting to receive something thrown in my direction. A boy and a girl from my PE class pumped their fists and gave me a thumbs-up. *Well, that's new*, I thought, awkwardly waving back and breathing a sigh of relief as I continued on my normal Friday route to first-period art.

I slipped into class just as the bell rang and took my seat toward the back. I flipped through my large sketchbook with my work for the semester. I wasn't the worst artist on the planet, but that's only because the planet had a *lot* of people on it. I was bad, and I was failing. While you got some credit for trying, doing your best to follow the techniques, and completing your work, a good 30 percent of your grade in Mr. Fritzberg's class was based on absolute skill. If you couldn't draw well, you weren't getting an A.

I scoped out the class and couldn't help but notice Liz Benson a few desks in front of me. A soft-spoken girl from the Video Game Club, she hunched over an epic pencil drawing of a dragon, delicately adding curling smoke from its nostrils. While I didn't want to cause her to fail an assignment, having that talent even for a class period could do wonders for my grade, not to mention that it would be flat-out amazing to experience.

"Okay, class, listen up, listen up," Mr. Fritzberg said, clacking a paintbrush against the side of his wooden easel like a judge pounding a gavel to bring order to the court. "Today we will be working on our self-portraits. This will constitute a full *twenty* percent of your grade. Do not cut corners. Do not rush this. When I was studying under the great French sketch artist Sébastien Chaufourier, we would spend the first forty-five minutes of the day staring at our own eyes in the mirror, studying the changes of our faces in the brightening light of the Paris morning, before even *daring* to lift a pencil."

I rolled my eyes. Of all the stories Mr. Fritzberg told of himself, he never seemed to include how, despite his illustrious training, he ended up teaching art in a Wyoming middle school. I swear half the class period was always in some way dedicated to inflating his ego. As if to prove my point, Mr. Fritzberg picked up a large sketch pad from behind his desk and propped it up on an easel for the class to see. It was his own self-portrait, expertly drawn and shaded, looking longingly off in the distance. All of Mr. Fritzberg's boasting aside, he was undeniably a talented artist.

"This took me one hour last night. And this"—Mr.

Fritzberg pulled up a blank sheet of paper—"will take me one minute." He set a timer on his phone and got to work, whipping his pencil across the page in smooth, practiced strokes. When the timer sounded, he had a drawing that, amazingly, very much resembled himself. "Do you see the difference when you don't take the time? When you're forced to cut corners? Seeing me do this is one thing, but doing it yourselves will cement the lesson into your brains. Flip to a new sheet of paper and get your pencils ready. I would also like a few students to come up and do it in front of the class. Caroline, David, and . . . Tiffany."

There it was. The curse wanted to pick a fight first thing in the morning, did it? Well, we were about to see what happened when I fought back.

I hadn't planned for this exact scenario, but I was ready nonetheless. When I took my easel and drawing pad to the front of the class I passed right by Liz. Her talent could bail me out of this for sure, but Queen Astrid, master strategist, had just devised a much better idea.

"Is everyone ready?" Mr. Fritzberg said, setting his timer again. I held my pencil tight and pressed down hard with my thumb until it snapped.

"Uh, Mr. Fritzberg," I said, holding up the broken pencil. "Can I borrow yours?"

Mr. Fritzberg looked annoyed but begrudgingly handed me his pencil.

"And . . . go!" Mr. Fritzberg said.

There was no thought, no deliberation, no time spent

figuring out what I would do. I just *knew*. My pencil scraped along the paper, not drawing a picture from its charcoal, but scratching away, *revealing*, a drawing that already existed in the paper itself. It was like nothing I'd ever felt before. Talent was no barrier. The only bottleneck for my creation was the time it took my hand to move the pencil. I didn't hear the alarm go off and didn't stop until Mr. Fritzberg tapped on my shoulder.

I turned from my paper and was met by a crowd of wide eyes and open mouths. My drawing, while still unpolished, was beautiful, a gray portrait with downcast eyes, the smudged pencil a haze of sorrow and shyness. It wasn't an image of how others saw me. It was how I saw myself. I was both proud of the drawing and a bit embarrassed, as if I had accidentally revealed too much about myself.

"That . . . is well-done, Tiffany," Mr. Fritzberg stammered. It was as much of a compliment as I had ever heard from the man.

I looked at my shoes and absently massaged one of my earringless earlobes. "Thanks."

I returned to my desk to finish my drawing over the next hour. I could think of nothing else until it was out of my system and fully onto its new home on the paper, where it could live a life of its own. Like nuzzling Merlin or belting angsty lyrics with Candace's singing talent, the process of expertly translating my emotions onto a piece of paper felt like I had offloaded a boulder of stress. It was a part of the talent I hadn't expected. I wondered if it had the same effect on Mr. Fritzberg, if he used it to soothe and communicate his emotions. When the bell rang, I reverently put my art supplies away before heading off to my next period.

So far, so good.

Score for the morning: Tiffany: 1, Curse: 0.

CHAPTER 9

Poster

I spent every spare moment in my next classes sketching and doodling in the back half of my English notebook. I drew pictures of me as Queen Astrid, my dad working at the planetarium, and random students in a variety of poses. One of my favorite pages was a grid of twelve small self-portraits, each labeled with a different expression: happy, surprised, shy, confident, anxious, victorious, and so on. Some of the faces looked much more familiar than others. I'd filled up close to five pages by the time the bell rang for lunch.

As I passed the band and orchestra rooms, I saw someone I would normally completely avoid, but not from some fear of getting bullied. Quite the opposite, actually. Today was different, however. I wasn't running from the curse anymore.

"Hey there, barbarian."

Simon turned and looked up at me, his round glasses, enormous bulging backpack, and pronounced overbite making him look remarkably like a human turtle.

"Tiffany?" He almost choked on my name. "You're here! I mean, you're always here in school, of course. You obviously know *that*, but you're *here* here, in person. Like, right in front of me."

"That I am, Simon." It took a lot not to crack a smile at his nervous rambling. I gestured from his head to his shoes. "I hardly recognized you without your bulging muscles, beard, and battle-ax."

He snorted a shy laugh and adjusted his backpack. "And you without your helm of champions." He referred to my character's crowned helmet I'd earned a few months back after being the last one alive during the troll caverns raid. "Actually, that's not true, Tiffany. I totally recognized you. I'd never *not* recognize you. Not that I'm always just hanging back recognizing you. Anyway. Does this mean there's no more, you know . . . curse?" He waggled his fingers spookily.

"Let's just say I've got a way to fight it now."

"I'd expect nothing less from Queen Astrid." He snorted again and I couldn't help but motion for him to talk a little quieter.

"Hey, what is that in your hair?" I asked, pointing.

"Huh?" Simon said, wiping his hand across his head. "Oh, it's sawdust. I just got done with woodshop. I don't have, like, mutant dandruff or anything. I mean, I sometimes do get a little dandruff, but this isn't it. I'm actually making a full-size treasure chest with a secret compartment in it."

"Really," I said. "I didn't know you did stuff like that."

Simon gave big exaggerated nods. "Oh yeah, when you're the youngest of seven kids, most of everything you get is hand-me-downs. See?" He pointed to his backpack, where the name "Tyler" had been embroidered on the top and then crossed out with a sharpie. Two other names were written and crossed out next to Simon's name, which was drawn in big silver letters. "If you want something of your own in my house, you basically got to build it, and if you want to *keep* something your own, you got to hide it."

There was a life lesson in there somewhere.

"Hey, you want to go have lunch?" I asked, nodding in the direction of the lunchroom.

Simon seemed to skip a breath. "With me? Uh, of course you're asking with me. Yeah, sure."

I had walked these halls hundreds of times, surrounded by hundreds of students, but I had always walked alone. Walking next to Simon, actually *with* someone, felt like I'd switched from endlessly swimming upstream to coasting with the current.

"Yo, Prison Break!" someone yelled. I turned to see a group of kids clustered in front of the bulletin board near the library. One of the kids was waving his hand and pointing in my direction. "You should totally do this."

Curious, I hesitantly walked over to see what he was referring to. A few kids parted and I saw they were staring at a poster. I read it under my breath.

"Help save our planetarium! Introducing the twelfth annual Shining Star competition . . . Partnering with club representatives from local middle schools . . . Participants judged on five categories: raffle ticket sales, intro video, costume, Q and A, and talent . . . Represent your club . . . Grand prize donated by Dr. Gordon Braithwait, professor of astronomy from University of Wyoming: the chance to name his newly discovered star."

I froze, trying to take in everything I was reading. *Save the planetarium. Name a newly discovered star.* How could I have missed this? My dad had even mentioned the fundraiser the other night. *Let the world see my Shining Star.* I could *literally* have my own shining star. This was it. It was the chance to fulfill my grandma's dying words, to show the world Mimi's Shining Star. I could deal the curse a death blow. On top of that, if I could somehow leverage my new power to do something extraordinary, it could also be my chance to save the planetarium, to save my dad. A rush of chills zipped up my spine. It was like the gravitational pull of this one central event held all my problems in its orbit. It had been right in front of me this whole time.

I flipped open my notebook and jotted down all the registration information next to some of the sketches I'd done. "Oh, sorry," I said as someone bumped into me, knocking my notebook to the floor. "Didn't mean to . . ." I trailed off. Candace Palmer glared down at me, loudly smacking her gum.

"And what's this?" Candace said, snatching up my notebook and thumbing through my drawings. She laughed and flipped the book around to show Martina, her other two dancer friends, and a few boys. "Cute sketches. Although that means they definitely aren't self-portraits." Her friends gave a chorus of chittering laughs.

"Please give it back." I felt myself flush bright red and

it took everything in my power not to make a grab for my notebook. That's what she'd expect, what she'd want.

"Yes, relinquish the book immediate—" Simon yelped as one of the boys next to Candace tugged on his backpack, sending him sprawling to the floor like an overturned turtle.

"Simon?" I turned to help him up, but Candace's friends still stood in the way.

"Oh, come on," Candace stuck out her bottom lip. "Give us your sad face. Look, it's right here." Candace held my sketchbook open to my emotional grid and pointed to my sad expression.

This was more than just embarrassment. I felt violated. It was like she was breaking into my bedroom and reading my diary out loud on a livestream. My sketches weren't self-expressions I wanted to share publicly.

"Hold on," Candace said, noticing what I'd just jotted down. She looked at the poster with a wide, sinful grin. "You can't honestly tell me you're thinking of doing this. You gonna beat me with a curtain-pulling routine? Oh, wait. Not exactly one of your talents, now, is it?" Her friends laughed again.

From what I remember, I actually pull curtains quite a bit better than you sing. In fact, I think I SING better than you sing. I thought the comeback over and over in my head but couldn't get myself to say it, or anything, for that matter. I just stood there and waited until Candace eventually dropped my book and walked away.

"Best of luck, Phantom," Candace called over her shoulder.

I bent down and helped Simon to his feet before retrieving my book with shaking hands.

"I'm sorry, Simon. You okay?"

Simon nodded, adjusting his glasses, but he didn't say anything.

"Thanks for sticking up for me." I took a deep breath. I felt worse for *him* than anything. I was the one who had brought him along. I'd told him I wasn't afraid of the curse, that I had the tools to fight it now. I wasn't so sure anymore.

CHAPTER 10

Talent Shopping

*W*hat in all that is sacred in the stars," my dad said, wide-eyed, nearly choking on a piece of burnt toast.

"What?" I said, acting as normal as possible as I walked into the kitchen and grabbed some orange juice from the fridge.

"Where is Tiffany and what did you do with my daughter?"

I put my hands up in defense. "*What?*"

My dad made a show of glancing at his watch, then tilted his head and looked out the window at the sky. "It's Saturday, Tiffy."

"Yes."

"And it's seven thirty a.m."

"Yes."

"And you're up."

I poured the orange juice into a glass and swirled it around as if it were some fancy alcoholic drink. "I'm not allowed to be up in the morning on a weekend?"

"It's not that you're not *allowed*," my dad said. "It's just that it's never happened. Like, ever."

"Well." I took a long swig, punctuating it with a satisfied exhale. "Maybe I'm turning over a new leaf."

My dad squinted his eyes, giving me a lingering look before shrugging and getting up from the table. "Well, let me know if you happen to find any meteorite fragments under the new leaf you're turning over, would ya? Me and Earl still haven't found so much as a space pebble while looking for leftovers from the big collision. Nothing would drum up business like getting our hands on a few of *those* fragments, let me tell ya. Just think of the exhibit we could make. I mean, I've seen some pretty decent rocks in other planetariums but not any that landed *right* next door. Heck, I wish the blasted things would have just crashed into the planetarium itself. Would have made national news. Could have rebuilt the place all new and fancy. Can you imagine? A planetarium built on a meteor crash site."

"Dad." I looked at him quizzically. "You were *in* the planetarium during the meteor shower."

"Oh, right." My dad's face contorted as he reconsidered. "Well, death by meteorite would be a pretty cool way to go."

"You are so weird." I shook my head.

"Without any fools there'd be no fun." My dad walked over and kissed me on the head. "I gotta go in to work. Valerie called in sick this morning and I could use the extra shift. I've got a decent-sized evening show at the planetarium after that as well, so Earl and I gotta go do some prep work. Cover up all the unfinished exhibits and the rest. What are you up to today?"

"Actually," I said, casually checking my nails. "I was thinking about going to the mall. Frank's birthday is coming up. Wanted to look around for gift ideas."

"That's sweet of you, Tiffy. Oh, hey." My dad put up his finger as if just remembering something. "If you're gonna go to the mall, I actually have a job for you."

I peaked an eyebrow. "You're putting me to work at the mall?"

"Oh, come on. There's five dollars in it for you." My dad rummaged through his pockets, finally pulling out two crumpled ones and a few coins. "Correction. There is . . . two dollars and eighty-five cents in it for you."

I puffed a laugh. "How could I refuse?"

"That's my girl," he said, hustling out of the kitchen and returning with a stack of large papers. "I need you to hang up some posters for the planetarium fundraiser. I got permission last week from the building owner to put them up at each of the entrances, but if you could ask some of the business owners to put them up in their stores, that would be awesome."

I took a moment to look it over again. "Dad, you never told me about the grand prize. Someone is gonna get an actual star named after them? That's incredible."

My dad shook his head in disbelief. "Tiffy, I told you last week during dinner. We had DiGiorno pizza. You complained I didn't get the stuffed crust."

I twisted my mouth. He was probably right. I did vaguely recall tuning him out during one of his rants about how awesome it would be to remodel the planetarium with reclining seats. "Oh . . . right . . . during the DiGiorno pizza. It's coming back to me."

"It's incredibly generous of Professor Braithwait. You know he grew up going to the planetarium. Said it's where he first fell in love with the stars." My dad got a wistful look like he was remembering Professor Braithwait's childhood himself.

"So I was thinking," I said slowly. "I've been working on a few things this last little while. I think I might want to participate."

My dad took about a three-second blink. He couldn't have looked more surprised had I told him I planned to join a traveling circus. "Really?"

"Yeah." I shrugged. "Why not? You've been so busy with the exhibits and everything. I figure I could do my part. We need all the help we can get, right?"

My dad nodded with a look that said "You have no idea."

"Plus," I added, "I think it's something that would make Grandma happy." *It would also be the perfect opportunity to epically humiliate Candace.*

My dad pressed his lips together and nodded, thinking he'd finally guessed my motivation for doing it. "Yes, I think it would."

"I read the flyer, but I'm still not too sure I know how it all works, other than you have to come up with a talent."

My dad beamed as if I'd just asked him to explain in detail why the planets in our solar system have different gravities. "Well, it's kind of evolved over the years, but there's five major categories: raffle tickets, intro video, costume, talent, and Q and A. The intro video is a minute long, and you're just supposed to introduce yourself. The costume is something that represents your club. The talent can be anything, really. Just whatever wows and impresses the judges. The question and answer is always fun. Definitely will make you think on your feet."

I scowled. Some of this, I could do. Getting a talent obviously wouldn't be an issue, and my plan was to spend the day at the mall shopping around for the best talents in town so Candace wouldn't stand a chance. I wasn't any good at editing videos, and I didn't have a clue about getting a costume together or how to think on my feet during a Q&A. Hopefully there'd be talents I could take for all of these.

"And the raffle tickets?" I asked.

"Ah yes." My dad held up a finger. "This is where the real money is raised. So each contestant goes around and gets people to buy their tickets for the raffle afterward. Lots of cool prizes get donated. Your name goes in the raffle one time for every ticket you buy, *unless* you buy your ticket from the kid who wins the competition. Then your name gets put in *five* times per ticket. So it really helps your sales as a contestant if you can convince people that you're the one who's gonna win. Even better, this year Professor Braithwait said he'd match the winner's raffle ticket haul. Very generous of him. The planetarium needs the money, Tiffy. I ain't gonna lie, this could be the big break in funding we need."

This was going to be harder than I thought. If there was one thing I hated more than standing in front of a crowd, it was trying to sell something to someone. The thought of canvassing the city and begging strangers to buy my raffle tickets instead of someone else's made my breath unsteady. I was suddenly back standing at my dad's hip, holding his hand, breathing in the smell of his wet unwashed jeans as we walked in the freezing rain. House after house of everyone we knew or barely knew, asking for money, a place to stay, the desperation eating through my gut like battery acid. I couldn't go back to that. No matter what powers the stars had magically given me, I just couldn't do the tickets. But how else was I supposed to compete in the fundraiser? How was I supposed to raise all the money we needed to actually save our home and not *literally* go back to that? It was a cruel catch-22, but there had to be a way out of it.

I grabbed a hat and packed the flyers in a backpack. I had a lot to figure out, but as far as today was concerned, my goal was pretty clear. It was time to go to the mall for some shopping—some *talent* shopping.

CHAPTER 11

Vinni G's

I had been to the mall plenty of times before with my dad and Mimi. I'd ogle the expensive jewelry, clothes, and shoes, check out the video games and toys, and smell the freshly baked cookies near the food court. I never got anything (except for the occasional cookie), but I honestly never *expected* to get anything. Items at the mall were for other people, plain and simple. They weren't for people like me. I had always been content just to take part as an observer, but this trip was different. This time I got to take something home, and I didn't even have to pay for it!

I stopped at the mall map and scanned the list of stores, segmented into categories: clothing, shoes, books and video games, restaurants, sports and outdoors, and so on.

"Come on," I mumbled to myself, trying to find a store that would have a unique talent I could have fun with . . . and maybe use to dominate Candace in the Shining Star competition. "Vinni G's Magic Emporium. Jackpot." I took off in a brisk walk, making mental notes of any stores I wanted to try later.

"Hey there, Tiffany," a familiar voice boomed. I spun to see Earl, my dad's good friend and fellow planetarium handyman, walking out of the comic book store. He had a big, boxy head, a potbelly that hung over his belt, and skinny legs with virtually no butt. Every time I saw him, I marveled at how a human could have such similar body proportions to Shrek.

"Hey, Earl," I said, anxious to get to the magic shop. I pointed toward the back of the comic book store. "You just finish playing some Dungeons & Dragons?"

"Yes ma'am," Earl chuckled, holding up several bags of role-playing dice like some five-year-old displaying a newly purchased goldfish. "Gotta get my reps in early today since I'll be helping your dad at the planetarium tonight. Actually putting on a show this time. Not just working on the exhibits, which is fine by me. Your dad is *very particular* about how these exhibits need to be."

Probably one of the main reasons that not a single one of them is complete. "Yeah, he takes his planetarium business pretty seriously."

"You know what?" Earl said. "You should come tonight. Your dad's doing a show on the stars in our galaxy. It's one of his very best."

My face twisted slightly, despite myself. "I'm going to be busy tonight, unfortunately. And you don't have to worry about me. I get enough of my dad's thoughts on the universe as it is."

Earl laughed again. "I suppose you do—"

Two teenagers ran past and bumped into Earl. He

clutched the bags of dice as if protecting a newborn child but let his car keys clatter to the floor. I bent down, picked them up, and stared at the keychain, a fiery orange bird.

"A phoenix?" I asked, handing back the keys.

"Pontiac Firebird," he said with a self-satisfied grin. "Nineteen ninety-nine. I'm borrowing it from my dad. It's got a 5.7-liter V8. Took me a while to learn stick shift, but you feel like you're in *The Fast and the Furious* when you drive it."

I raised an eyebrow. However much Earl was my dad's best friend, the guy talked and acted like he was about sixteen instead of his midforties. Although I had to admit there *was* something cool about driving a car named after my favorite fantasy creature of all time. Something that had a bit of raw power. Something you could really feel push you back into the seat as you smashed the accelerator to the floor and aggressively shifted gears in perfect concert with hitting the clutch.

"Well, I gotta run," Earl said. "Starting a *Doctor Who* marathon with my dad. On to the Seventh Doctor now. Sylvester McCoy was a highly underrated Doctor, if you ask me. Anyway, don't want to be late."

"Right," I said, nodding. For the first time in my life, I found myself inexplicably jealous of Earl. Not for the *Doctor Who* marathon, but because he got to drive that awesome car on the open Wyoming roads. "Yeah, I gotta run as well. I'll see you around."

"Sure thing."

I turned and jogged off, not stopping until I stood in front of my destination. Vinni G's Magic Emporium was a strange blend of authentic, old-timey merchandise and cheap plastic gags. Turn-of-the-century magicians' posters, leather-bound books, and antique collectibles were in stark contrast with the L-shaped glass counter that looked like it belonged in the prize section of a Chuck E. Cheese. Back when Mimi was still healthy enough to get around, Vinni G's had been her go-to spot for things like tarot cards, gemstones, and incense.

I made my way to the back of the store, where a skinny man stood behind the counter performing a magic trick for a mother and son. I hadn't been here in a few years and didn't recognize him. He whipped out three plastic cups and a small red ball and handed them to the boy for inspection. Satisfied, the boy handed them back, and the man placed the ball under one of the cups and began sliding all three of them around in a well-practiced dance. He stopped and the boy pointed to the cup in the middle. The man lifted the cup to reveal nothing. The boy chose another one and it was empty as well. The man lifted the third cup and the ball wasn't there, either. He reached back behind the boy's ear and the red ball appeared in the man's fingers. He was actually pretty good.

"Whoa!" the boy said, looking to his mom and back. He held up a huge box that looked to be a beginner's magic set. "Mom, we *gotta* get this."

"Maybe next time, sweetie," the mom said, motioning for her son to put the box down on the counter.

The clerk tried to hide his disappointment, but he was a better magician than an actor. "Now, remember, son," the man said, tapping on the box. "The art of magic is not in the cups or the ball. It's in *practice*." The man held out a flat palm and flicked his wrist, instantly producing a business card that he handed to the mom. "I also provide private lessons for willing magicians in the making."

The mom gave a forced smile and took the card as I approached the counter. I wasn't exactly sure how my power even worked, so today was going to be a bit of trial and error.

"And what can I help with today, young lady?" The clerk's Adam's apple protruded like he'd tried to swallow the biggest rough-cut gemstone in the store.

"I was wondering if you could teach me some magic today."

"Teach you?" The man produced a coin and smoothly walked it across his knuckles. With a flick, he made it disappear and then reappear in his other hand before rolling it across his knuckles again. "I can *show* you magic and sell you items to help you learn, but the only true teacher of magic is time, focus, and dedication." He dramatically waved his hands and the coin was gone. This guy was amazing.

"Do you mind if I give it a try?"

With a flashy wave of his hands, the coin plunked onto a black felt cloth on the counter. "I would never deny an eager apprentice."

I plucked the coin from the table and weighed it in my

hand. I didn't exactly know how I was supposed to absorb the talent, as it had just kind of happened automatically the other times before. The man smiled, looking on. I licked my lips, squinted my eyes, and stared at the coin. And I immediately knew what to do.

I pinched the coin between my thumb and index finger and undulated my fingers like a wave rolling across water. The coin effortlessly tumbled over my knuckles until it reached the end and fell over my pinky. I carried it across my palm with my thumb and brought it back over my pointer finger, where it started all over again.

"Like this?" I asked. "Is this it?"

The man's jaw dropped and a rush of chills went all the way up to the top of my head. I had known how to perform the man's trick when I touched the coin, but it wasn't until I *did* the trick and saw the reaction on his face that I understood *why* he did the trick. People had been surprised when I shot the dodgeball and sang Candace's song, but this was different. What I had shown this clerk was impossible. One minute he was positive that a girl couldn't do his trick, and then I had changed everything with a simple coin. That was the power of magic: the gift of wonder. In a weird way, being amazed by a simple yet impossible trick was a form of hope. If you were wrong about what could be done with a coin, then maybe you were wrong about other impossible things in your life. Maybe there was an elegant and magical solution to your problems after all.

I flicked my wrist, making the coin disappear from view

before looking up with a smile. "What other tricks can you show me?"

We moved on to card tricks, cutting a rope that re-formed, and even a bit of juggling.

"How long did you say you'd been doing magic?" the man asked as he put away his juggling balls.

I gave a small shrug. "Oh, I just kind of recently picked it up."

"Well, if you ever want any lessons—" The clerk flicked his wrist and sent his business card tumbling to the floor.

"I've got your info," I said, repeating his motion and producing one of his own business cards between my fingers.

He smiled and ran a hand through his hair, shaking his head. "Maybe I should just have you back to put on another show for folks. Heaven knows I need the business."

I furrowed my eyebrows, not exactly sure what he was getting at until I turned around to see a group of no less than twenty kids and parents scrunched into the store, including the boy and his mom from earlier. I must have been pretty involved with my magic tricks not to notice an *entire* crowd form behind me. I instinctively hunched my shoulders and felt my cheeks blush. It was one thing to perform a trick, but it was another thing to perform in front of complete strangers.

"How can I learn to do that?" the boy asked. His eyes couldn't have been wider if I had just floated down through the ceiling.

I bit my lip. I didn't want to lie to the kid or give harmful advice. I had no idea what to say until I saw the beginner's magic set from earlier. "A magic set, a good teacher, and lots of practice. Oh, and come to the annual planetarium fundraiser!" I reached into my pack and handed him a flyer.

He gave large, exaggerated nods and thanked me. By the time I wove through the gathered crowd, the clerk was ringing up the first in a long line of customers.

Candace had better come prepared to the Shining Star, because I was just scratching the surface.

CHAPTER 12

Breaking Bread

By early afternoon, in addition to being able to do more magic tricks than Houdini, I could play the guitar like Taylor Swift and make a stuffed animal like ... well, Jennie, the manager of Build-A-Bear (wasn't sure what I was going to do with that one, but you gotta make hay while the sun's shining, so I took it). Whether these were going to be the talents I used to help save the planetarium, I didn't know, but for now, this was all just practice. I'd worry about the strategy and game plan once I had more pieces to the puzzle. For the moment, I actually had a more pressing issue. I had passed by the food court about seven times, and if I had to smell any more fried food and warm donuts, my stomach was going to revolt and eat itself.

I walked to the food court, pulled out the change in my pocket, and sighed, inwardly apologizing to my stomach. The mall food was notoriously overpriced, but there had to be *something* I could buy. I wandered around, passing everything from burgers to pizza to Korean barbecue to fancy salads. It all sounded good, but I wouldn't be able to get anything super filling.

"Cool trick," some kid said as he walked by.

"What?" I turned around, at first not even sure he was

talking to me. He pointed to my hand and I glanced down to find myself absently rolling a quarter back and forth across my knuckles. I didn't even realize I was doing it. "Oh, you're welcome."

You're welcome? That didn't even make any sense. He wasn't *thanking* me for doing the trick. I gave an awkward wave and pocketed the quarter, turning away. Why was I such a doofus around everyone? I could probably be doing table-side magic right here in the food court to earn all the money I needed for food, but borrowing talents unfortunately didn't come with the confidence to perform them in front of a crowd. If I was going to perform at the talent show, I would either need to learn some confidence or find a way to borrow that as well.

At the end of the row of fast-food restaurants, I saw a sign that made my stomach grumble with approval: FREE SAMPLES, PLEASE TAKE ONE. I hustled over and stood in front of the curved glass counter of Northern Baked Goods, a bakery I'd never noticed before. The scent of warm bread swirled together with freshly baked cookies, and I thought I was going to pass out right there at the counter. I lifted the bowl-shaped lid from a plate of pink sugar-cookie bites and sneaked two pieces before putting the lid back on.

"Can I help you, ma'am?" a man's voice said from behind the counter.

"Uh, no I didn't," I stammered, thinking for a second that he was accusing me of taking too many cookie pieces. "I mean, why, yes. You can."

I rubbed my chin, looking over the items on display as if heavily weighing my options. What I was *actually* doing was trying to find something under three bucks.

"Our cinnamon-swirl sourdough is today's special," the man said. "Would you like to try a sample?"

"Yes, please!" I said a little too eagerly.

The man smiled, and for a second I felt like I recognized him, although I was sure I'd never seen him. It was a weird sensation. He turned around and grabbed half a slice of the warm bread and handed it to me.

"Now, be warned," he said, pointing a finger. "One bite of that bread and you won't be able to think about anything el—"

"Dad," a voice called from somewhere in the back of the bakery. "Someone's calling about a catering order and they're asking for a better discount."

The man failed to suppress a frustrated eye roll. "One moment, please," he told me as he made his way to the back. When he spoke to his son, he wasn't as far out of earshot as he probably expected. "A *better* discount? What kind of discount did you offer in the first place?"

"I said I'd give them ten percent if they could pick it up and we didn't have to deliver it."

"Brady," the dad said in a low growl. "We have been over this before. You need to clear those things with me *first* before you just go sweet-talk someone into a deal. Go help the girl at the counter, please."

Wait a second. That man's smile. Brady. Oh my gosh.

"Sorry about that. How can I help you?"

My heart seized like gears without grease. It was none other than Brady Northrup. His apron was splattered with flour and colorful smudges of frosting, and he casually rested a rolling pin on one shoulder like some warrior would his battle-ax. Would he even notice me? Normally, I'd say he wouldn't know me from a department-store mannequin, but after what happened at dodgeball, I figured there was a chance. I was wearing a hat and I wasn't in gym clothes, but maybe . . .

"I . . . I'm not sure," I said nervously. I could hardly meet his eyes. I knew who he was, he didn't know who I was, or at least I wasn't sure if he knew. The awkwardness was overwhelming, and since he didn't seem to notice, it was like I was carrying the awkwardness for the both of us.

"Well, let me give you some options," he said, flashing his easy, wide smile. There was little doubt as to why all the other girls fawned over this kid. "I could help ring you up if you've already made your decision. I could help you select something if you *haven't* already made your mind up. Or I could let you off the hook if you just stopped by for the free samples."

I withdrew my wad of cash and coins and plopped it on the glass counter. "I need help figuring out what's the most filling thing I can get for two dollars and eighty-five cents."

Brady looked down at the money and bit the side of his cheek. "Two eighty-five, huh? Hmmm. This might take a while to figure out. We better have something to tide us over." He glanced back at his dad before grabbing a choc-olate chip cookie from behind the counter, breaking it in half and handing me a piece. He stared up at the prices and absently ate his cookie, acting as if he was deep in thought.

I hesitated. Would I get in trouble for taking this? I mean, an employee *was* offering it to me, but I was pretty sure said employee's boss (or in this case his dad) wouldn't be all that pleased about it. My stomach grumbled loudly, as if trying to shout down any second guesses, so I took the cookie and disposed of the evidence in my mouth as quickly as possible.

"Yeah, I think it might be the large banana-bread muf-fin," Brady said, nodding. "Definitely isn't the chocolate chip cookie. Darn thing wasn't filling at all. I just want another one."

"Sounds good to me."

"That you want another cookie or the banana-bread muffin?

"Uh . . . both?" I shrugged, not knowing if I was pressing my luck. A part of me didn't actually want him to give me another cookie, didn't want to make his dad mad. But then there was another part of me that kind of liked the thrill of eating an illicit chocolate chip cookie. There was also another part of me that really liked cookies and yet another part of me that was starving, so it was kind of three parts of me against one.

Brady set his rolling pin on the counter, grabbed both a huge banana-bread muffin and another cookie, and placed them into a paper sack. I broke off a chunk of the muffin and popped it into my mouth and just about melted into the floor. I couldn't remember ever tasting anything so good. I didn't even *like* bananas. What wizardry did one possess to turn mushy old bananas into this absolute wonder?

"Pretty good, huh?"

"It's *amazing*," I said around my mouthful. "Your dad's a talented guy."

Brady gave an overexaggerated look of being offended. "Excuse me, Miss, but *I* bake the banana bread around here. Mom does the recipes. My dad's just here to get mad at people and crack the whip."

I laughed and let out an embarrassing little snort, but Brady only flashed his perfect smile. He seemed so cool. Too bad he didn't seem to recognize who I was, although being unmemorable had kind of been my goal for the past two years, so I couldn't exactly blame him.

He went to the register and rang me up. "Twenty-five cents is your change." He handed me a quarter, and instead of simply taking the change, I grabbed it, walked the coin across my knuckles, and made it disappear with a flick of the wrist.

"Whoa, what?" Brady did a double take. "Do that again."

I had hardly even meant to do the trick. It was so second nature to me that I'd simply done it without thinking. "Do *what* again? Buy a muffin? I only had two dollars and eighty—"

"I will *give* you another muffin if you do that trick again."

Brady looked expectantly from my hand to my eyes. "Consider it like getting paid for a performance."

"I can't, actually." I clicked my tongue.

"Why not?"

"Quarter keeps on disappearing," I said, acting as if I were going to hand him the quarter, only to have it vanish. It wasn't just that my moves were smooth. My performance, banter, and misdirection were smooth. Maybe it was all part of the magic-act talent.

Brady blinked in amazement. "Please tell me you're not gonna pull it out of my ear."

"I can't do that, either," I said, reaching across the counter to the side of Brady's head. I pulled my hand back to reveal a handful of muffin crumbs. "Too much muffin crammed in there."

Brady gawked. "What in the—"

"Brady, need you back here, please," his dad called from the kitchen.

"We'll have to continue this later," Brady said, looking down at my hand of crumbled muffin and shaking his head as if still trying to figure it out.

After he left, I stood there a moment, trying to process what exactly had just happened. If you had given me a hundred years, I wouldn't have guessed my talent shopping at the mall would result in a conversation like that with anyone, let alone Brady friggin' Northrup. And from what I could tell, it was an entirely curse-free interaction.

Before leaving, I noticed he had left his rolling pin on

the counter. I stared at it. Such a simple tool that could help make some of the most amazing things. I picked it up to tell Brady he'd left it but froze just as I opened my mouth. I suddenly got the overwhelming desire to make banana bread, which was weird because I didn't know the first thing about making banana bread . . . or did I? I glanced around the bakery at the ingredients and baking tools. I wanted nothing more than to climb the counter and get to work on some improvised baked good. But that meant . . .

"Oh dear." I gingerly set the rolling pin down and craned my neck to see if Brady or his dad had seen me. "What do I do? What do I do?" I took a deep breath and did the only thing I could think of. I took a few slow steps away from the counter and sprinted away like I'd just stolen all the cash from the register.

CHAPTER 13

A Taste of Things to Come

I couldn't remember ever riding my bike home so fast. In fact, by the time I got home, I could hardly remember the bike ride at all. I'd experienced lifetimes of talents all in a few hours. I had talked to Brady. Brady had talked to me. I knew how to play the guitar, do magic tricks, and bake ridiculously good bread and cakes. And this was after just one afternoon goofing around. This was only the beginning.

I flew through the front door and went straight to the kitchen, pulling open cupboards and instinctively grabbing pans, mixing bowls, and measuring cups. I had no idea what I was doing . . . except I did. We didn't have very many ingredients, but I could improvise. I knew exactly how much flour to add, how to substitute butter since we had no vegetable oil, and how to expertly crack an egg without getting the shells in the bowl or yolk on the counter. I'd *never* done that before. Not even once. I loved eggs, but never made them out of fear I'd explode the shell and make a wild mess. I greased the pan and preheated the oven, and it wasn't long before the house was filled with the wondrous aroma of white cake.

While I waited, I went to the hallway closet and pulled out an old guitar I'd seen my dad play all of one time. Someone had apparently left it in the planetarium lost and found years ago. Never could figure out who would bring a guitar to a planetarium, or even better, who would *leave* a guitar at a planetarium.

I wiped the dust off the scratched-up guitar body and took a seat in the kitchen, experimentally plucking the strings and wincing at the discordant twang. Without thinking, I started to hum and twisted the tuning pegs back and forth, taking less than a minute to bring the instrument into perfect pitch. I absently plucked the strings and gradually slipped into a few classic rock songs: "Stairway to Heaven," "Hotel California," and "Back in Black." Much more my dad's taste than mine, but playing them felt like second nature. Must have been what the old dude at the guitar store was most familiar with. I didn't miss a note. The guitar was part of me. It was like taking Candace's singing talent and mixing it with Mr. Fritzberg's art talent. I could use my hands and fill a previously quiet room with smooth rhythms, complex solos, and hypnotizing harmonies. All this from a hollow wooden box with six strings. Pure magic.

"Hey, Tiffy," my dad said from the entryway, shutting the front door behind him.

I jumped to my feet, standing like a soldier waiting for

inspection, as the guitar flipped off my lap and onto the floor. "Hey, Dad!" My reply came out about three times louder and more suspicious than it should have.

My dad poked his head into the kitchen to see me standing like a statue, his old guitar unceremoniously discarded on the ground. "I heard some music when I drove in. If you're trying to play along to some songs, Sparkles, I'd suggest something a bit easier than 'Stairway.' Might wanna try, like, 'Mary Had a Little Lamb' or something first."

"Yeah, that's good advice, Dad." I bent down and picked up the guitar to return it to the closet, but hesitated. There was a part of me that wanted to play right then and there. To shred those strings like a rock star and blow my dad away. The reaction would be priceless. But how exactly was I going to explain myself? I had gotten lucky with the singing. My dad knew I carried a tune like an injured cat. He also knew that most people played the guitar better with their feet than I did with my hands, so what was I going to say to him when he suddenly saw me able to play like an expert? My dad had more than enough on his mind without introducing his daughter's newfound magical ability into the mix. He'd never been a big fan of Mimi's astrology and mysticism, anyway.

"Everything all right, Tiffy?"

"Uh, yeah," I said, snapping to and putting the guitar back in the closet.

"You get a chance to hang up any of those posters?" My

dad rubbed his face and yawned as he picked up a copy of *Astronomy*, absently flipping through the pages.

"Quite a few, actually," I said. "Lots of people were excited."

"Really?" My dad looked up from his magazine, and his face lit up like I'd just told a first grader that Santa was about to walk through the door. I meant it as an offhand comment, but seeing my dad's hopeful face reminded me of just how desperate he was for this fundraiser to go well.

I nodded. "I think this year is going to be something special, Dad."

"I certainly hope so, kiddo. Hey, is that *cake* I smell?" He leaned down and quickly stole a peek inside the oven. "Did you . . . *make* that?"

"Well, it didn't fall out of the sky." The expression was typically my dad's, so he gave me a raised eyebrow. "I was trying out a recipe for a birthday cake for Frank. I should have some extra."

"You don't say," my dad said, frowning with interest.

"It's just a taste of things to come, Dad." I flashed a grin and nodded.

"Turning over a new leaf, indeed," my dad said, and went down the hall to our one bathroom to get showered before the evening planetarium show.

I pulled the cake out of the oven and tripled the next batch. Would have gone quadruple, but I wanted to save some milk for breakfast. After another half hour, I stood in the kitchen, shirt and hands dusted with flour and crusted with dried batter as I admired my cakes. This talent thing was *actually* working. It wasn't a dream, a figment of my imagination, or some misremembered memory. It was real. The throbbing in my fingertips from way too much guitar playing was real. Those cakes were real. And while baking cakes and strumming on the guitar wasn't going to save the planetarium, it gave me hope that it could be done.

CHAPTER 14

Through the Screen Door

*I*t was close to noon when I finally rolled out of bed, not out of the norm for a Sunday morning. Before I even brushed my teeth, I took a quarter from my nightstand and tried to roll it across my knuckles. I gave up after fumbling it to the floor three times in a row. All my talents from yesterday were definitely gone. And I never even got to make a stuffed bear.

I stumbled my way into the kitchen like a zombie to find yet another note from my dad. "Gone meteorite hunting with Earl."

I yawned and grabbed a bowl of cereal, catching a glimpse of my reflection in the microwave door. Did *everyone* have bedhead like this or was it just me? I tried running my fingers through my knots to straighten it all out, but it was like trying to untangle a ball of Christmas lights with a garden rake.

I wandered back through the front room, munching on cereal and tunelessly humming a song I'd played on the guitar yesterday. I really needed to make it a point to try every musical instrument I could get my hands on. I remember watching TikTok videos for like an hour of this one guy who could do a saxophone solo for like any—

I looked toward the front door and gasped, half choking on my Cap'n Crunch and coughing milk out my nose. Standing on my steps, hand raised to knock, was Brady Northrup, glaring at me through the front screen door.

I hurriedly wiped the milk from my face as my body went as cold as Pluto. What on earth was Brady doing at my front door? How did he even know where I lived? My bedhead! I was still in my pajamas. Pajamas that consisted entirely of one of my dad's NASA T-shirts. I literally wasn't wearing any pants! I slammed my eyes shut, *praying* this was one of those bad dreams when you showed up to school in your underwear and you had to take a test on a book you'd never read. I opened my eyes. Nope. Brady was still at my front door, and I still didn't have any pants on.

Brady finally lowered his hand and spoke slowly. "Knock, knock."

I flashed an awkward half grin and failed one last time to straighten my hair as I walked to the front door, cereal bowl still in hand.

"Unique place you got here," Brady said as he glanced around and very deliberately lifted his foot over the broken middle step.

I coughed a few more times and tugged the bottom of my pajama shirt as far down as it would go. "Well, ya know . . . my dad does a lot at the planetarium, so it's just super convenient."

"Makes sense," he said as if he would have made the same decision himself in my dad's shoes.

"You . . . should try it." *You should* try *it*? What was I saying? I looked around for a place to put my cereal down but finally settled for the floor. I had never felt more awkward in my entire life. And that was saying something. However bad things had gotten, I had at least always had pants. Other than that one time when I got pantsed, of course.

"I need to talk to you."

Butterflies swarmed in my stomach. Rabid, vampire butterflies. Was this bad? Was this good? *How* could this be *good*? It *had* to be bad. But what would Brady actually want to talk about? The dodgeball thing? Maybe he just really wanted to see another magic trick.

"Like, right here?" I gestured to the floor.

He craned his neck to look over my shoulder. "Anyone home?"

I shook my head. "My dad's out looking for meteorite fragments."

"You know." Brady waggled a finger. "I didn't recognize you at first when you came to the bakery."

"Me neither. I mean, I recognized myself. I mean you. I didn't recognize you at first, either. With, like, your apron on and stuff." I winced at my own blabbering.

"Right," Brady said, squinting. "Well, you see, when I went back to talk with my dad, he left me in charge of the bakery to go take care of that catering order. And a really weird thing happened."

"Oh yeah?" I gulped. I tried to remain calm but was sure I had a facial expression like I was trying to brace for a head-on collision.

He continued, "Yeah, I kind of—I don't know how to put this—suddenly lost the ability to bake stuff. Which was kind of unfortunate since I had to improvise a custom birthday cake and make a turtle bread that afternoon. Do you know how those turned out, Tiffany?"

"I do not," I said slowly, bracing myself for the answer.

"Well, after several failed attempts, two small kitchen fires, and somehow getting dough in the ceiling fan, I ran out of time to make anything better. The turtle bread is currently trending on the 'nailedit' subreddit because it looks like a blobfish and my dad got a text that only *one* of the birthday guests even managed to swallow a single bite of the cake."

"Hey, at least *someone* liked it, right?" I winced as I said the words.

"They threw up," Brady said flatly. "The one person who ate it threw it up."

"Oh."

Brady's stare intensified, but his complete lack of anger was so disarming that it made me feel like I was missing something. "Do you know when it was that it finally came to me who you were, Tiffany Tudwell?"

I smacked my lips together several times, dry as moon dust. "I do not, Brady Northrup." *Well, at least he knows my full name.*

"It wasn't until I went back on our security camera footage to erase my mistakes before my dad saw what on earth I was doing, that I saw *you*, picking up my rolling pin, looking confused, setting it down, and running away. The same girl who miraculously, out of nowhere, managed to *dominate* PE dodgeball just as I, yet again, suddenly lost all my ability to so much as bounce a ball on the ground. Same weird thing happening, same—"

"Weird girl?" I couldn't stop myself from finishing the sentence.

"Yeah," he drew out the word.

I swallowed hard again. "That *is* weird." I never imagined anyone would connect the dots, and especially not back to me. Not this fast.

"So, I don't know what's going on, but I'm willing to bet that you do, and I think I deserve some answers."

My mouth worked soundlessly up and down, as if it instinctively knew it should reply but my brain hadn't quite gotten onboard with the idea yet. "I don't know what you mean."

"You sure?" Brady's voice cracked, his flawless demeanor wavering just a tad. "Then how do you have three of my white cakes on your dining table?" He pointed over my shoulder toward the kitchen.

I winced. That one tiny little scrunch of the face was all it took to completely confess my guilt. It was a look that said I knew something and he'd caught me. Of my precious few natural talents, being a convincing liar was not among them.

"I gave you free cookies, Tiffany. During an hour of

need. And in return, I spent two days thinking I was losing my mind. You know what it's like to spend an entire evening trying to hit a *single* free throw?"

"Actually . . ."

"You know what it's like for *me*, then?" Brady replied quickly. "I need to know what's going on. Now."

I was trapped. He knew something weird was up. Well, he didn't *know* know, but he knew that I knew. I didn't have a lot of options. You never did when you were caught with your pants down . . . or off, as the case may be. I needed a strategy here. I was good at that. I just needed to calm down and come up with a plan. There was no way I was going to *lie* my way out of this. One, I was a horrible liar, and two, what lie would even make sense? But if I told the truth, he would . . . huh. What *would* he do? That just might be it.

I straightened myself, trying to look as dignified and calm as possible given the circumstances. "All right. I will tell you, but you can't tell anyone and you can't freak out. This is going to seem . . . strange."

"Fair enough," he said, visibly relaxing, his easy smile returning. "I promise."

"Okay, so you remember that meteor shower from the other day?" Brady nodded. "Okay, well, I was watching from my backyard and made a wish because of all the shooting stars, but when I did, those two meteors exploded right above me. I was, like, literally showered in stardust."

"Uh-huh."

"*Well*," I continued, "ever since then, I can kinda, you know . . . take people's talents for about a day."

Brady drew his eyebrows together and paused for a few seconds. "What?"

"Look." I held my hands up as if trying to calm a dangerous animal. "I'm not quite sure how it all works yet, but it seems like I can kind of . . . borrow someone's talent from them if I touch an object they used that talent with."

"You wished upon a star." Brady stared at me blankly before bursting out in laughter. "You sure you didn't just blow out any birthday candles or find a four-leaf clover? C'mon, what's *really* going on here?"

"Well, how *else* do you explain how I was able to play dodgeball like that, bake those cakes, or do all those coin tricks?"

Brady tilted his head a fraction. "How are you actually doing this? Are you, like, some kind of hypnotist or something?"

I twisted my face, my emotions rising. "Yep, you got me. I'm actually Mysterio. I got bored fighting Spider-Man so I chose to live in a trailer behind a planetarium and perform mass hypnosis on middle school kids in Wyoming. Look, I told you what happened, what's happe*ning*."

"I don't know," Brady said defensively. "I'm supposed to believe you got magical powers from wishing on a star?"

"If you had a better explanation then I'm guessing you wouldn't be standing on my doorstep. Here," I said, walking back to my kitchen and grabbing one of the cakes. "Tell me this doesn't taste exactly like something you would make."

"I don't want to try your cake."

"But it isn't *my* cake," I said, opening the screen door and backing Brady onto the grass. I was on offense now. "I made it with *your* talent, after all."

Brady backpedaled away as I pursued him, cake in hand like I was some priest wielding a cross to cast a demon from my yard.

"Eat the cake, Brady."

"I don't want to eat the cake."

"Just taste the cake!" I shoved the cake toward his face, but he caught my wrist. I tried to pry his fingers off with my other hand but ended up grabbing at his wristwatch. I paused. "What the . . . ?"

Brady stopped as well, more confused than ever. "What the what?"

I pulled my hands free and jabbed my finger at Brady. "Where'd you get that watch?"

"My dad gave it to me for my birthday."

I knew it was a lie. In my struggle to break free, I'd inadvertently absorbed a talent from his watch. If it was my first time taking a talent, I probably wouldn't have noticed, but there was no mistaking the sudden urge to stealthily pick Brady's pocket. It was a thrilling challenge, to see what I could take from someone without them noticing.

"You stole that watch." I pushed him away, smashing the cake into his chest.

"Hey!" he said, wiping at the crumbs. "What are you doing?"

I looked for some surprise or guilty glint in his eyes, but he just stood there, staring at me. He was good.

"You like to steal, don't you? In fact, I'd bet it's what got you sent off to Thunderbird Intermediate for a while. You steal so much that you're actually pretty good at it. I'd even say . . . talented."

Brady shook his head. "I think I'm gonna leave now."

"Fine, leave," I said. "But you sure you wanna go without your phone?"

He stopped and reached into his jacket, only to pull out a crushed chunk of cake. "What the . . . ?" He whirled and saw me holding up his phone, brandishing it like I'd gotten the last roll of toilet paper in a pandemic.

"How many more talents of yours am I gonna have to borrow before I get you to believe me?" I tossed him his phone, which he plucked from the air.

He looked back and forth from his phone to the handful of cake, confusion seeming to sink in deeper with every second.

I stood so triumphantly, I nearly put my hands on my hips and posed like some kind of superhero. Any second now, he'd be forced to accept the truth of what I was saying and—

"What are you?" Brady said, stumbling backward a few

steps. He didn't look angry. He was worried. He was actually afraid of me.

"I . . . uh." I actually didn't know what to say. All I knew, as I watched Brady run away, was that I was pretty sure I'd made a big, big mistake.

CHAPTER 15

Birthday Cake

I tried to calm my nerves as I grabbed my visitor's badge from Gabriela and made my way down to the Sunny Vistas rec room. It was Sunday afternoon, and I hadn't seen Eleanor, Frank, and Stefano since I ran out after the card shuffling incident on Wednesday. I was sure I had left them more than a little confused and possibly thinking they had done something wrong. I had no idea how I was going to set this straight.

"Bellezza!" Stefano said, throwing his hands up as I approached. "How are you?"

I walked over to receive my customary Italian cheek kisses while Eleanor gave me a warm hug, her small frame still strong despite her years.

"Where's Frank?" I looked around to see if he was playing billiards or watching TV as I took off my backpack and removed the Tupperware container that held Frank's birthday cake.

A strange look washed over both Eleanor's and Stefano's faces, as if they were unsure how to explain what they needed to say. My heart jumped into my throat.

Probably sensing where my mind was going, Eleanor

reached out and grabbed my hand. "He's fine, dearie. Just a bit late is all."

I relaxed, knowing he hadn't suddenly passed away or had a heart attack or something, but I knew there was still something that she wasn't telling me.

"And what do we have here?" Stefano lifted his cane and tapped the top of the Tupperware container.

I popped off the lid like some magician performing a grand reveal. "A little something I made myself."

Despite a pair of skeptical looks, they each accepted a piece and took a bite.

Stefano's eyes popped open and he brought his fingers to his lips, releasing them with a kiss. "Buonissimo! All this time you've come here and kept this talent from us? Shame on you, Tiffany. Bless you for the cake now, but shame on you."

I laughed as he took more bites, each time shaking his empty fork in my direction like he was scolding me for having done something wrong.

"Mmmm, yes," Eleanor said, taking a nibble. "Truly splendid. Well done, Tiffany. I would love to know your recipe."

"What's this?" a voice said from behind.

I turned to see Frank in his customary tweed suit and flat cap, shuffling over to the table.

"Tiffany here brought you a birthday cake," Stefano said, finishing off his piece.

"I can see that it's a birthday cake, Stefano," Frank grumbled. "I'm half-deaf, not half-blind. I'm just used to the person with the birthday being there for the birthday cake. I *have* only been to over ninety of my own birthdays, though, so what do I know?"

I stood and gave Frank a hug, handing him a piece of cake as he took a seat at the table. "Happy birthday, Frank."

"That's very kind of you, dear, thank you. I didn't get so much as a phone call from two of my three kids and yet my deceased friend's granddaughter hand delivers me a cake. You're an absolute gem, kiddo."

"Now, Francis," Eleanor cautioned just as Frank was bringing a forkful of cake to his mouth. "You aren't supposed to have gluten after two p.m., remember?"

"Dadgummit, woman." Frank lightly pounded his fist on the table. "I'm ninety-four blasted years old. If I haven't lived long enough to do what I want, then I don't know when exactly that's gonna happen."

Eleanor gave me a quick wink. One of her favorite things in life was getting Frank riled up.

"You had a good birthday, Frank?" I asked.

He took his first bite of cake and immediately dug in for another. "Well, the head scans all came back clear, so I guess that's about as good a birthday present as you're gonna get at my age."

"Head scans?" I asked. "What head scans?"

"You didn't tell her?" Frank said, wiping his mouth as he looked from Eleanor to Stefano.

"Tell me what?" My heart jumped back up into my throat.

Frank rolled his eyes at his two friends and shook his head before he turned to me. "I ain't one for sugarcoating it, kiddo. After my little . . . episode with shuffling cards, they were concerned I'd had an aneurysm or a stroke or something like that. Scans came back clear. They don't have an explanation for it. I don't know. But hey, if I can't manage to shuffle a deck of cards, then I at least won't have to lose to Eleanor anymore."

"You had to get your brain scanned?" I asked. My heart now dropped from my throat to the bottom of my stomach.

"But everything is fine now," Eleanor interjected. "*Right*, Frank?"

"Well, don't know, Eleanor," Frank said. "We ain't exactly spring chickens, you realize. Losing motor skills like that probably means the wheels are starting to fall off."

What had I done? Tears welled in my eyes and I struggled to keep myself together. I had gotten Brady to think I was some kind of monster, and now I had gotten my friends to think they were *dying*. But what was I supposed to do? I couldn't just tell them about my powers, *could* I? It hadn't exactly gone all that well with Brady, but I also didn't want Frank to live under the assumption that there was something seriously wrong with him.

My anxiety must have been showing through because Eleanor reached over and grabbed my hand again. "Are you all right, dear?"

I gave a weak smile. "I'm doing just great, Eleanor."

"We know the planetarium's not doing so hot," Frank

added, apparently not convinced by my answer. It always amazed me how much information and gossip these three knew from the confines of their assisted living facility. And they didn't even use the internet.

"Well, we've got the fundraiser coming up soon," I said. "And my dad's been spending a lot of time out trying to find pieces of that meteorite collision from a few nights back. So hopefully he can cash in big there."

The comment drew a lot of slow nods. Apparently relying on a talent show and hunting for rocks didn't seem like the best of plans to save a failing business. And to be honest, after hearing myself say it, I didn't blame them.

Frank pulled out a bottle of pills and fumbled at the cap with his shaky hands, cursing colorfully. "They want me to take three of these blasted things a day now. I swear I swallow more pills in a day than I do bites of actual food."

My stomach twisted and soured, and for a moment I thought I was going to throw up. I couldn't let Frank go on like this, regardless of how badly things had turned out with Brady.

"I have a confession to make," I blurted. I took a deep breath and looked at the table.

When I didn't speak, I felt Stefano's hand on my shoulder. "It's okay, Tiffany. There's nothing you can't tell us."

I took a very slow and measured breath. "You've all been very kind not to bring it up, but I'm sure you remember last time when I ran out blabbing about a curse."

"Oh." Frank vaguely waved his hand around. "Maybe

a little. Hard to remember specifics about anything these days."

I gave a smile that let him know I appreciated the olive branch. "So, I know this is gonna sound kind of ridiculous, but I promise you I'm being one hundred percent honest here. A lot's happened in the past few days."

"Go on," Eleanor said, leaning forward with a look of genuine interest.

I tried to stop bouncing my leg under the table and noticed my heartbeat had somehow migrated to my ears (my heart seemed to be traveling around a lot during this visit). "I was talking to Mimi during the meteor shower the other night, asking her for help with my problems, with the struggling planetarium, just kind of everything that's going on, ya know. Well, right when I was done, those two meteors collided in the sky above me, and ever since then, I've kind of had the ability to, uh, ya know . . . take people's talents for a day."

All three froze, staring at me with unblinking eyes, until Stefano reached up to his ear and fiddled with his hearing aid.

"Scusa, Tiffany. Could you repeat that one again? Don't think I heard you correctly."

I sighed. I knew this wasn't going to come easy. "Frank, when you suddenly lost the ability to shuffle cards, I'm willing to bet your ability came back the very next morning, am I right?"

Frank shrugged. "Yeah, but things tend to come and go when you're ninety-four."

"But things don't come if you've never had them to begin with," I said.

"I'm not sure I follow, dear," Eleanor said.

"It wasn't just that Frank lost the ability to shuffle cards, it was that I *gained* the ability. And it's happened over and over again with stuff like singing, playing dodgeball, doing magic tricks, and," I said—pointing to the cake—"baking."

I could tell my three friends were caught between trying to believe something that was, well, *unbelievable* and wanting to give me the support I obviously needed. Just telling them stories and feeding them cake wasn't going to cut it. I was going to have to show them.

"Stefano," I said curiously. "How many times have I beat you in a game of pool?"

Stefano gave me a broad, toothy smile. "The good Lord has blessed you many ways, principessa. Playing billiards was perhaps not one of those ways." That was Stefano's way of saying "never."

"Come play me in a game and watch what happens."

He looked to Eleanor and Frank before standing up with his cane and hobbling over to the billiard table. I racked the balls into a triangle at one end of the table and set the white cue ball at the other end.

"Here you go," I said, handing Stefano a cue. "And don't go easy on me. I want you to give it your best."

He gave a warm smile and nodded. Despite his age and having to move around with a cane, Stefano was robotic with the pool cue, chalking the tip, lining up his initial shot, and sending the cue ball flying across the table. With a *crack*, the balls went zipping around the table, with one striped ball disappearing into a corner pocket. He repeated the process two more times, each time knocking in another striped ball, before finally missing.

"You ready for this?" I asked Stefano, holding my hand out.

"I'm not sure what I'm supposed to be ready for, but I'll say yes," Stefano said, handing me the pool cue.

The moment I touched the cue, I could tell something was different. The balls weren't just randomly laid out on the table. There was a geometrical pattern that started with the white cue ball and extended to the surrounding solid color balls. There were options, angles, and spin so that I wouldn't just hit a ball in, but ensure that the cue ball was well positioned to hit the *next* ball in. The game had a chess-like beauty to it that I had never seen until now.

I lined up my shot and did a few practice motions with the cue before bringing it forward sharply. The white ball shot across the table, colliding with the solid green ball and sending it directly into a side pocket.

"You've been practicing," Stefano said, waggling a finger.

I hit three more balls in before purposefully missing my last shot so I would line Stefano up for a relatively easy straight shot across the table. I passed the cue back to

Stefano. "If I've been practicing, then you need to explain to me why you're going to miss your next shot as bad as you've ever missed a shot in your entire life."

Stefano raised an eyebrow as he took the cue back to take his shot. Motioning the cue forward and backward, I could already tell he had lost his practiced stroke. He shot the cue forward for a hard hit but completely missed the ball, jerking the tip upward.

"What the devil are you doing, man?" Frank said, looking on with Eleanor.

"I slipped," Stefano said, although he didn't sound too sure of himself. He took the shot again and this time sent the white ball flying off the table. We all watched as the ball clacked on the ground and rolled out to the hallway. Eleanor, Stefano, and Frank stared at me slack-jawed.

"Anyone else got any other talents I could borrow?" I asked with the best "I told you so" face I could muster.

Frank broke an extended silence, pointing to Eleanor. "She's really good at cards."

CHAPTER 16

To-Do List

With one final push on my bike pedals, I crested the top of Galaxy Hill just as the last sliver of sun disappeared behind the western horizon. A light was on at the planetarium and my dad's car was in the parking lot. It didn't take Sherlock Holmes to guess what he'd be up to.

I pulled my bike to a stop and walked up the fourteen stone steps to the front door, my legs feeling like Jell-O after the steep climb on my bike.

"Dad?" I called out as I stepped into the large lobby area. There were probably no less than a dozen COMING SOON signs posted in front of half-finished or fully covered exhibits. Anything from a moonlike landscape with three remote control lunar rovers tipped on their sides to touchscreens with wires dangling out of the back. The largest one was the infamous moon-walker rig. The thing took up nearly half the room, with pulleys and bungees hanging from the ceiling all converging on a harness that was supposed to allow someone to walk and bounce around like they were on the moon. Dad and Earl had spent the better part of a year working on it, and it still wasn't ready to go.

I got a whiff of fresh popcorn and saw that the lights were on at the ticket counter and the concession stand. I swear my dad could probably get all the money he needed and more to save the planetarium if he and Earl stopped helping themselves to the snacks.

"Dad, you there?"

The only sound was the echo of my own voice.

I walked down a curved hallway to the left, passing older space and science exhibits that lined the entire length of the wall. Anything from dioramas of the moon landing, to explanations of a black hole, to a hand crank that rotated tiny models of the planets in our solar system around a glowing orange ball.

Halfway down the horseshoe-shaped hallway, I reached the double doors to the main theater room. A hundred and seventy-eight seats sat beneath a huge domed ceiling where people came to see laser shows and educational movies. I had sat through all of them dozens of times, listening to my dad give the live narration. Toward the front of the room was an open area in the floor where guest speakers would theoretically stand to address the audience. It was also where the contestants would perform during the Shining Star competition. The thought caused my stomach to do a somersault. My dad was in the middle of the room at the control board he'd tricked out to look like he was manning the helm of the Starship *Enterprise* every time he conducted a show. He wasn't running a show now, though. He was sprawled out over his chair, breathing loudly, dead asleep.

I walked up to see a bird's nest of wires sticking out of

the bottom of the control board, various tools, parts, and manuals littered on the floor along with two crushed Red Bull cans. A sheet of white paper on the console caught my eye. Half of it was a to-do list with no less than twenty items. Things like "calibrate lunar rover touchscreens," "balance tension on moon-walk rig? Figure out how to reinforce metal frame," "graphic designs needed for each exhibit," "build 2x4 frame for meteor impact simulation," and "women's toilet is leaking."

The other half of the paper was a mess of scribbled math and dollar signs. I'm sure it all made sense to my dad, but I couldn't follow it other than a bolded "375" circled multiple times at the bottom.

An alarm went off on my dad's phone, and he shot forward in his chair, almost falling out of it.

I screamed, which caused my dad to scream.

"Sparkles, what are you doing here?"

"Geez, Dad!" I said, placing my hand on my chest. "Just coming to check if you were alive."

"Oh, well, I am now," he said, rubbing a bit of life back into his face. "Just taking a little power nap was all. Could hardly keep my eyes open, which kind of makes electrical work a little tricky."

"Well, don't hurt yourself, Dad, okay?" I said, patting him on the shoulder. There was no use in telling him to slow down or to stop or to take a break. None of those things would save this planetarium and none of those things would save our home.

"How'd it go last night?" I said. "I never got a chance to ask you."

"It *didn't* really," my dad grumbled, shaking his head.

"What do you mean? Did they not show up?"

"Did *they*? No, *they* showed up. It was *Earl* who didn't show up. Exhibits were a mess and not covered up. Tried to do everything myself. I was frazzled. Half the group walked out. They *walked out*, Sparkles."

"I'm sorry, Dad." I scrunched my face. "But what happened to Earl? I bumped into him at the mall. He seemed pretty excited . . ." I trailed off. *The keys.*

"Yeah, well, he was apparently *so* excited that he drove his dad's car over a curb and into a light pole. He said he thought he was in reverse and floored it forward. Can you believe that?"

I swallowed hard like I was trying to muscle down a sea urchin. "That is . . . unusual."

"Just my blasted luck."

"Is he okay?"

My dad waved his hand dismissively. "Yes, as long as you don't count emotional distress from missing his *Doctor Who* marathon, he's perfectly fine."

I couldn't believe it. I nearly choked on the realization that after all my worrying and concern about how I could use my power to help save this place, I'd only managed to make it worse. Someone could have gotten hurt. I wanted to scream, to take some cage fighter's talent and punch a hole through a wall.

"I just don't get it, Sparkles," my dad continued. "We can't afford stuff like this. Like we *literally* can't afford it."

"It'll all work out, Dad," I said, rubbing his shoulder and consoling myself as much as I was my father. "We'll get the money from the Shining Star, and you and Earl can take the time you need to finish the exhibits. You can beat a Tudwell up, but you can't keep a Tudwell down, remember?"

My dad took a long, worrying breath.

"What's the matter, Dad?"

He waited a moment before finally responding. "We need the exhibits done in time for the Shining Star."

"Wait. *What*?"

"Mr. Myers called again," my dad said, pressing his palms to his eyes. "He said he wants all the exhibits done in time for the Shining Star."

"But . . . but that's in two weeks," I stammered. "He can't just demand that! He hardly even pays you for all this extra work. How can he just *demand* that?"

"He owns the place, kiddo. He can do whatever he wants. He said he received a lot of complaints about the planetarium being under construction. He got more complaints after last night. It's the reason people don't come. We're gonna have a lot of people coming for the Shining Star. He sees it as our big opportunity to show folks things have changed, to make an impression." My dad paused and shook his head repeatedly. "I screwed up, Tiffy. I tried to take on too much, fix and upgrade too many things. I wanted it all to work out so badly, I just got in over my head."

"So what does this mean?" I asked quietly, as if I was afraid he'd hear and actually give me the answer. "So the money we raise at the Shining Star doesn't matter?"

"Oh, it matters," my dad said. "We need every last cent of it to keep this place open, but Mr. Myers doesn't want to depend on a fundraiser to run a business long-term. I don't blame him, Tiffy. He wants it making money, pulling in crowds and schools. He told me if we can't finish the exhibits and prove this place has a future, then he's going to sell the planetarium."

I had braced for the answer, but the words still hit me like a kick to the stomach. I knew better than to complain that "life wasn't fair." My experiences had taught me that "fair" should never be an expectation, but this was just cruel.

"Is it even *possible* to complete the exhibits in time?" I asked meekly.

"No." My dad picked up the paper from his console and gently shook it. "Not unless you happen to know an electrician, a welder, a graphic designer, a computer technician, a carpenter, and a plumber who all want to work for free."

I took mental notes as he read through the list. If my dad could put in overtime and work two jobs to save our little family, then I could do it, too. I could use my power to win the Shining Star *and* get the skills my dad needed to finish the exhibits.

"Dad, what's three seventy-five mean?" I said, pointing to the paper.

"Huh?" he said, flipping the paper around. "Oh, well.

Just to paint an even sunnier picture for you, it's the number of raffle tickets the winner would have to sell for us to stay open *if* Mr. Myers decides not to sell the place."

"What about Professor Braithwait matching the winning raffle-ticket sales?"

My dad winced. "That *is* factoring in him matching the winning ticket sales. And we'd still need the other contestants to pull their weight as well."

"I'm guessing three hundred and seventy-five is a lot?" The thought of selling just one ticket almost had me breaking out in a sweat, let alone nearly four hundred.

My dad pressed his lips together in a flat smile. "No one has ever sold more than a hundred, Sparkles."

"Ah," I said, knowing full well that my dad was certain the situation was hopeless. He would never finish the exhibits, and there was zero reason to believe they would even come close to the necessary raffle-ticket sales. And even knowing all this, he smiled and patted me on the head. It was why I loved my dad, and it was why he didn't have to worry about pulling this whole thing off by himself. Because someway, somehow, I was going to do it for him.

CHAPTER 17

Sidekick

On Monday at school, Brady couldn't keep his eyes off me. I wish I could say it was because of my supermodel attractiveness or irresistible charm, but his expression looked more like he was trying to summon the dark side of the Force to strangle me. I waited the entire morning for a sign of retaliation—whispered comments behind my back, a note in my locker, a text, or a post online—but nothing came. By the time lunch rolled around, I felt like I'd been holding my breath the entire morning.

I sat by myself in the lunchroom at my normal spot by the trash cans and pulled a peanut butter and honey sandwich from my backpack. I looked over the students as I flipped open my notebook and scanned the list of talents I'd written down for the Shining Star.

In the history of talent shows around the world, I was probably the only person ever to have the problem of not having to work on a talent. My problem was simply to pick the right one, or two . . . or three talents. I jotted down where I thought I could get them, if I'd taken them already, and how much I had enjoyed them. To be honest, most entries scored a perfect ten out of ten on that last part, with the exception of making a Build-A-Bear.

"Queen Astrid, may I join your merry company?" I looked up to see Simon, holding a sack lunch in one hand and pointing at the seat next to me.

"As long as that backpack grants you advanced curse resistance of some sort." I gestured toward the seat and scooted over a bit.

"Would never leave home without it." He slipped off his massive bag and dropped it on the ground with a heavy thump, like some kind of backcountry backpacker getting ready to set up camp for the night.

"Looks like you packed your home *in* it."

He snorted, pushing up his glasses as he took a seat. "I just like to be prepared. If I need something, I'd rather be looking at it than looking for it, ya know. Working on the next raid strategy?" Simon leaned over to inspect my book.

I gave a little sigh. "No. Just trying to figure out what I want to do for the Shining Star. Aside from needing to raise, like, more money than anyone in the history of the competition, I also have to directly compete against Candace, which is actually probably more daunting than trying to raise—" I stopped, Simon's eager, goofy stare interrupting me more than words could. "What?"

"So you're actually gonna do it?" He spoke through a huge smile.

"Yes," I said, a bit offended. "Are you so surprised?"

"Surprised? I'm giddy. I'm rapt. I'm ..." He turned around, fished a small pocket thesaurus out of his backpack, and flipped to a page. "I'm . . . jubilant! Tiffany, you'll be officially representing the VGC!"

"The what?"

"The Video Game Club! You'll be representing the Video Game Club. This is amazing. We've never had a rep at the Shining Star in our storied five-year history. I can't wait to tell the others. This is gonna be great. Knowing Queen Astrid, I bet you already got your whole game plan together. Costume, video, talent. Oooh, are you gonna draw?"

"Am I gonna *draw*?" Keeping up with Simon when he was wound up was like being the last person on your team and trying to catch every dodgeball thrown your way, a feeling I was quite familiar with.

"Yeah," Simon said, as if the connection was obvious. "I saw your self-portrait hanging up in Fritzberg's class. I had no *idea* you could draw like that. Not that I pay attention to how you can draw, or that I wouldn't because you're really good and deserve to be paid attention to . . . I mean your drawing does . . . not that *you* don't." The longer Simon talked in circles the redder his face got.

"I understand what you mean," I said, putting a hand on his knee to calm him down. He went still as a statue at my touch. It wasn't an effect I was used to having on people. "So it sounds like you know a bit about the Shining Star."

"Sure," he said, slowly regaining his composure. "I've been to every one for the past seven years."

"Wait, really?"

"Yeah, I've got six older brothers and sisters, remember, so there's always been someone participating. Debate, improv, drama, chess. And the one year I *didn't* have a sibling doing it, I still had to go because my second-oldest brother dragged me along to see his girlfriend. She was representing the Rock Paper Scissors Club, I kid you not. When my brother asked me if I thought she had a chance of winning, I said about one out of three." Simon snorted at his own joke.

"You're not gonna hold up the family tradition?" I asked.

Simon shrugged. "I've always been kind of the runt of the litter, so I don't think anyone's really expecting me to. They don't expect a lot out of me, to be honest. I'm also not much of a performer, anyway."

"That's just because they haven't heard your pump-up and victory speeches during *Warcraft of Empires*."

"I am pretty good at those speeches." Simon looked down, but couldn't suppress an embarrassed smile. "But that's just because I'm around the crew. I've seen how bad people can crash and burn at the Shining Star. Nooooo thank you."

"Wait," I mused. "So you've got a pretty good idea of what works and what doesn't?"

"Oh sure." Simon nodded, pushing up his glasses. "I have quite a good memory for that kind of thing. In fact, I have all of *The Princess Bride* memorized. That's not, like, a hyperbole or anything. I literally have the *entire* movie memorized. Wanna hear a little bit?"

"Maybe some other time." I held up my hands to intervene before I got a ninety-minute monologue. "I do need some help with the competition, though, if you can."

"As you wish." Simon paused expectantly. "It's from *The Princess Bride*."

"Got it."

"Well, yeah, let's see. I mean, I don't think I can help much with the raffle tickets since I'm not much of a people person, and I'm not really creative when it comes to making videos and stuff, and I've used the same Ash Ketchum costume for the last three Halloweens so I'm not very inventive when it comes to *that* . . ." Simon trailed off, scratching his head. "I'm not making a very good case for myself, am I?"

I gave a short laugh. "It's okay if you can't physically do any of it. I just need your advice on what's worked and what hasn't. I don't even know where to begin and I'm going up against Candace."

Simon winced as if the name was a doctor's-needle poke in the butt cheek. "Yeah, that's quite the final boss, Queen Astrid. If Victims of Candace was a club, it'd probably have the biggest membership in history. Good news is, you'll probably have a lot of support, especially from the VGC. At any rate, from what I remember, the best contestants in the past had, like, super over-the-top costumes, but they had to be related to their clubs. Their talents were pretty unique but well practiced. It doesn't pay to just do something goofy for laughs. It actually has to be a talent. Videos have been all over the place. Let me see. Videos come toward the beginning, so they sort of set the tone to introduce you, so just make a good first impression. Q and A boils down to who can think on their feet. I remember my brother, Jake, got big points for, like, a three-word answer once, but another time this drama dude gave like a whole speech and he won, so I guess it just has to be good. Raffle tickets should be . . . well, more than everyone else's."

I took a deep breath. "You don't happen to have, like, a few hundred raffle tickets bought and paid for in that pack of yours, do you? Or, like, the Q and A questions so I could study them? Or a spare costume?"

"I'm afraid not, my queen." Simon humbly bowed his head and spoke in his British fantasy-game accent. "But never fear. The VGC will come to your aid. I will consult with our party posthaste and devise the proper course of action! We shall level you up so that you may face and vanquish the final boss."

"Thank you, seriously." I couldn't help but laugh every time Simon did one of his improvised speeches. He seemed like a totally different person when he turned it on. "By the way, you got some of your woodshop dandruff on you again."

Simon looked over at his shoulders and brushed his shirt and hair, covering his food in sawdust. "Oh crud."

I bit the inside of my cheek to hold in my laugh. "I hear wood shavings are high in fiber," I said. "For how good you are at building things out of wood, I'd think you'd be used to . . ." I trailed off, an idea forming.

"I'd be used to what?"

"Hey, do you only work on your project at school?"

"Yeah, we don't have hardly any of the tools at home, so I've got to do it all at woodshop. Why?"

"No reason," I said, trying to act casual. "I was just thinking about maybe helping my dad with something at the planetarium. Would you be able to show me some of your tools after school?"

He shook his head. "Inconceivable!"

"What?" I said. "Why?"

Simon remained serious for all of three seconds before failing to hold back a smile.

"Oh my gosh," I said, recognizing the look. "*The Princess Bride*?"

"There's hope for you yet."

I absently spun my combination lock, mulling over each of the elements to the Shining Star. The money, the tickets, Candace. It was overwhelming to think about. I tried to keep my mind on what I *could* do. I could use Simon's insight to select the perfect talents. I could maybe use my talents to make a—

I popped open my locker and a folded-up piece of paper fell out, bouncing off my shoe. I picked it up and saw my name scrawled across the front.

Fully expecting some social death threat from Candace, I opened it and read it quietly to myself.

"Meet me under the stage after your rehearsal. We need to talk. Urgently. Brady."

CHAPTER 18

Beneath the Stage

*P*laces, everyone," Mrs. Willard announced, clapping her hands, her numerous turquoise bracelets clacking. "Final run-through for the day. Let's make it flawless, my beauties. In two days, the whole world will be watching!"

It was a very Mrs. Willard thing to do, to embellish the significance of a middle school play. The "whole world" was really a couple hundred students who had to be there and a dozen or so parents who probably wish they weren't. Not exactly the Super Bowl halftime show.

My nerves nipped at me like a swarm of blood-starved mosquitoes. I hardly paid attention to what was going on as we ran through the play. Not with a secret meeting with Brady looming over me, or directly *beneath* me, as the case may be.

I was also chomping at the bit to make it back home and start working on the two-by-four frame for the meteor impact exhibit. After a quick stop with Simon to the woodshop right before rehearsal, I couldn't stop thinking about the exhibit I needed to build. Leaving it undone felt like purposely leaving my zipper down. I was itching to set it right. Every talent I took was different, but that immediate desire to want to use the talent was always the same. I'd already drafted up sketches to not only finish the exhibit, but also *improve* it.

I hardly even noticed when it was finally Candace's turn to perform her Lost Boys musical number. Mercifully, she didn't so much as look in my direction. After our little confrontation in front of the Shining Star poster, I had been bracing for her to pour on the abuse. Bullies liked coming back to easy targets like raccoons liked rooting through open dumpsters for easy pickings. From what I could see, however, she had just gone back to not knowing I existed. Fine by me.

It was weird to stand there and not just dream of how it would be to sing like her, but to know *exactly* how it felt to sing like her. Watching the beauty and grace of her backup dancers, listening to the magic of Candace's voice, it almost made me forget how much I wanted to lock them all in an overfull porta potty and tip it over.

The performance finished without a hitch, and I pulled the main curtains shut.

"Just marvelous, dears," Mrs. Willard said, giving a solo standing ovation. "All that's left is to share your talents with the world. You all have tomorrow off. Find your centers. Spend time communing with your inner performers. Until then, my beauties."

"Good job, everybody," Marco said through the headset.

"The fade to black on the spotlight was a nice touch. Solid work, Enoch. Tiffany, try to be smoother on the final curtain close, please. It looked a little uneven in the middle."

You look a little uneven in the middle. "Okay," I squeaked. Short of stumbling across a professional pirate and stealing his rope-pulling talents, I didn't think there was anything I could do to please Marco. Trying to get on his good side was probably a lost cause.

"Hey, thanks for your help, Tiffany."

I turned and almost fell over when I saw *Candace* standing next to me, beaming with her perfect smile. It took me a moment to register that the compliment had actually come from *her*.

"Uh, thanks," I stammered, still trying to grasp the monumental change in behavior. Maybe there was some hope after all—

"If *everyone* was talented," Candace said, interrupting my thoughts, "there'd be no one to pull my curtains and cue my music."

There it is. In a way, the insult was a relief. Not that I preferred it or anything, but it was much less difficult to understand than a suddenly nice Candace. "You're welcome." *Way to stand up for yourself there, Tiffany.*

Candace gave a surprised laugh. "So glad to see you actually know your place, Phantom."

I stood there nervously, rubbing my ear piercing and trying to keep her from noticing my trembling knees. She shook her head and walked away, her annoying little laughs echoing off the cavernous stage walls. It wasn't for another ten seconds that I finally unfroze enough to actually take a breath. How was I ever going to compete against her without absolutely wilting?

I took a bit longer than usual to tidy up my ropes and curtains in order to buy some time for everyone to clear out before walking over to the west-end trapdoor. I pulled it open and took two deep breaths, gazing at the staircase that disappeared into the darkness below like a scene straight out of a cliché horror movie. I didn't bother turning on the lights in case someone saw them and came down to see what was going on. I was sure that Brady's whole point in choosing this spot was so we could meet in private.

I pulled out my phone and turned on the flashlight. "Out of the frying pan and into the fire," I said to myself as I crept down the stairs, the wood creaking with each step until I got to the bottom. I panned my light from left to right, casting long shadows off the dozens of vertical support beams that held up the stage above.

"Brady?" I hissed. "It's me. Tiffany."

A few seconds passed and a light flicked on about four columns away. The top half of Brady's body floated in the darkness. I fought down my rising nerves and made my way over to where he stood.

"You got my note," he said.

No. I was actually looking under the stage for someone else named Brady. You seen him? "Yeah, so what's up?"

Brady looked from side to side as if expecting to see someone spying. "I want to apologize."

My eyes went wide and I braced myself for a follow-up jab like I'd gotten from Candace.

The silence stretched on until Brady spoke again. "Honestly. I do. I'll be straight with you. I'm on thin ice with my dad after coming back from Thunderbird Intermediate. He's strict with me in the first place, and completely botching two custom orders and getting our family business's name trending on Reddit was not exactly a bonding moment between the two of us, as you can imagine. And then you claimed to have this, like, cosmic superpower, and it was . . . a lot to take in."

It was hard to tell in the low light, but something told me he was being sincere. "Well, I may have overreacted by chasing you out into my yard, shoving cake into your chest, and pick-pocketing your phone. I wasn't wearing any pants, and it's hard to think on your feet when you've got nothing on your legs."

There was a life lesson in there somewhere.

Brady contorted his face, probably a bit confused by my last comment. "Look, I'm sorry. Truly. It was my first time having my talents magically stolen."

I squinted one eye, trying to detect any signs of deception. "For the record, I didn't *mean* to take your baking talent, and I had no idea it would cause you to make a blobfish bread. And the dodgeball thing just kind of happened. You threw a bunch of balls at me first. I took your talent in an act of self-defense."

"For the record," Brady said, repeating my phrase and holding up his hands, "I don't remember ever actually hitting you with a dodgeball that day. And when you took Candace's singing ability, was that in self-defense as well or were you maybe playing a bit of offense there?"

"Wait, how do you know about that?"

"So that *was* you." Brady snapped his fingers. "I thought so."

Dang it! This Brady guy was crafty. "What gave it away?" I asked again.

"Candace suddenly loses her singing voice for a day, has an epic meltdown, and you think I wouldn't hear about it?"

I hadn't heard about the epic meltdown, although it didn't surprise me in the least. Despite Brady talking like I should know more about the connection between him and Candace, I wasn't actually sure what it was. I knew they used to be boyfriend and girlfriend, but that had been before Brady got sent to Thunderbird.

"That one with Candace was more of an accident as well," I said.

"Is that right?" Brady said, his tone not quite believing. He pointed up at the stage floor. "I heard how she talked to you. I see how she treats other people. You sure taking her singing wasn't a bit of payback?"

"I never said I was *unhappy* with the accident."

Brady gave a quiet laugh. "I guess not. So, how well do you actually control this thing? How much do you understand about what you can do?"

I paused a second, not sure of exactly how much I should reveal. "Enough."

"Okay, so how many talents can you take at once? Do you get anything other than their talents, like their personality or memories? Is there a time limit between when people use the object and when you can touch the object to take their talent? When multiple people use an object and you touch it, can you, like, scroll through and select the one you want? Can you take a talent and then put it back into a different object and pass it along?"

I tried my best to mask the "deer in headlights" look that was almost certainly plastered all over my face. Instead, I deflected with a question of my own. "Why do you want to know all this?"

It was his turn to look surprised. "Three separate times I'm the victim of an *actual* supernatural power, granted to a girl in my school by two exploding asteroids, and you're confused why I might want to learn a little bit more about it?"

"They were meteors," I corrected. "But okay. You've made your point. So, what, I give you the answers and that's it? Everything's good between you and me, and you won't tell anyone else?"

"I want more than just answers," Brady said, tilting his head.

"What, then?"

A knowing smirk crept up one corner of Brady's mouth. "By the look I just saw on your face, you don't actually know the answers to any of the questions I asked. I want a front-row seat to this thing. See it in action, test its limits."

I searched Brady's eyes, trying to guess at his game. He could read me like a picture book, but all I saw was what he showed me. He seemed afraid when he was afraid. Truly sorry when he was apologetic. Sincere when he opened up. Every side of him seemed authentic, but I'd seen how good a liar he was when I confronted him about stealing his watch. I needed to be careful here.

"And if I do this—include you in figuring this whole thing out—what's in it for me?"

He held his hands out wide. "Name your price."

However much it might complicate things going forward, being owed a favor from someone like Brady was like getting a wish from a genie. He had influence, both with the people in the school and online.

"What's it gonna be?" Brady spurred me on. "How about I make you a star?"

Make me a star . . . a star. "Wait, what?"

"In one of my videos. It wouldn't be hard. Not with your ability," Brady said. "Steal the right talents and I'm positive we could make something go viral."

"Make me a star," I mused. His videos, his confidence, his huge following. This was it. It was everything

I needed. It was almost too good to be true. I locked eyes with Brady. "And I need you to help me win the Shining Star competition. And win *big*."

"Oh, is that all?" He raised his eyebrows.

"Hey, if that's too much to ask from the great Brady Northrup, then I could always just take my magical meteor powers to someone else, I guess." I twisted my mouth, pretending to be lost in thought. "Maybe someone with a slightly bigger YouTube following. I think there's this one guy who—"

"Whoa there." Brady put his hands up. "I'm in. I'm in. We'll have a lot to coordinate here, so what's your Snap?" Brady pulled out his phone and waited on my reply.

"Yeah, I don't have Snapchat. I'll just give you my number."

Brady slowly lifted his gaze from his phone to me, a confused expression frozen on his face. "You don't have Snapchat?"

I folded my arms. "Who am I gonna snap, Brady? My friends at the old-folks home? I communicate with the Video Game Club through Discord."

Brady released a prolonged exhale. "We've got some work to do."

CHAPTER 19

Equipment Shed

*T*he next morning, keeping my eyes open during second-period math while my teacher droned on about y-intercepts was like trying to lift Thor's hammer. I had worked furiously the night before at the planetarium to finish the wood framing for the meteor collision exhibit. At 2:22 a.m., just as I was looking over my work, my abilities had vanished with a snap. By the time I'd cleaned up, dusted myself off, and climbed into bed, it was actually closer to 3:00 a.m., but at least we were one step closer.

At lunchtime, I completely fell asleep, only to be awakened by a text from my dad asking if I had seen anybody in the planetarium the night before. He had found a window open, and while nothing was stolen, he was thoroughly confused by the fact that the intruder was apparently very generous with his time and talents. I told him he most likely had an infestation of planetarium fairies and to leave out bowls of milk. He told me he was leaning toward elves.

As the final bell rang, my phone buzzed with an incoming text message. It was Brady this time.

Since you're not using Snapchat, I hope you get this text. If not, I can send a telegram or maybe a messenger pigeon. Meet in the old equipment shed. ASAP. I got a plan.

I rolled my eyes. This guy certainly had odd meeting spots. After a quick trip to my locker, I went and got my bike from the front of the school and rode it back around to the far side of the soccer fields to the old equipment shed. One of the doors was already propped open.

It was dim inside, and the immediate smell of motor oil, sweaty football pads, and spray paint was almost enough to make me pass out. Brady lounged on the seat of a riding lawn mower, his feet kicked up on the steering wheel.

"I got your messenger pigeon," I said, inspecting my surroundings. "First we meet under the stage, now we're in the equipment shed. Was the abandoned coal mine all booked up or something? I'm beginning to think you don't want to be seen with me."

"Oh, come on," Brady said, playfully dismissive. "I think it's cozy."

I rolled my eyes. "Let's get on with it. I'd give it about five minutes next to these old football pads before I either barf or go unconscious."

Brady sat up, greedily rubbing his hands together. "First things first, we need to conduct a few experiments. I'm going to need to know exactly what I'm working with. Here, toss me one of those old footballs out of that bin over there."

I walked over to where Brady was pointing, pushed a bin of baseball bats out of the way, and picked up a football. I lofted it to him, but the ball fell well short and ricocheted off the side of the lawn mower, bouncing into a nearby stack of yard tools.

"Interesting," Brady said as he hopped down and tossed me the football, which passed straight through my hands and nearly smacked me in the face. He squinted his eyes. "Well, at least we know we're starting from scratch with football talents."

I scowled at Brady and picked the football back up. This time I felt like I had a better understanding of what to do with it, but it wasn't like the other times I'd taken a talent. There wasn't an overwhelming sense of new ability. I tossed the ball back in a near spiral, which Brady attempted to catch with one hand, but dropped.

"I think the talent has to be fresh or I can't absorb it," I said, looking at my hands.

"Yeah," Brady said, returning the ball to the bin. "Plenty of talented people have played with these footballs over the years, but it doesn't seem like you got anything before I had touched it. And even then, I feel like you didn't steal all my talent. Maybe because I didn't really put that much into it? So is there anything in particular you have to do to take the talent? Is there any kind of sensation when it happens?"

"I don't really *do* anything." I twisted my face, thinking. "It just kind of . . . happens when I touch an object."

Brady shook his head. "Nah, that's not right, you gotta be doing something."

"And what makes you say that?" I folded my arms, a bit annoyed that he professed to know more about my power than I did.

"Because if you weren't doing *something* special, you'd be taking talents from nearly every object you came into contact with."

I opened my mouth to reply but stopped. He had a point. I didn't just absorb every available talent around me, or I'd constantly be leaving a wake of bumbling and confused people wherever I went. I tried thinking back to each time I had taken a talent. Candace's singing through the microphone, Brady's dodgeball talents through the ball, his baking talents through the rolling pin, Frank's shuffling talents through the cards, Earl's driving ability through his keys, and so on.

"Every time I had just kind of touched an object." I shrugged. "It's not like I'm chanting some spell or waving a wand or anything."

"Yeah," Brady said, snapping his fingers as if he'd just gotten an idea. "But you are *focusing* on the object."

"Okay," I said, not quite convinced yet that he was onto something.

"Here," he said, handing me a rake. "I'm gonna throw you this tennis ball and you try and bat it out of the air."

"With a rake handle?" I said, *really* not convinced he was onto something.

"Just humor me."

I reluctantly agreed and flipped the rake around. Brady tossed me a tennis ball, and I swung as hard as I could. The rake swished through the air and out of my hands, causing Brady to dive for cover.

"Perfect," Brady said from the floor.

"And what was so perfect about almost getting a rake to the face?"

"You couldn't hit the ball because you weren't focused on taking a talent."

I raised an eyebrow. "What talent was I supposed to have taken from the rake that would make me be able to smash a tennis ball out of the air?"

"None," Brady said, smirking. "But there's plenty in those baseball bats you pushed out of the way to get the football. And those were just used by the baseball team not an hour ago."

"Huh," I said, walking over and picking up one of the bats. I focused on it this time, imagining someone swinging it through the air and crushing a baseball back into the sky.

"I don't think it worked," I said, trying my best to look confused.

"Really?" Brady said, brow furrowed.

"Toss me another tennis ball."

Brady grabbed another ball and underhanded it in my direction. I bent my knees, brought the bat back over my shoulder, rotated my hips, and sliced the bat forward, crushing the ball back toward Brady.

"Ahh!" Brady flinched backward, covering his face as the tennis ball zoomed past his head and smashed into the metal siding of the shed with a deafening clang.

"Never mind," I said, inspecting the bat. "I'm good."

Brady didn't seem a fraction as amused as I was. "You sure you don't get a bit of personality to go along with those talents? Some of those baseball guys are real turds."

I tilted my head, considering. "I mean, I *was* super full of myself when I learned how to bake bread that one time."

"Geez," Brady said. "You're brutal."

I smiled. I was pretty sure that I *didn't* get any personality when I took the talents; I think it was just that I finally felt comfortable. I'd spent so long living under the shadow of the curse that I'd all but forgotten what it was like to express myself. I had gone from one extreme to the other, from inhibited self-expression to one of near infinite possibilities.

"Okay," I said, leaning the bat on my shoulder. "What next?"

"Next," Brady said a bit warily, "we need to get you a bunch of awesome talents to make a video that I can post on my channel."

I tilted my head, looking at him skeptically. "We have to meet under a stage and in an old shed and now you want to jump straight to posting about me on TikTok?"

"We're gonna kill two birds with one stone here, Tiffany. We make your video for the planet aquarium—"

"Planetarium."

"For the *planetarium* competition, and after we post it

on my channel, you won't have to ask *anyone* to buy a raffle ticket. They'll be asking *you*."

However much I suspected Brady of having some ulterior motive, his solution just worked too well to turn it down, especially with all the time I'd need to put into finishing the planetarium exhibits. Plus, I'd give my left arm not to have to go door-to-door selling raffle tickets, and here he was promising that people would come to *me*. "Okay, so what are we gonna do for this video?"

"Leave that to me," Brady said. "I'll have a bunch of stuff ready for you to try."

I raised an eyebrow. "Stuff you got lying around the house, or stuff like your wristwatch? You know, stuff that your 'dad gave you for your birthday'?"

Brady paused long enough that I knew what the answer was already. "Help me understand the rules here. You're allowed to steal someone's talent and I'm allowed to . . ."

"Borrowing. I'm *borrowing* their talent. They get it right back."

"Okay, and I promise to abide by the same rules." Brady stood up straight and put his hand on his heart. "I will return anything I take once we are through, and talents will only be *borrowed* when we're pretty sure they won't be noticed. Deal?"

A part of me felt like I was making a deal with the devil, but if Brady was going to be out getting items, then he might be able to solve another one of my problems. "Deal, but I've got a couple of requests of my own as far as items."

"Anything. What do you got?"

I took a notebook out of my backpack and read from the list I'd prepared earlier. "I need talents from the following: electrician, welder, graphic designer, computer technician, plumber, painter, and someone who can lay carpet."

Brady's eyebrows shot up. "Is that all? You sure you don't want to build a rocket or perform brain surgery this weekend?"

"Maybe after we fix up the planetarium. Oh, and make sure it's not, like, an expensive item that you're taking, okay?"

"Any *other* requests?" Brady said with mock patience. "All the items don't have to be, like, a certain color or brand or anything?"

"Look." I shook my bat menacingly. "Giving you a list of items to steal, even if you *are* going to put them *all* back, already makes me feel more like a crime boss than I ever wanted to, so you gotta cut me a little slack here."

"I get ya," Brady said in a tone that showed he understood.

"We have a powerful tool here," I said. "Gotta be careful not to do more damage than good. We've only got a couple of weeks before the Shining Star, so hopefully that's enough time to get everything sorted out."

"You see." Brady shook a pointer finger. "That's where you're wrong."

"What do you mean?"

"The competition's already started, Tiffany. It *started*

when Candace saw you looking at that poster. She's already playing mind games, trying to intimidate you, get you to doubt yourself. It's why she makes little comments like she did before we met under the stage. That's how people like Candace *always* win, because she's always playing the game. You're waiting for the game to start and she's already five points ahead. Time to get on offense, Tiffany."

I scratched my head. I still wasn't sure about the history between Brady and Candace, but his advice did kind of make sense. "Okay, so what do you suggest we do?"

"After you showing her up when you took her singing talent and outshining her at dodgeball, I'll guarantee she's more threatened by you than anyone else in the whole school. Now we need to throw her off her game, have her doubting her ability to perform before she ever sets foot in that planetarium. We need to win before it starts."

I narrowed my eyes. "So what are you suggesting? I keep taking her talent or something?"

Brady shook his head. "I was thinking of just once."

"Once? You sure that'll be enough?"

"It will be if it's during the play tomorrow." Brady's smile widened. "Now show me what you can do with this basketball."

CHAPTER 20

Phantom of the Auditorium

my goal in tech crew had always been to make every performance as flawless as possible ... until today.

The play was in an hour, during sixth period, and I'd never been more nervous for a performance in my entire life. And I wasn't even the one in front of the crowd.

I still wasn't quite sure *exactly* how I was going to take Candace's talent at the right time. There was no final dress rehearsal or anything, and I needed an object that I could use to hijack her singing ability. I'd need to stay alert and have the guts to jump on any opportunity that presented itself, all the while not creating any suspicion that I was up to something.

Captain Hook and Tinker Bell passed me in the hallway. They didn't pay me a second glance. No one ever did. The second you put on one of those headsets and black tech-crew shirts, you blurred into the background.

My phone buzzed and I pulled it out to see a text from Brady.

I got the stuff. Come to my house after school to make the video. But for now: DON'T. BACK. DOWN. We win this round.

I stared at the words as I walked. Brady had hardly known me a couple of days, but he already knew me well enough to guess I'd be entertaining second thoughts about going through with this.

I turned the corner and skidded to a halt, my sneakers screeching on the tile floor as I nearly ran into a group of girls.

"Sorry," I said instinctively, keeping my eyes low as I shuffled to the wall.

"No worries," a familiar voice said. "We actually thought you'd pass right through us. That's what *phantoms* do, isn't it?" I looked up and blanched. Martina and the other two backup dancers stood shoulder to shoulder, taking up the entire width of the hallway. Their exaggerated performance makeup, Lost Boy costumes, and ultra-stylized hair drew an even starker contrast than usual between me and them. They looked like they were sixteen-year-olds going to the fairy prom, while my black turtleneck and jeans made me look like I was some dollar-store mime.

The other two laughed and for a moment I wished I *was* a phantom, able to just phase through the wall and disappear from view.

"Looks like you skid-marked yourself," Martina said,

smacking her gum and laughing as she pointed to the ground where my shoes had left a pair of black streaks on the floor. "And, oh my gosh, look at those *shoes*! I didn't know Walmart had a clearance section."

I didn't know stereotypical, pick-me popularity hacks were on clearance for three-for-one. I felt my skin heat up from ghost white to solar red. "Can I please get by?" I couldn't even meet their eyes.

They stood there awhile—I'm sure just to let me know that they were in control—before Martina finally moved to the side. "Just make sure you pull the curtain on time, Phantom."

I walked past them, trying with everything I had not to let my emotions snowball, not to give them any bit of satisfaction. You didn't dump blood in the water around sharks. You put pressure on the wound until you could seek medical attention and soldier on.

Then I felt it. Three taps on the back of my head. I froze. I didn't need to hear the chorus of cackles to know what had happened. I reached back and felt three sticky masses embedded in my hair. I tried to pull the gum free, but the more I touched the pieces, the worse they got stuck.

There was a life lesson in there somewhere.

I turned to see the three girls snap pictures of me with their phones. "Good thing you stick to the shadows," Martina said before all three disappeared around the corner.

I swallowed down the desire to cry and felt the emotion concentrate until it transformed into something else entirely: rage. I hated how people like Candace and her friends had this kind of power over me. How I could literally inherit a magical power from outer space and still feel less than them. I cracked my knuckles and took a deep, shuddering breath. Brady was right. "We win this round."

I stormed off, not knowing where I was even walking, just that I was walking with bad intentions and the power to do more than put one foot in front of the other.

"Hey, Tiffany, I was wondering if you could—"

I didn't even know who it was that I blew past. If it was important, they could find me later. I strode through the center of the hallway, propelled by some unseen force. I eventually found myself standing in the girls' dressing room, which was empty save one girl who was adjusting her pirate bandana in the mirror. I scanned the room until my eyes stopped on three identical duffel bags, each with a matching dance insignia stitched on the outside.

Bingo. I didn't even bother looking over my shoulder as I scanned the bags until I found the one with the name MARTINA embroidered on the side. I unzipped the top and grinned at a pair of white high-top Nikes. These girls thought always making fun of people like me made them strong, but they were wrong. It was their weakness. If you spent your life going around punching down at everyone you saw, you were eventually gonna hit the wrong person, someone who was in the right mind to punch back. *Ladies, you can beat a Tudwell up, but you can't keep a Tudwell down.*

I reached out and touched the sneakers. It took a bit longer than in times past, but I eventually sensed the talent. My eyes shot open and I stumbled back a few steps before catching myself and smoothly transitioning into a shuffle I remembered seeing on a TikTok a couple years earlier. I *had* it!

"Sick shuffle."

I looked up at the pirate girl, unable to suppress the look on my face like I was a toddler caught with my hand in the cookie jar. "Uh, thanks."

"I'd forgotten about that one." The girl pointed at my legs.

"Yeah," I said slowly. "*Just* remembered it."

"You know you got something in your hair—"

"I'm aware," I said woodenly.

"Oh okay," the pirate girl said. "Well, best of luck tonight."

I gave a small wave and then hurried out of the dressing room and back toward the stage, where my fellow techies were busy with final preparations. My heart thumped in my chest and my brain hovered in a haze of adrenaline. No going back now. The wheels were in motion. I'd made my move. I was on offense. Scoring points. I felt good, amped up. It was like I'd just chugged two of my dad's Red Bulls. I *floated* to my position backstage by the curtains.

I fiddled with the ropes and constantly paced back and forth as we neared the start of the play. I felt like I could bike up Galaxy Hill ten times in a row.

Actors and the stage-prop kids busied about, doing

last-minute checks and walk-throughs. I waited until finally, from the other side of the stage, Candace arrived. She was radiant. Sparkling fairy-dust makeup, stylishly unkempt hair, a formfitting dress of fake fur and leather. She was primed to steal the show, and I was primed to steal it from her.

Trailing behind Candace were her three backup dancers, looking for all the world like triplets, except in the way they carried themselves. I could spot it immediately. One was hiding something, or trying to, at least. It was a worry, that panicked worry you'd have in a dream where you were the star of a play and you'd forgotten all your lines. She'd try to tell herself it was just preshow jitters and that her dancing ability would come back. Because it always had.

"Not this time, sweetheart," I mumbled. I would have tilted my head back and let out a villainous "muahahaha" had I been sure no one would hear me. I checked the time and peeked out at the audience. Only ten minutes to go. My window for getting at Candace was closing. I marched over to the sound cart, grabbed a microphone, and walked it to one of the sixth graders.

"Hey, Dexter," I said, tapping him on the shoulder and holding out the microphone. "Can you go do a quick sound check with Candace?"

"Huh?" He looked like I'd asked him to go hand-feed the microphone to a *T. rex*.

"You gotta hurry. Parents are coming in and she's been super bugged about not getting the chance to do a last-minute check. Go be her knight in shining armor."

Dexter perked up at this and jogged the mic over to Candace. I watched from the shadows as she grabbed the mic, sang a few lines that sounded over the loudspeakers, then handed the mic back. Dexter stood there confused as to what to do next. He looked in my direction, but I ducked back behind the curtain.

"What was *that* all about?" Marco's voice came over my headset.

"Uh, just needed to double-check one of the mics is all," I said as if I was a bad actor reciting my lines.

"Well, keep it down," Marco hissed. "We've already got parents in the audience. We need to keep this thing professional. Seamless. You hear that, everyone? We're gonna make this thing *seamless*."

No, I thought as Dexter came back and handed me the mic. *We're not.*

I put the microphone back, but not before I sang myself a little tune. I could tell immediately that I hadn't transferred the same degree of singing talent that I had last time. It was probably because she'd only used the mic to sing a few lines instead of belting out an entire song, but I had a feeling it'd still be enough.

Within minutes, the seats were filled to capacity with students and parents, ready for Wyoming's most ambitious middle school rendition of *Peter Pan*. I hardly paid attention to any of it. Peter Pan prancing around in green tights, Captain Hook running away from someone in a cheap crocodile costume. It just faded into the background. Any opening and closing of curtains was done entirely by reflex—until we approached the Lost Boys musical number.

Peter, Wendy, and the Lost Boys retreated to the back of the stage as the auditorium lights went dark. The audience fell predictably silent. The time for second-guessing was over. I'd pushed this rock downhill and there was no stopping it now. The spotlight popped on, illuminating a perfect circle at center stage. I felt my heart in my throat. Candace walked into the center, grabbed the mic, and parted her lips. A note rang out over the auditorium speakers. A completely plain, mildly passable, slightly flat note. I peeked out and saw the audience collectively shift in their seats as if twisting their bodies could somehow bend the note back in tune. Another ten seconds of her singing and I gladly, most gladly, *never* more gladly, pulled open the back curtain to reveal Candace's Lost Boys backup dancers.

The two outside dancers strode confidently forward in rhythm, but Martina stood as still as a cornered mouse. After the first few moves, the other two dancers cast surprised double takes back in her direction, pleading with their eyes for her to move. I smiled as Peter Pan finally gave Martina a little nudge forward, forcing her to awkwardly shuffle over to the other girls with all the grace of my dad jamming out to Nickelback. She looked at her friends and tried to imitate their moves but only managed to crack one of them in the nose with her elbow. Laughter bubbled up from the crowd, and Candace faltered, a rare look of uncertainty twisting her beautiful face.

Desperately trying to keep up with her friends, willing her body to perform a routine she'd probably done a hundred times, Martina tripped. She stumbled forward, windmilling her arms as she tried to regain her balance. The audience saw it coming, the cast saw it coming, but Candace didn't. She was like a parked car on a railroad crossing.

"Watch out!" Mrs. Willard yelled from the audience.

Candace glanced backward just as Martina barreled into her, sending them both tumbling to the ground. It should have been one of those moments where I winced and turned away, overcome by secondhand embarrassment, but I only smiled and rubbed my hands together like some Disney villain. The music played on for a few more seconds until I heard Marco bark the order to shut it off, which was a small pleasure in and of itself.

I hung back in the shadows, soaking in the hushed whispers of the audience like they were my own standing ovation. "My power over you grows stronger yet," I sung softly. The Phantom of the Auditorium had come to play, and she had just taken the lead.

CHAPTER 21

Dummy

*O*nly a few days ago, it had been Brady standing on my front porch, and now here I was standing on his. The situation was very different, however. It was the afternoon, I was invited, and I was wearing pants.

I took an unsteady breath and gave a light knock on the front door. I fiddled with my hair—now in braids—as I waited. Even after freezing the gum and lathering my hair in peanut butter as soon as I got home, I had still had to resort to cutting some of it out before rushing over here. At least the braids hid the worst of it, sorta.

The door opened and Brady stood there, flashing his signature wide smile. "Way to win the round today, Tudwell. Video of Martina crashing into Candace is flying around online, and I can confirm that Candace is not pleased. I see you, uh . . ." Brady gestured to my head ". . . changed your hair."

"Gumbushed by the backup dancers," I said flatly.

Brady nodded as if it were a story he'd heard many times before. "Looks like they didn't go down without a fight. Come on in."

I followed Brady as we walked through his house to the back door. A pair of little Brady clones played *Super Smash*

Bros. on the living room TV while Brady's mom was in the kitchen surrounded by scores of mixing bowls, ingredients, and note cards.

"Oh hello," Brady's mom said, wiping her hands on her apron before she extended one toward me. She was effortlessly beautiful. Blond, thin, her face warm with expression. "I'm Carol. Sorry about the mess. I would say that it's rare, but this kitchen is always undergoing some kind of baking experiment."

"Tiffany," I said, shaking her hand. "Your home is perfect, Mrs. Northrup." Her expression deepened further, as if she'd just been handed the world's cutest puppy.

"That's very kind of you, Tiffany. Oh, and Brady." Mrs. Northrup grabbed her phone off the counter and tapped the screen a few times. "Your father sent me a text earlier. Wanted to make double sure that your make-up essay was done and that you'd already finished the extra dribbling drills he showed you. Thirty minutes' worth."

"Yeah, Mom." Brady took a short, calming breath. "He texted me as well. All done."

"Good boy."

Brady rolled his eyes and opened up the back door. I waved to Mrs. Northrup and went out into the backyard, which I instantly recognized from Brady's TikTok and You-Tube videos. A half-court-size concrete pad, complete with spray-painted basketball lines, took up most of the backyard itself. Two adjustable basketball hoops were cemented into place at either end, while the patio table and chairs were pushed off to the side next to a pair of expensive-looking cameras on tripods.

Brady shut the door behind me and thumbed back toward the kitchen. "What was *that* all about?"

"What do you mean?" I asked.

"I thought you were gonna shed a tear there for a second."

I gave a long, heavy glance back through the glass door. I didn't look at Brady when I spoke. "This might sound kind of weird to you, Brady, but I don't actually go into a lot of other people's homes. Yours seems very nice."

Brady shook his head. "Don't let that fool you. Most of the time my brothers are chasing each other with scissors and my mom's two steps behind with a wire whisk."

I let my thoughts linger for a moment longer on what it must be like to live in a house like this, with a family like this. I'd thought a lot about how things would be different if my mom had never left, if I'd had siblings and it wasn't just me and my dad. I hadn't really *seen* it, though, hadn't *felt* it until now.

"Come on," Brady said, pulling back the warm blanket of my thoughts. "We've got work to do." Brady grabbed two duffel bags from the base of one of the hoops and brought them over.

"Okay, this one"—Brady patted the smaller bag of the two—"is most of what you asked for, minus a couple things like the computer technician's keyboard. That'll be tricky."

"Thank you." Nothing made you feel quite like a spy-movie villain like taking a duffel bag full of stolen items.

"I'll get started on these tonight and get them back to you as soon as I can."

"Or not."

"What do you mean, 'or not'?" I said, a bit offended. "That was the deal."

"I know, but I was thinking. How cool would it be to have, like, a whole shelf or closet full of talented items? You'd be like one of those assassins in the movies with a secret weapons room where they have all their guns on display and select their favorites before a mission. You want to sing one night, boom. It's right there. Kick a soccer ball, fix your AC when it breaks, juggle bowling pins while riding a unicycle. Whatever. It could all just be right there. Weapons room, Tiffany. Think about it."

"I'm not going to have a closet full of stolen items from all over the city." Although it did sound *amazing* to have instant access to be able to do anything I've ever wanted.

"You could always just replace them with a similar item. I take a mechanic's wrench full of talent and leave a brand new one in its place. Problem solved."

"Huh." This Brady guy was slick. "Okay. I'll think about it."

"Good. Now let's get started." He took the bigger bag and unzipped it, pulling out objects and placing them on the patio table. A violin case, a paintbrush, a dart, a jump rope, a bow and arrow, a worn-out baseball glove, a Rubik's cube, a basketball, a deck of cards, a coin, a creepy-looking ventriloquist's dummy, and a huge zucchini.

"A zucchini?" I asked, scratching the back of my neck.

"It's for the deck of cards," Brady said, as if the answer were obvious. "Now that we've got Candace second-guessing her talents, and the whole *school* second-guessing her talents, it's time we move you in to take the spotlight. You ready?"

"Not really," I said. "But I don't think that matters much at this point."

"That's the spirit." Brady patted me on the shoulder. "I've got some stuff that should be fun to play around with for the video, and then I've got some other stuff to continue our experiments. What do you want to start with?"

I scanned the items and picked up the vintage ventriloquist's dummy. He wore a little suit with a bow tie and had plastic hair parted to one side. "This has to be the creepiest thing I have ever seen. Whose nightmare did you have to break into to find this thing?"

"Believe it or not, it actually belongs to my uncle. He still does shows every—"

"Who you calling creepy?" the dummy said, turning its head until its lifeless eyes rested on me. I jumped back, acting startled. "Have you seen *your* hair? When you were cutting the gum out of it, I think you could have done us all a favor and just shaved it all off."

"I'm so sorry," I said to the dummy. "I didn't know you could hear me."

"I'm *always* listening," the dummy said ominously, this time turning toward Brady. I knew exactly what sound substitutions to make to prevent my lips from moving when the dummy spoke. I knew how to speak from my diaphragm and force air through my nose to make the dummy sound completely different from me. The effect, combined with the right motions and personality from the dummy, made it seem like he had a life of his own. "I've heard what you've said about me, Brady."

"Okay, that's enough of that one," Brady said, putting his hands up as if to keep the dummy from suddenly attacking him.

"Brady." The dummy's eyelids drooped down before flicking wide open. "I will find you while you sleep!"

"Oh my gosh, Tiffany, stop it."

I burst out laughing as I put the dummy back on the table. "I think we've got a winner there."

"Yeah, that's a hard pass for me." Brady grabbed the dummy and stuffed it back into the duffel bag.

"You'll pay for this, Brady." The dummy's muffled voice seemed to come from inside the duffel bag.

Brady gave me an exasperated stare. "Are you done yet?"

I couldn't contain my smile. "I was just getting warmed up."

Brady shook his head and handed me the bow and arrow.

The next half hour was pure bliss. Each talent came with its own unique satisfaction. Seeing the arrow thunk into the bull's-eye from all the way across the yard, hearing the snap of the net on a swished three-pointer, the rhythmic tic of the jump rope passing perfectly under my feet and above my head, flicking the playing cards so fast that they stuck into the side of the zucchini. I wasn't sure if anyone on the planet had ever or *could* ever have done all these things in one afternoon.

After Brady said we'd gotten enough footage for his video, I started on a few of the experimental items he'd collected. The dart had talent, but it was fuzzy, too mixed together, used by too many people for me to grab ahold of anything and use it. The same was true of the paintbrush. It took me a while to dig out the talent from his dad's old baseball glove, but it was still there.

The violin was something special, however. It was mesmerizing. It was different from the guitar, more fluid. My whole body swayed to the music as I drew the bow across the strings, rocking more intensely with each emotional swell. The vibrations started in the instrument, but passed through my body as surely as they carried on the early evening air.

"Whose violin is this?" I said, holding it out and unexpectedly having to swallow down rising emotions.

"It's my aunt's," Brady said. "To be honest, you could probably borrow it for a while, as long as my parents don't see you leave with it. She doesn't really play much anymore."

"Why on earth not?"

"Car accident." Brady clicked his tongue. "Can't do much with her left arm anymore. She hasn't played it since I was little."

"That's horrible," I whispered. I could sense the years of practice and sacrifice she had put in to get that good. My heart broke for a woman I'd never even met. I reverently put the violin back in its case.

Brady shrugged. "Yeah, well, such is life."

I took a step back from the table. "We have to be careful with this thing."

"I'm pretty sure I could throw that case off a roof and it wouldn't—"

"Not the violin," I interrupted. "My power."

"Tiffany, as I said, we'll only ever borrow the talents when they're not being used and to stick it to people like Candace, who deserve it. Deal?"

"Well, who's that exactly?"

Brady looked at me in disbelief. "You're telling me you don't have a list in your head right now of ten people who deserve a bit of bad luck?"

Man, I really wish I was better at lying. It *had* felt awesome to get back at Candace and her dancers. "Maybe, but who are we to make that decision?"

"Who are we *not*, Tiffany?" Brady said, holding his hands out wide. "You just gonna keep waiting on life to one day teach people like Candace that she's not God's gift to humanity?"

"Isn't that, like, her parents' job?"

Brady scoffed. "Her *parents*? Who do you think gave her a thousand-dollar cell phone when she was seven? Who do you think allows her to Snapchat whoever she wants? Who doesn't monitor her TikTok? Who buys her designer clothes? Her parents enable this garbage. If we don't do this, there's *no one*, Tiffany. Before I go edit and post this video, you gotta decide right now whether you want to be a doormat for the rest of your life."

I froze, taken aback by his sudden emotion. Brady was right in a lot of ways, but I still felt like I was being pulled along by a swift current in a direction I wasn't sure I wanted to go. Things were finally happening for me, though, and I didn't think I could swim to shore even if I wanted to.

I locked eyes with Brady and gave a resolute nod.

"All right, then." He clapped his hands. "Next stop, stardom."

CHAPTER 22

Night Shift

The lights were off. Crickets chirped outside like nature's metronome as I lay in my bed and counted the glow-in-the-dark sticker stars on my ceiling. I already knew there were 143; I was just waiting for the signal that the coast was clear. It was a sound I usually dreaded, but tonight it meant that I could finally get working. After a few more minutes I heard it: the deep rumble of my dad's snoring.

I grabbed my duffel bag of items I'd gotten earlier that day and climbed out my window, jogging over to the planetarium under the cover of darkness. I might as well have been on the run after robbing a bank for how hard my pulse whooshed in my ears. I even wore all black. It just seemed to fit the occasion.

I used my spare key to unlock the front double doors of the planetarium and slipped inside. I kept the main lights off, opting only for the ones by the concession stand. I didn't want to draw suspicion if my dad happened to wake up to go to the bathroom or something and looked out at the window. Luckily, he had an early shift tomorrow and had, for once, chosen a reasonable hour to go to bed. It was only 9:15 p.m., which meant I had a solid five hours before I'd lose my talents at 2:22 a.m. and have to call it a night.

I unzipped the duffel bag and laid out the items Brady had gotten for me: a pipe wrench, a paintbrush, a computer mouse, some funky-looking pliers, and something that looked like a glue gun on steroids with a long length of black tubing coming off the bottom. How on earth did Brady get all these things in only a day?

"Well," I said, rubbing my hands together. "Let's see what I'm dealing with here."

I went through them one by one, picking them up and focusing on the object until I suddenly knew not only what it was, but exactly how to use it. The paintbrush was pretty self-explanatory. In fact, I was pretty sure he had just taken this one from Mr. Fritzberg. I wasn't sure how I knew, but it was almost like his particular artistic ability had its own unique signature. The pipe wrench was a plumber's, the mouse was from some kind of graphic designer, the pliers were an electrician's wire strippers, and the weird glue gun thing was a welder's MIG welding gun.

I slowly surveyed the planetarium foyer. In the low light, the contours of the sheets haphazardly covering the exhibits gave me a feeling like I was standing in a haunted house or a morgue. But there were no chills up my spine. I was far from afraid. I was the mad scientist here. I now knew how to bring almost every single one of these suckers to life. My only question was where to start.

The hardest part of the night was just staying focused

on any one thing. With so many new talents and passions swirling inside me, I wanted to give each one a turn. After testing, stripping, and terminating wires under the *Star Trek* console for an hour, I took a bathroom break, only to get distracted with working on the women's toilet. After pinpointing the problem to a leaking toilet anchor flange, I went to the foyer to see if Earl had a replacement stashed somewhere and caught sight of the blank wall behind the moon-walker exhibit. I *had* to do something about it. Leaving it blank would be like seeing a pristine blanket of snow and not jumping in to do a snow angel. I immediately broke out a pencil to quickly sketch the outline of a kid in an astronaut suit riding on the back of a rocket ship as it blasted through space filled with planets, aliens, and swirling galaxies. We had a few buckets of paint to choose from, but I was going to need a lot more colors as well as some better brushes to actually make it work. I could also speed up the process with a number of cleverly applied stencils, so I'd need to either get some or make some.

I hadn't brought my laptop to be able to mess around with graphic design, but I ended up walking around to each exhibit and sketching out what I thought were cool symbols and logos for each one. The welding tools were the only things I left completely alone for the time being. Welding out the moon-walker rig braces seemed like it needed an evening of its own.

I didn't know if it was my adrenaline or the passions connected to my new talents, but I didn't so much as yawn until the time when I suddenly had no idea what I was doing, right in the middle of twisting on a wire connector. One moment I understood exactly what needed to be done and had the talent to do it. The next moment . . . nothing. It was so strange not knowing how to do something I'd just been able to do. I could remember doing it, even still feel the satisfaction from doing it. I just couldn't actually do it anymore.

I checked my phone. 2:22 a.m.

"Looks like the night shift is over," I said, stretching both arms to the ceiling and twisting to pop my back. I cleaned up my various work fronts to leave as little evidence as possible that I had even been there, beyond the products of my expertly skilled labor, of course.

I went to turn off the light above the concession stand and looked over the exhibits one last time. I'd left notes on each exhibit requesting any additional materials or tools I'd need to finish the job and signed them "The Planetarium Fairy." There was still a lot to do, but in one night, with the right skills, I had made a serious dent in the to-do list.

"You know," I told myself, "I think this might work."

When my morning alarm clock buzzed less than three hours later, I had a *very* different opinion on the matter.

CHAPTER 23

Three Words

I was a zombie the entire next day. Every time I sat down, I risked falling asleep. If my head leaned against a wall or on a desk, it was automatic. Simon said something to me at lunch about costumes or something, and Brady sent me a text telling me the edits for the video were coming together nicely, blah, blah, blah.

I trudged through the hallway, staring down at my feet as they took me automatically along my Thursday route to my last class period. However tired I was, I was going to have to go back to the planetarium again tonight, and probably *every* night leading up to the Shining Star. I could try to take naps in the afternoons and evenings, but that didn't leave much time for school and actually getting ready to *compete* in the Shining Star itself. *One problem at a time, Tiffany*, I told myself. I just had to gut this out. If I could just hang on then it would all be over in a few—

A phrase from the surrounding hallway chatter hit me like a Taser. I stopped so hard my shoes squeaked on the tile floor. Three words I had been running from for two years like some escaped convict trying to ditch the FBI.

I'd done everything to leave those three words attached to someone who no longer existed, and yet here they were: "Ugly Cry Girl."

I panned around, trying to see where it had come from, not wanting to confront it, but simply needing to know. Ten feet away, two girls and a boy huddled around a phone, glancing from the screen to me as if to check that I matched the description on a WANTED poster. When they noticed me staring, they glanced away, doing a poor job of hiding their laughter.

I turned and hustled to class. *What was going on?* I took my seat and had no trouble staying awake now. Focusing on what my history teacher was saying, yes, but not staying awake. I noticed a few other students during class do the same thing: check their phones, look in my direction, and fail to conceal smirks and laughs. I shrank in my chair, nowhere to go or hide. I felt like a zoo animal.

"May I please use the hall pass?" I said, shooting my hand into the air.

Mrs. Schoonmaker nodded toward the door and I launched out of my seat, grabbed the hall pass from the wall, and slipped out the door. I briskly made my way to the bathroom to splash some water on my face. What was going on? As if in response to my question, my phone buzzed. I yanked it out of my pocket. A text from Simon. I read it under my breath.

You doing okay? I mean, who cares what Candace thinks, anyway? She's just nervous that Queen Astrid and the VGC are going to dominate the Shining Star, especially after her Peter Pan performance. Don't even waste your attention on it. Bees don't waste their time explaining to flies that honey is better than poo. I'm not exactly sure what that means, but my older brother told it to me once and it seems like it would apply.

I read the message a few times, then asked Simon what he was talking about. A few seconds later, I got a link to a TikTok posted from Candace's account along with a message from Simon that I should "maybe not read the comments." Not knowing what I would see, only that I knew it wouldn't be good, I took a deep breath and clicked on the video.

It started off with the original clip of me with my green hair, toilet-seat earrings, and bright Spider-Man tie-dyed shirt, reading my poem about Mimi. The video slowed down and then freeze-framed on the infamous "Ugly Cry Girl" still image. The foundation for so many memes and jokes, all at the expense of one of the most vulnerable moments of my life. I felt light-headed, foggy, like it wasn't even me in the video, or even me watching me.

"But where did she go?" the video asked before fading to black. Pipe-organ music faded in—*The Phantom of the Opera*. The next scene was of me the night of the *Peter Pan* play, turning around, disgusted look on my face as I pulled at the gum in my hair. It paused at the perfect moment to capture my contorted face, half-covered by a snarl of hair. "Ugly Cry Girl has come out of hiding to evolve to her next form: Phantom of Auditorium!" The video ended with a dramatic chord.

I numbly put my phone back in my pocket. I took Simon's advice. I didn't read the comments. I only saw that there were a lot.

How could I ever go back to class? How could I ever even come back to school or show my face anywhere when it was synonymous with a joke? When people looked at me and laughed?

I went into a bathroom stall, sat down, and waited for the last bell of the day. A flurry of students rushed into the bathroom and left shortly after. I waited another hour before finally peeking out, recovering my books and backpack, and making my way to the bike rack. I didn't so much as open my mouth to talk to anyone until that evening when a FaceTime call from Brady woke me from a nap. Looking at my phone before I answered, I saw that I'd apparently missed a few messages from him as well.

"Hello," I croaked.

"What ya up to?" Brady asked, far too upbeat for my current emotional state. He appeared to be sitting down at his computer in his bedroom.

"Hiding from a world that hates me. What are you doing?"

"Just about to post our video, actually. Wanted to give you a heads-up."

"I'm kind of done with internet videos of me for the day, in case you didn't see."

"Oh, I saw it," Brady said, not the least bit troubled. "Couldn't have been better timing for us, actually."

"Couldn't have been *better*?" I shot up. I usually liked Brady's relaxed attitude, but I could have reached through the phone and strangled him at that moment. "I was thinking 'never' would be better timing for me. Maybe you've never been down the Candace-viral-video road before, but I have. It doesn't end well. She wins. I don't care. I can't compete with someone like her, cosmic superpowers or not."

Brady motioned for me to calm down. "I've been burned plenty by Candace. In this case, though, this is a good thing. Trust me."

I clenched my jaw, forcing myself to match Brady's emotions. "Look, I've got a long night ahead of me of working on toilets and murals, so you'll have to forgive me if I don't see how becoming a school-wide laughingstock is a good thing, Brady."

"Two people." Brady flashed a pair of fingers. "Machine Gun Kelly and Eminem."

I raised an eyebrow to suggest that I was listening but had no idea what he was talking about.

"They're two rappers," Brady explained. "A while back, Machine Gun Kelly made a song dissing Eminem and then

Eminem responded with his own song dissing Machine Gun Kelly. Go see how many views those videos have compared to their other videos, especially Machine Gun Kelly, who is much less known. They exploded. People love good drama. They want to see the battle. She didn't mean to do it, but Candace just set the stage for us. All eyes are on you now, and this evening, with our video, we clap back . . . loudly. Again, trust me."

"Do I even have a choice at this point?"

"Not really," Brady admitted. "Go magically fix your exhibits. I'll do the same to your social life."

CHAPTER 24

A Star Is Born

Why couldn't we wear hats to school? Or, you know what, *masks*. A mask would be even better. Whatever would best hide Ugly Cry Girl from the world and the world from her. After yet another long night working at the planetarium, it was hard enough getting out of bed *without* the prospect of facing another day of snickers and stares. I thought about faking sick, staying home, and hoping the whole thing would blow over. But that would only make my situation worse. With all the late nights I would need to pull at the planetarium, it was going to be a struggle to keep up with school as it was. I couldn't afford to miss a day. And, to be honest, if all my efforts to try to hide from my reputation for the past two years hadn't worked, then I didn't know what another day was going to do.

I locked up my bike and stared at the ground as I headed into school, trying not to focus on the dread that bore through my stomach like a power drill.

"Yo, Prison Break!"

"Shoot for the stars, Tiffany!" Someone patted me on the back as I passed. I quickly inspected myself for gum or a sticky note or something before turning to see a kid I recognized from my art class, smiling and giving me a thumbs-up.

"You got my vote!"

"Save the planetarium, Tiffany!"

I looked around. Were these kids talking to me? They *were* talking to me. And the comments kept coming. It was like I'd come back to my hometown after winning a gold medal at the Olympics.

"Sick collab with Brady!" someone else said as they walked by. "Been holding back on us, huh?"

Brady. He'd done it. Just like he'd promised. Overnight, *literally* overnight, my social standing had gone from zero to hero. I was in the spotlight now. This was real. No need to hide behind a video game avatar or worry about what route I'd take to class. I couldn't have imagined there would ever be a reason for people to adore me, and yet somehow it magically came.

I walked through the halls, books held close to my chest, dressed the same as I always was, hair still in braids to cover up the chunks I'd cut out, and yet everyone treated me differently. Gone were the whispered snide remarks, the sinking feeling in my stomach like the curse was lurking behind every corner. I felt a thousand pounds lighter.

"I bow to you, Queen Astrid."

I spun to see Simon standing beside me and gently lowering his head like some monk in prayer.

"Oh hey."

"You were *amazing* in that video. Not that you aren't amazing *outside* the video—" Simon stopped abruptly, tilting his head quizzically. "Are you okay?"

"Honestly, never better. Why?"

"You look a little tired," Simon said, an expression of genuine concern written across his face.

"Just lots of late nights helping my dad at the planetarium. I'm good—*great* actually."

"Do you remember that one raid when we stayed up until five a.m.? We were stuck in the time loop of Cryzax, and you figured out that the only way to survive the anomaly was actually to have us all *die* in the Citadel of the Maker and then *respawn* outside the loop? That was so friggin' awesome. I'm just glad other people are finally waking up to what the VGC has known about you for a long time. Speaking of the VGC, we've been working hard, pounding the pavement. Sold thirteen raffle tickets for you. I've got even better news than that, though. Remember I was telling you yesterday about the costume? Well, I wanted to show you a couple sketches we have. We've still got over a week until the Shining Star, so we've still got tons of time to make it all work. You know what? Let's just chat it over with the group on Saturday, early afternoon, online. That work?"

"Uh, yeah, sure," I said, trying to keep pace with Simon's avalanche of words.

"There's a special questing event for the Vault of the Demon Queen that we can—"

"Hey there, superstar," Brady said, appearing at my side and playfully slugging me on the shoulder. "What did I tell you? Already got like fifty people wanting to buy raffle tickets for Tiffany 'The Talent' Tudwell."

"Seriously?" My face lit up and I turned to Brady. "That's incredible."

"Man, that is great!" Simon sprang back into the conversation. "Those raffle tickets can be a *real* pickle. Kept my oldest sister from winning seven years ago. We've been able to sell a whopping thirteen. I think it's awesome that you're backing the Video Game Club, Brady. An unlikely party coming together, huh?"

"Yeeeah." Brady drew out the word. "Love the energy. Hey, do you mind if I borrow Tiffany for a second? Thanks, buddy."

Brady didn't wait for a response and led me away by the arm, leaving Simon alone in the hall. I looked back over my shoulder only to see his expectant face disappear in a sea of students.

"That's gonna happen to you for the next little bit," Brady said, a sucker stick protruding from his mouth like a cigarette.

"*What's* gonna happen to me?"

"You know." Brady gestured over his shoulder. "The admirers. Come in all forms. Gotta take the good with the bad, the weird with the cool. Trust me. You should see some of the comments I get online. Lotta psychos out there, Tiffany. Lotta psychos."

"Simon's not a psycho, Brady," I said, trying to keep up

with him as we walked the halls. Now that we were walking together, people weren't just making comments, they were parting out of the way. They were stopping and staring. I thought I saw one person even pull their phone out and take a picture. Usually a very bad sign, but not today, not with Brady at my side.

"Yeah, it's hard to tell." Brady waved my comment off. "Hey, I was going to ask you. I think we should make another video."

"*Another* video?" I said. "You don't think the first one was good enough?"

"Quite the opposite," Brady said. "I think we should follow it up. Build on the momentum. I know how these things go, Tiffany. You gotta ride the wave when it comes. We can make this one more geared toward the planetarium, if that helps. Make one that should score you some serious points at the talent show. Plus, it should help us get even more support. I've got a basketball game on Saturday afternoon, but I'm free after that. You in?"

"Uh, yeah, sure. Of course, if you think it'll help," I said, both relieved and surprised that Brady wanted to do more stuff with me. "You already got more stuff for me to borrow talents from?"

"Working on it. You just show up and do what you do best."

"Sure thing." I probably had some big goofy grin on my face, but I couldn't help it. Brady made the first video because that was part of our deal. He didn't have to ask for this second one, and if he was asking, then I was answering, especially if it could help out raffle sales even more. "Oh, and we still need to work on my Q and A. I'm not sure I can borrow a talent for that one, so you'll just have to help me figure it out."

"Deal. I'll text ya later. Oh, and I got you a couple of things for your weapons room," Brady said, pulling out a pair of metal scissors and handing them to me.

"You got me a pair of scissors?"

"From the most expensive stylist in town," Brady said. "After the whole gumbush thing, I thought if you were going to be cutting your own hair, you might as well have a bit of help. And don't worry, I swapped the scissors out for a new pair. Doing it the right way, just like you said. She'll never know they're even gone. Just don't steal the talent until after six o'clock or there's like a five percent chance my mom could end up with a mullet. And I got you this as well."

Brady pulled out a makeup brush and handed it to me.

"Okay, now I'm feeling judged," I said, taking the brush. I mean, my hair was a wreck, and my makeup was more or less nonexistent, but other people weren't supposed to *notice* that stuff. And they definitely weren't supposed to *say* anything about it. But then again, if I had something stuck in my teeth, I'd want someone to let me know and hand me a toothpick.

"I just figured they'd be something any girl would want, especially since you've got the Shining Star coming up. For the makeup brush, just don't use it super early in the morning and you should be good. If I ever see my aunt looking like a clown, I'll let you know you used it too early. Oh, and I'm still working on a computer programmer's keyboard. I haven't forgotten."

"You're a regular Robin Hood," I said, pocketing the scissors and the brush. "Stealing from the talent rich and giving to the talent poor."

Brady nodded appreciatively. "Makes me seem very noble when you put it like that. And speaking of stealing from the talent rich, I was thinking about how we're going to go about taking Candace's singing ability during the Shining Star. What you did at the play was okay, but if we want to go in for the kill, then we're going to have to make sure she does a proper warm-up. One where she really puts her talent into it, you know."

"Yeah, sure," I said. It was hard to say no to Brady, to question his methods when he'd been so right about everything and helped me with so much. I knew that draining Candace of her talent was the smartest strategy to ensure she didn't win, to get her back for what she'd done to me, but something about it felt wrong. It felt like cheating, which may have been a bit weird since I was still going to use my cosmic ability to get talents, but there still felt like a difference between using my ability to get a talent and using my ability to sabotage someone else's. Even with Candace being as nasty as she was, there was something about "going in for the kill" that just wasn't . . . me. But then again, being me didn't seem to really work out all that well. Maybe I was due for a change.

"Candace is proving to be a bit harder to discourage than I thought," Brady said. "I was asking around at a few of the other businesses at the mall to see if they'd want to buy some raffle tickets. Almost every one of them had already bought some from Candace. She'd apparently been very convincing in getting people to believe that she'd win."

The bell rang and cut my conversation with Brady short. I thanked him for the scissors and the makeup brush, and we went our separate ways to class. This was all happening so fast. Less than two weeks ago, I'd been a cursed nobody. Now Brady Northrup was inviting me over to make viral videos and giving me gifts. And above all this, a viable plan to save the planetarium *actually* seemed to be coming together. I knew it was risky, I knew it was tempting the fates, but in that moment, I allowed myself to ever so briefly believe that I was going to pull this thing off.

CHAPTER 25

Planetarium Fairy

merlin?" I called as I came into my room. "Merlin, where are you, buddy?" I checked under my bed but found only a pair of old sweats and a lot of dust. Looking for Merlin was actually one of the main reasons I didn't pick up after myself very well. I knew how much he loved hiding away in different spots and I just couldn't bear the thought of denying him the pleasure. I opened my closet and noticed the top of my laundry basket wiggling.

"There you are," I said as I bent down and extracted him from his burrow of dirty clothes. "You are not gonna believe what happened at school today, Mr. Merlin." I took a seat at my desk, turned on my computer, and pulled up Brady's YouTube channel. My video already had twelve thousand views, and triple that on TikTok. I figured I'd add a few more to that total since I had some time to kill before my dad was done at the planetarium and I could sneak back in to work on another exhibit. I thought I'd finally try my hand at welding tonight. My dad had the Saturday morning shift at Best Buy tomorrow, so he wasn't going to be up very late tonight. I clicked play and watched my handiwork again.

"Hi, my name is Tiffany Tudwell. I'm representing the Video Game Club at this year's Shining Star fundraiser. But gaming is the least of what I do," I said in the video, before launching into a series of basketball trick shots, followed by playing the violin, solving a Rubik's cube while jump roping, hitting a bull's-eye with an arrow at forty yards, making a coin disappear, and finally throwing a bunch of playing cards into a zucchini. After watching the video several more times, I did what I had sworn off doing years ago and dared to read the comments on a social-media post about me.

> Dude, Nintendo girl got game!

> Wait, this girl goes to OUR school?
> Where'd you find her, dawg?!

> Should have tried throwing the cards with one hand, doing the Rubik's with the other . . . all while jump roping.

> Girl can solve a Rubik's cube in under a minute but can't solve how to do her hair.

I closed out of the screen. "Welp, back to never reading comments again." The comment only hurt because it had some truth to it. Having to chop out a bunch of gum hadn't helped, but my hair problems were bigger than that. I didn't like my forehead, so I had to cover it with bangs, but my bangs grew all weird, and it wasn't like my dad had ever had the money to take me to some fancy stylist to figure it out. I literally cut my own hair with the same scissors we used to open Amazon boxes, and it showed. Solving this problem was long overdue.

I checked the time: 6:24 p.m. It was probably okay to pull out the scissors Brady had given me, but I wanted to make extra sure. If this person was supposedly some high-profile hairstylist, then having them lose their ability to cut hair right in the middle of an appointment could be pretty devastating. The last thing I wanted to do was give my hair problems to someone else.

I bided my time by making a Friday-night bowl of ramen noodles and grabbing some extra mirrors from around the house and setting them up in the bathroom before finally getting the scissors out of my backpack at 7:15 p.m. Go time.

The talent in the scissors wasn't just fresh, it was also deeply embedded. It took virtually no effort to absorb the talent.

I stared at my reflection. I'd never really liked what I saw, but I'd never really known how to do anything about it . . . until now. *What* had I been thinking with this haircut? Even without having taken chunks out for the gum, it was wrong in so many ways. My bangs weren't straight, my hair wasn't layered right, it wasn't textured right, it wasn't right for my face shape, it wasn't *anything* right. But it could be fixed. There was enough stone here to make a sculpture. In fact, my thick hair was an advantage. I had tons of options.

There was no rush, no nervousness, just the methodic snip of the shears and hair hitting the floor. With each pass, more and more of my former hairstyle melted away, leaving behind something I'd only ever seen in a magazine or on the pretty girls at school, but never me. When I was done, I must have stared at myself in the mirror for ten minutes straight.

"Saturn's rings," I said in awe, tilting my head from side to side, half expecting that it was all the work of some beauty filter that would turn off at any moment. It was such an odd sensation. Was this the real me? In a weird way, it felt like some kind of strange betrayal of who I'd been before, but I didn't know why I should forever have to sport horrible hair. Why couldn't *this* be who I was?

I took a quick shower, dried my hair, and got dressed. I inspected the results again in my bedroom mirror, making sure it wasn't going to take some extra-special styling ability to look presentable every day.

"What do you think, Merly?" I asked, looking down at my rabbit. "Could maybe use a bit of my old green hair dye, but I think this will do for now."

A sudden snort sounded from the other room, causing Merlin to dash back into my pile of clothes. It was my dad's snoring, the signal that it was time to start the next phase of my evening.

"Merlin, it's time to move on from evening hairstylist to late-night welder." I paused, considering the sentence. "You know, I highly doubt anyone has ever said that exact phrase."

I grabbed my duffel bag, opened my window, and crept out toward the planetarium.

I concentrated on the bright, sizzling spark as it inched along in the darkness. It was like my own little star, created and controlled by my hand to forever fuse two things into one. I released the trigger on my MIG welding gun and watched through my tinted visor as the spark disappeared and the molten orange of the adjacent weld metal faded away. I lifted my welding helmet and inspected my work. There was something incredibly satisfying and even beautiful about making a proper, uniform weld bead.

"Tiffany?"

I jumped at the sound of my dad's voice and turned around, welding helmet flipped up, half-mask respirator covering my nose and mouth, and welding gun in hand.

"Oh, hey, Dad," I said, voice muffled through my respirator before taking it off and setting my helmet to the side. I knew my dad might eventually catch me in the act. *Just play it cool, Tiffany. What would Brady do?* "Whatcha doing?"

"What am *I* doing?" My dad couldn't have looked more dumbfounded had he discovered Santa Claus welding on the moon-walker rig frame. "It's one in the morning . . . and you're welding . . . with a new haircut."

I went over to the metal cylinder of shielding gas and twisted the knob closed. "Well, I'll tell ya this, Dad. I would have been outta here forty-five minutes ago had someone done an ounce of weld prep. A little wire brushing goes a long way to cleaning up some of this old base metal. And who set up your weld machine? Voltage was sky high, wire speed was almost twice what it should be, and the polarity was reversed. Can you believe that? Rookie mistake stuff, Dad."

"Tiffany." My dad stood there, unblinking. "I'm not sure I understood a word you just said. How did you . . . where did you learn how to do this?" He gestured vaguely at the metal frame.

"Oh, you know," I said, trying to play it off. "Picked up a little bit in tech ed at school. Knew you needed the help."

My dad shook his head as if trying to wake himself from a dream. "Has this been you the whole time? All this planetarium fairy stuff?"

"*Me?*" I pointed to myself and gave an incredulous laugh. "How could this all be me, Dad?"

"I don't know, Tiffany." My dad scratched the back of his bald head. "I also didn't know you moonlighted as some night-shift welder until about thirty seconds ago, so I'm thinking there might be a few other things I don't know."

"Okay," I breathed out. I didn't want to lie to my dad, but I didn't have to tell him the full truth, either. Not right now at least. "Look, even before Mr. Myers told us we needed to finish the exhibits, you were working yourself way too hard. The last two weeks have been ridiculous. I'm not only terrified about what's going to happen to us if we don't fix this place up, but I was worried about what's going to happen to *you* if you tried to keep doing it by yourself. I know you're protective of this place, Dad. You want stuff done a certain way, but I wasn't going to stand by and watch you work yourself to death just to fall short."

"You didn't have to hide it from me, Tiffy."

I raised both eyebrows, gesturing with the welding gun. "Oh, so you would have been fine letting me run the MIG welder on the moon-walker rig?"

"Okay," my dad conceded. "I see your point. And the other stuff? The woodworking, the electrical work, the mural?"

"The women's toilet."

"Aaaaand the women's toilet, apparently."

I paused, choosing my words carefully. "A bunch of people have lent their talents to help. I'm sorry, Dad, I just knew if I didn't do it like this that you'd try to oversee everything and end up working even harder. I'm just trying to help."

"Ain't that something." My dad pressed his lips together and shook his head in awe. "You know, it's amazing to see a community come together and pitch in like this. I know better than to mess with something that's working, so carry on, I guess. I won't look a gift horse in the mouth. Tell everyone thank you if you ever see them."

"I will, Dad," I said, breathing an inward sigh of relief.

My dad let out an extended yawn. "I gotta get back to bed, Sparkles. I'd tell you not to stay up, but I don't think you'd listen, and I'd try to give you some safety advice about welding, but I actually don't know the first thing about welding. So, I guess, be safe and I'll see you tomorrow."

"Get some sleep, Dad. I'll take it from here."

CHAPTER 26

Makeover

*I*t was close to noon before I extracted myself from my bed and staggered into the kitchen to make myself a very late breakfast. Even though my dad was at Best Buy and I would have the planetarium to myself, I couldn't risk taking any of the talents to work on the exhibits until night-time, so there was little reason to get going at a respectable hour on a Saturday. Plus, today and tomorrow were going to be my only chances to rest up. The Shining Star was exactly one week away, and we still had several exhibits to get up and running before then.

I found a sticky note stuck to an overturned bowl on the kitchen table.

"For the planetarium fairy," I read, lifting the bowl to find a stack of cold pancakes and four strips of crispy bacon. Every morning I had to remind myself that my lingering thoughts weren't actually the echoes from some super realistic dream. I was living this stuff. I really *had* been the popular kid at school on Friday. I had a viral video (well, I had technically had *two* of them, but I tried to forget about the first one). I had finally gotten rid of my awkward hairstyle, and I'd welded out the entire moon-walker frame and been caught as the planetarium fairy. My life was absolutely bonkers.

I finished breakfast, took a shower, and fiddled around with my hair until it looked halfway decent. Since I was supposed to go over to Brady's in the evening after his basketball game to work on the next video, I hunted around in my closet for the only name-brand shirt I owned. Shopping at Goodwill was like panning for gold; you did occasionally find a nugget.

I went over to my dresser and rooted around for the shirt before I saw something that made me pause: an old wooden jewelry box that Mimi had given me. I ran my fingers over the astrological Virgo sign etched on top, wiping off a layer of dust. I opened it to reveal a treasure trove of my old earrings. Anything from dangling tacos to little dinosaurs that looked like they were biting your earlobe when you wore them. This was a part of me I'd long since sacrificed, a part that Mimi had loved.

I sifted through the box, smiling softly at how absolutely goofy some of these earrings were. I went to grab a pair of orange glow-in-the-dark phoenix earrings, but stopped. I couldn't think of a single other girl in the entire school who wore earrings like this. That was probably a sign. Plus, what if Brady didn't want them in the video tonight? I was moving forward, not backward. "Maybe next time, Mimi," I whispered as I shut the box and returned it to its spot in my dresser.

I finally found the shirt, balled up under my bed. I sniffed it, shook out the rabbit fur, and tossed it in the dryer to freshen it up a bit. I went to the bathroom and poked around at my odd assortment of dollar-store makeup like I was a toddler pushing around vegetables on my plate. I had no idea what I was doing. Tens of thousands of people were going to see this next video, maybe even more than that. If I could fix my hair, then I could fix this. I went to my room, pulled out my special makeup brush, and got to work.

While I would have preferred to use something that wasn't off-brand makeup, it would have to do. The principles were the same. The lines I had to contour for my given face shape, the angle of the wings on my eyeliner, the color phasing of my eyeshadow, the smooth, light blending strokes to pull it all together.

"Whoa." I laughed, despite myself. Where my new hairstyle felt like it was fixing a problem, this felt like I was wearing a popular-girl costume. Did people actually do this every day? It seemed . . . excessive to me, but it was more in line with the kind of people I saw on social media, so it was probably the right call.

"I'm not so sure about this one, Mr. Merlin," I said, twisting from side to side to inspect my new face.

Merlin stared up at me and twitched his nose before taking a few slow hops toward my feet.

I looked at my phone. "All dressed up and nowhere to go until Brady's done with his basketball game. Unless, of course, I *went* to the game." I had never been to a school basketball game. In fact, going to *any* kind of school event (other than to pull curtains) had been strictly off the menu for the last two years.

I looked down at Merlin, his black eyes staring blankly up at me. "What? Why shouldn't I be able to go to the game? *Lots* of kids go to the game, Merlin. They do. Plus, the Shining Star is a whole week away. We've got plenty of time to pick a final talent and practice for the Q and A, so don't tell me I can't take an afternoon off."

I took one final look in the mirror and headed for the door when my phone buzzed with an incoming message. It was from Simon, reminding me of the online questing event he'd mentioned the other day. We were supposed to talk about my costume. I looked back over my shoulder at my computer and headset, then at the clock. I felt bad leaving Simon hanging, but if I didn't leave right now, then I wouldn't make the start of the game. I also knew myself well enough to know that there was no such thing as hopping online for just a few minutes, especially when Simon was involved.

"What should I do, Merlin? I haven't seen Simon in a while and I do need to talk to him about my costume. On the other hand, I'm all dolled up with my cosmic superpowers and I'm feeling brave enough to challenge the curse and go to a friggin' basketball game. And that, like, never happens. Ever." I mulled it over, tilting my head from side to side, weighing the options. I didn't want to miss either, but if I had to choose, then maybe I should strike the one iron that rarely got hot. I didn't *want* to leave Simon hanging, but it wasn't like he was hard to get ahold of. I didn't think he had ever taken more than about six seconds to respond to any of my messages, no matter the hour. I typed out a quick reply to Simon.

> Hey, Simon. Sorry I can't hop on right now. I had something come up. Let's definitely do something soon though, k? Don't level up too much without me.

His reply was almost immediate.

> Troll boogers! I know that not idly doth Queen Astrid abandon her post, so I hope everything is okay.

I read the text, then took a deep breath, trying to fold and contort my emotions into a position that wouldn't make me feel so bad. I glanced down at my rabbit.

"Don't you look at me like that, Merlin." He stared up impassively. "Things are more complicated now. I've got a lot going on, in case you haven't noticed."

Merlin bounded over and disappeared into a burrow of clothes.

"Conversation over, apparently. Well, time to go make an impression."

CHAPTER 27

Halftime Show

I entered the school to the sounds of squeaking sneakers and the murmur of a distant crowd echoing down the hallway. I still had five minutes to spare, so I knew they'd just be doing their warm-ups. I wiped my palms on the back of my pants and took a couple slow breaths. I was surprised at how nervous I was. What were the other students going to think when I just wandered in alone, all done up, looking totally different from how I normally looked? I didn't blend into the background like I used to. People recognized me now, for all sorts of reasons. Maybe this whole thing was just setting myself up for failure.

"Hey, I figured *you'd* be playing today."

I turned to see a group of three girls and two boys I recognized from school.

"Uh, no basketball for me today," I said. I never knew what to say when I was put on the spot like this.

"Maybe some trick shot for the halftime show," one of the boys said.

"I guess you'll have to wait and see."

They waved and walked past me on their way to the game.

That wasn't so bad. They didn't make fun of me or tell

me I looked weird or anything. Maybe I could do this. Marshaling my courage, I stepped into the gym. Other than in the movies, I had never actually seen a live high school sporting event. Students filled the bleachers immediately to my left, while parents took up most of the spots farther down the way. On the other side of the court, a much smaller group was gathered for the opposing team. Both basketball teams were in the middle of their warm-ups, taking shots and running quick plays. I had no idea where to sit, so I just walked along the base of the bleachers looking for an open spot.

"Prison Break!"

"Yo, PB!"

I looked up and waved randomly, not sure where the calls were coming from in the noisy gym. Eventually I found an open section next to the parents where I wouldn't have to awkwardly cram myself between a bunch of students. I took a seat and pulled out my phone, pretending to respond to about a dozen text messages that didn't actually exist.

The horn blared, and within a minute the game was underway. Brady was all over the place, hitting outside shots, driving to the basket, grabbing rebounds, making steals. It was interesting to see him play against other kids who were almost as good. I'd only ever seen Brady dominate in gym class and hadn't really seen him have much competition. By the end of the first quarter, our team was up by five.

"Tiffany?"

I turned to see Brady's mom sitting just a few seats down from me. "Oh, hello, Mrs. Northrup."

"Tiffany." Brady's mom threw her hand over her heart. "You look gorgeous, honey. Where'd you get your hair done?"

"Thanks." I flushed red. Getting compliments for how I looked was about as strange and foreign an experience as being suddenly able to drain a three-pointer. "I actually did it myself."

"What?" She looked around at her friends in amazement. "Well then, I'm overpaying for my stylist, let me tell ya. I might need to have you do my hair next time you come over for a video. You all ready for next week's Shining Star competition?"

"Still some things to work out, but Brady's been helping me, so I'm in good hands."

"Great to hear, Tiffany." Brady's mom turned to one of her friends. "Oh look, Sasha, Colton is going in for Brady."

Sasha, another pretty mom who could have passed for Mrs. Northrup's sister, shook her head. "Let's hope he doesn't just randomly act like he's never touched a basketball in his life like he did at the scrimmage, for Pete's sake."

"He'll do great, Sasha," Mrs. Northrup encouraged her friend. "I'm sure he's just adjusting after his last growth spurt. He must have shot up half a foot since last season."

My blood went as cold as deep space. I leaned over to Brady's mom. "I'm sorry, what was that about Colton and the scrimmage?"

"Oh, boys being boys." Sasha turned to me and rolled her eyes, talking to me like I was just one of the ladies. "He came home from their big scrimmage earlier this week complaining that he couldn't even dribble a ball. Airballed every shot, apparently. Coach benched him this game, and he's been all emotional about it. Honestly, Carol, Brady's just been playing better ball since coming back, and Colton was looking for an excuse."

My mind spun. How many basketballs had I touched? Every single one was draining *Brady* of his talent, right? Could Brady have been faking? But when did I take a basketball talent early enough in the day to mess up something like an afternoon or evening scrimmage? I thought through all the times I'd ever taken a talent.

The day in the equipment shed. He'd thrown me a basketball.

"Was the scrimmage on Tuesday, by chance?" I asked.

Sasha thought about it for a second before nodding. "Yeah, that sounds about right."

I bit down and ground my teeth. Brady had *used* me to outperform Colton at the scrimmage so he could get a starting spot. He'd lied to me. He'd played me and I fell for it. I completely and utterly fell for it. I immediately felt like the eyes of the whole crowd were fixed on me, like they knew what I had done, how I cheated Colton out of his starting position. I would have left right then and there had an idea not crossed my mind. I sat there, blood boiling, as I waited for the half to be over and teams to shuffle off to the locker rooms. I made my way down to the court floor and stood there, seething, biding my time until the teams came back out.

Eventually, Brady led his team back out onto the floor and began taking warm-up shots. I waited until a ball bounced in my direction.

"Ball," Brady called out casually, holding his hands up. When I didn't toss it back, he looked over, eyes flashing wide. "Tiffany, hey. Glowing up. Nice. What are you doing down here on the court?"

"What happened to Colton during Tuesday's scrimmage, Brady?"

For the first time since I'd known him, I saw Brady speechless. He actually stammered. He looked back and forth between my face and the ball in my hands like I was holding his child hostage. He tried to keep calm and spoke in a sharp whisper. "I can explain, Tiffany. If you just give me the ball back, I will explain everything after the game."

"Oh, I'm sure you will. Have a great second half, Brady," I said, pulling up and draining a three. The onlooking students burst into applause as I turned and walked out of the gym.

CHAPTER 28

A Little Bit of Faith

I burst into the house and ran straight to the bathroom. I washed my face over and over, scrubbing my eyes and cheeks until every bit of my phony, ridiculous TikTok-girl makeup was gone. I felt used, gullible, stupid. How could I have been suckered so badly and just blindly trusted Brady like that? Where was he getting off handing *me* a makeup brush? What about all those other talents I had taken? Were *all* his stories made up? What about all the tools I was using to fix the planetarium? What if the electrician who owned the wire strippers was working a night shift somewhere? Or the welder? Or the carpenter? I hadn't allowed myself to entertain those thoughts because I had trusted Brady, because I had been selfish. What emotional damage had I done to people? What physical harm had I caused? Who had I let Brady turn me into? I felt sick. I couldn't breathe. I needed air. I needed—

I dropped to my knees and retched into the toilet bowl until I got rid of every bite of the morning's pancakes and bacon. I flushed the toilet, slumped to the floor, and burst into tears. I couldn't do this. The curse had won. For years,

I had learned to stay out of the spotlight, work from the shadows, avoid attention. I'd changed my hair, my clothes, my activities, all so I'd avoid detection. I'd gotten good, and so the curse had to bait me with something I couldn't refuse. It gave me the one thing I'd wanted most: a taste of all the talents I had to watch others perform while I hung back behind life's curtains. And I had swallowed that bait, hook, line, and sinker. This thing hadn't come from Mimi at all. It was just one giant cruel trick, the ultimate checkmate from a wretched, cosmic curse.

I peeled myself from the bathroom floor, walked to my room, and collapsed on my bed. There was no way I'd be able to perform for the Shining Star. I already struggled enough with my confidence, but there wasn't a talent on Earth I could take now without second-guessing myself, without worrying what damage I might cause to someone else. And one of the worst things about it was that even if I knew who I had hurt, I could never apologize to them. How exactly was that conversation supposed to go with Colton, for example? "Hey, remember when you randomly lost all your basketball skills and then got robbed of the starting position you'd worked so hard for? That was me. I magically drained your talent through a basketball when I was mapping out my newfound cosmic superpower in the old equipment shed with Brady."

My pain and disappointment wasn't from knowing that I'd come so far only to come up short; it was from the fact that I'd climbed so high, for all to see, only to fall.

I'd allowed myself to think I could do this on my own, to have hope that a Tudwell could set things right. After putting myself out there, making a name for myself, letting the world see my shining star just like Mimi had wanted, I now felt like I'd built all my success on a foundation of lies and stolen goods. I never wanted to take a talent from anyone ever again as long as I lived. Which, unfortunately, meant one thing: the planetarium, my dad, my house, myself . . . we were all doomed.

It was times like this that you needed a very old and trustworthy friend. Luckily, I had three, and it was still visiting hours.

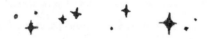

The back patio of Sunny Vistas Assisted Living was a pleasant area with umbrellaed tables, benches, horseshoes, a pickle ball court, a firepit, and two boccie-ball lanes. My friends sat dealing cards at one of the tables. Eleanor had a cup of tea, Frank a glass of lemonade, and Stefano a small cup of coffee.

"Eccola! Tiffany!" Stefano announced as I approached the table. After giving everyone their customary greetings, I pulled over a metal chair and sat down. "Your hair is bellissimo!"

"Thanks," I said, reaching up and touching my bangs. "I did it myself . . . kinda."

Frank plucked a card off the top of the deck and froze

just before sliding it over to me. "I'll deal you in as long as I'm not going to suddenly lose the ability to dress myself when I try to shuffle the deck."

"You have my word," I said, crossing my heart.

Frank nodded and dealt me into the hand.

"To what do we owe the pleasure, my dear?" Eleanor said, taking the tiniest of sips from her teacup.

"Tiffany does not need a reason to visit us," Stefano said.

Eleanor set her cup down with a clink. "She doesn't *need* a reason, but she has one today. Call it a woman's intuition."

I didn't know if Eleanor was just that perceptive or if I was wearing my emotions on my sleeve, but there was no reason to avoid what I had come here for. "I need some advice."

Suddenly the cards were forgotten and I had the full attention of the table. I recounted everything that had happened with Brady, the experimenting with my ability, the play, the video, my planetarium fairy work, and finally the basketball game. I rubbed my face with my hands as if trying to massage away my anxiety. "I can't do the Shining Star. I can't take another talent. I can't finish another exhibit. I don't know what to do."

"What are your choices, as you see them?" Frank said, leaning back in his chair and folding his legs.

"Well," I said, pursing my lips. "If I want to win the Shining Star, beat Candace, name a star after Mimi, defeat the curse, and raise enough money to save the planetarium, my dad's job, and our home, then my best bet is to patch things up with Brady and have him help me steal a bunch of super impressive talents."

"Sounds like a good option to me," Frank said.

"But can you not see?" Stefano said, pinching his fingers together and shaking his hands in his classic Italian gesture. "She does not want to take another talent. It has brought pain to others and would allow Brady to prevail. It would be a betrayal of her heart to use her power again."

While Stefano had definitely said it differently than I would have, he was right. Taking more talents to accomplish my goals felt selfish now. I was spreading my curse, robbing people, using them—like Brady had used me—to get what I wanted. Brady had convinced me that we could do it ethically, take talents only from the jerks and people who wouldn't be using their skills, but I couldn't trust that anymore. I couldn't trust *him*.

"You know, kid, life's a lot like cards," Frank said. "There's almost never a black-and-white decision. You read the field and you play the odds. Sometimes you win, sometimes you lose. If you have to play against someone like Eleanor you *mainly* lose, but you always have to make do with the cards you have. Now look here. You're going to give up on everything you and your dad need just because this Brady kid tricked you? You got swindled a bit. Good. Now you know better. Now you're gonna be a bit more savvy this next go-round. You don't learn nothing from the times you get it right, kid."

"I just don't want to hurt anyone else." I let out a sigh I

felt like I'd been holding inside my body for a week. "I just wanted to get rid of the curse and honor Mimi's last words to me. I just wanted to feel special, but now I've screwed everything up, and I'm afraid I don't have what it takes to fix it before it's too late. Maybe the point of getting the power was to resist it and not use it. It just seems like the universe is telling me to use it *and* not use it. I just don't know what to do."

I felt Eleanor's soft, wrinkled hand take my own and give it a comforting squeeze. "I think you're right, dear."

"About which part?"

She shrugged. "Maybe all of it. I don't know why all of this has come to you. But the only antidote I know for uncertainty is a little faith. You have a beautiful heart, my dear. It pushes you to save your father, connect with your grandmother, and not want to hurt other people. It doesn't seem like you can do all three right now. But I don't think this thing was given to you to torture you. Test you, per-haps, but not to torture. Stay true to your heart and have a little faith."

"So I just hang back and believe that it'll all work out?" I asked.

Eleanor gave me a warm smile. "I remember when I was almost your age, Tiffany. It was the beginning of the war. They were afraid the Germans would bomb our cities, so they rounded up millions of British children and evacu-ated us to the countryside to supposedly keep us safe and have us avoid the horrors of war. *Just* the children were evacuated, mind you. Our parents stayed behind to work. So there I was, all of nine years old, two hundred miles from home, clutching my knapsack with one hand and my little brother's arm with the other. They lined us up with all the other children, and the host families would come inspect us like puppies at the pound and then choose one or two to take home. I didn't know where I was going or if I'd ever see my parents again."

"That's horrible." My mouth hung open at the hardship Eleanor had to endure, and at such a young age. I would never complain about getting picked last in dodgeball ever again. "What did you end up doing?"

"I just moved forward and never stopped." She took another sip of her tea and patted me on the hand. "I needed faith, but faith without works is dead, my dear. Keep moving forward, Tiffany. Don't stop. Don't give up. Don't give in. And trust that the answer will reveal itself."

"That strategy hardly ever works when you're playing cards, by the way," Frank said. "But she's right. If you don't know what to do, then get busy on what you *do* know how to do."

I took a deep breath and nodded. "Well, the good news is that without being able to take anyone's talents, that should be a pretty short list."

CHAPTER 29

Call for Aid

*W*hen I went back to school on Monday, there was a part of me that wanted nothing more than to fade back to obscurity, for no one to notice me, talk to me, or expect anything from me. The shout-outs and compliments in the hallway and in class seemed like they were meant for someone else, someone I was ashamed I'd ever been. They were reminders that I'd not only been taken advantage of but that I'd hurt innocent people by being so careless.

Despite sending me sixty-four unread messages, Brady hadn't tried to come talk to me in person. I figured he'd gotten the message to keep his physical distance from someone who could remove his talents with a touch. I'd learned that soon after I'd left the game, Brady had "sprained his ankle" so he couldn't play the second half. The kid was clever, I had to give him that.

Every time I thought about Brady, I was tempted to ditch class, bike down to his backyard, steal one of his basketballs, and keep it so I could randomly drain his talent whenever I felt the urge. We'd see how much he liked the idea of a weapons room after that.

Brady's video had only gone more viral since the weekend.

More people had bought raffle tickets. More people would be there. This was all exactly what I had wanted, but only if I was anchoring it with a cosmically powered talent. Without that, it just served to set them up for a bigger disappointment and set me up for a bigger embarrassment.

But there was so much at stake if I failed. The planetarium, my dad's job, and my house, and yet all I wanted to do was curl up into a ball, close my eyes, and wait for the whole thing to pass over me like a bad storm.

After the final bell rang, I went to my locker to drop off some books and was met with a familiar voice.

"We missed you on Saturday, Queen Astrid." I turned to see a hesitant Simon standing next to me.

Simon. Just seeing him stung. If there was anyone I'd neglected and treated poorly by following and trusting Brady, it was Simon.

"I know, I'm sorry. I've just been super busy with everything."

"It's okay. We all just ended up getting mauled to death by a roving pack of dire wolves." Simon snorted. "Or at least half of us did."

"Actually," I said, "that's only a half-truth."

"No, we really did get mauled to death by dire wolves. I swear. You can ask Allison."

"No, I mean what *I* said."

"Oh." Simon blinked heavily through his thick glasses.

"Brady promised me a bunch of help with the Shining Star, and I got caught up in it and it turns out it wasn't the right kind of help, so now I'm totally behind, I don't have a talent, I'm going to be a complete disaster at the Q and A, I'm stressed out, I don't know how to help my dad complete the exhibits, and I might lose my house if we can't save the planetarium and I know you promised me a bunch of help too and I haven't been treating you right." I took a huge breath. "I'm sorry, Simon. You're a good friend. You've always been there, and I shouldn't have taken you for granted like that. I honestly don't deserve you."

Simon opened his mouth to reply, but my last sentence hit him like a phaser set to stun. He made a series of disbelieving grunts and croaks before finally forming a sentence. "*You* don't deserve *me*?"

"No." I shook my head. "I really don't."

"How could you even say that?" Simon looked around as if he was going to find a crowd of people nodding their heads in agreement. "You've helped me countless times. You remember the Butcher of Crow Haven raid? How I got taken prisoner and was bleeding out and the whole group was panicking, but you got everyone to focus and came up with the plan to use poisoned dragon meat to incapacitate the butcher so you could rescue me. Or the time—"

"Okay." I held a hand up. "Sure, maybe I've helped you in the virtual world. But coming up with a strategy to slay a dragon or solving a dungeon puzzle in a game isn't exactly helping you in real life, like, where it actually counts."

"Tiffany," Simon said, his expression somewhere between disappointment and disbelief. "The VGC is everything to me. You're the glue that holds it all together. You weren't there before you were there. Okay, that's kinda obvious, but what I mean is that everything changed when you joined the VGC. It went from chaos, every man for himself, to being a group that could come together and have fun and actually accomplish something. They're my clan, my crew, my people, my *only* people. I don't really get that anywhere else, Tiffany. Yeah, it's virtual, but I promise you it's as real as it gets for me and it actually counts." Simon gave a small pained smile. "Ah, I'm not making any sense."

It was my turn to stand there stunned. "No, no, it makes sense. I just didn't . . . know, I guess. Thank you for telling me."

He nodded and we both stood there a moment in silence, as if not to disturb this new layer of our friendship as it settled.

Simon was the first to speak. "So you still need help for the Shining Star?"

I gave a deep sigh followed by a desperate little laugh. "As much as you can give me."

"Our queen calls for aid," Simon said, his eyes narrowing intensely. "And the VGC will answer!" Simon thrust his finger skyward and I didn't even care about all the odd looks nearby students were surely casting in our direction.

"Let me guess. *The Princess Bride*?"

"That one's actually *The Lord of the Rings*. But close enough. So what exactly do you need?"

"Well," I said, scratching the back of my neck. "A lot."

"Don't worry," Simon said, unslinging his massive backpack and fishing out a notepad and pen. "I come prepared."

CHAPTER 30

Reinforcements

I was alone. In complete darkness and perfect silence. With the press of a button, the sky was dotted with twinkling stars, swirling nebulae, and the green spectral glow of the northern lights. I stood in the center of the planetarium's domed auditorium, feeling for all the world like I was in the center of the galaxy itself.

I tilted my head back and gazed at the artificial sky. A universe of hundreds of billions of galaxies, each filled with as many stars. It was impossible not to feel both completely insignificant and that there were an infinite number of possibilities beyond your wildest imagination.

"Mimi," I whispered. "I'm closer, but I still don't feel like I'm close. I've done what I thought was right, what I thought you wanted me to do. I've made some mistakes. And it's all gotten me here. I'm not seeing how it could possibly all come together, how I can fix this place, raise the money, win the Shining Star, but I'm taking your friends' advice and working hard, having a little bit of faith. They miss you, by the way. If you're looking for things to do and you've got anything left in your cosmic bag of tricks, I could use a boost this week. If not, that's okay, too. I just want you to know that I miss you and that I hope you've found your place in the stars."

I closed my eyes and listened.

There was no explosion of meteors this time, only the quiet, constant hum of the projector . . . followed by the distant sound of the front doors opening.

"Tiffany?" a voice echoed from down the hallway.

"Uh, in here," I called out, not sure who my visitor was. I waited in the middle of my projected galaxy until, a few moments later, Simon poked his head into the auditorium. "Simon?"

"Whoa." Simon's jaw dropped as he stepped into the auditorium. He almost looked funny without his shell of a backpack. "This is epic."

"Simon, what are you doing here?"

Simon got distracted looking around at the projected universe before finally answering my question. "I told you at school today. I'm coming to help." Simon looked at me like he was confused about why I was confused.

"I appreciate it, Simon," I said, glad that he was kind enough to show up, but unsure of what he'd actually be able to help me with. "I'll take all the help I can get at this point."

"Good thing." Simon snorted. "'Cause I brought reinforcements."

"What do you mean . . ." I trailed off as I heard the front doors again. I followed Simon out of the auditorium, down the curved hall, and into the foyer to see no less than a dozen other kids, all from the Video Game Club.

"All right, everyone," Simon said, clapping his hands together. "You saw the list from earlier today. No time for grand speeches and pleasantries. We've got work to do to restore the kingdom of Planetarium to a newfound glory. Cole and Sydney, grab your laptops and figure out how to program those lunar rovers. Eli and Zeke, I need you installing the rest of the touchscreen interfaces and troubleshooting any that don't work. Riley, can you see if you're able to take the sketches of the new exhibit logos and cut metal signs from your CNC machine? Also, keep an eye out for any other things you think you could make to spruce up the place. Liz, the mural is all yours. The rest of us, let's try to figure out this moon-walker rig. Let's roll!"

I stood there in stunned silence before finally reaching out and grabbing Simon by the shoulder. "They know how to do all this?"

Simon shrugged. "Let's see. Sydney and Cole speak C++ almost as well as they speak English. Eli and Zeke build battle robots and took second place in the university tournament last summer. They lost to a pair of girls from Gillette, but try not to mention it. Still kind of a sore subject. Riley makes a few thousand dollars a year running his own manufacturing business from his garage. You know Liz can paint, of course. She's in your art class. I've got Grant working on doing a few reedits on your video. What you did with Brady is beyond awesome, but from what I've seen it needs to match the theme of your club, so he's doing his best to put a video game spin on it. Every one of us is still pushing raffle tickets." Simon stopped and studied the moon-walker rig. "I've got no clue how that thing is supposed to work, though, so I guess we don't know how to do *all* of it."

"S-Simon," I stammered. "I don't even know what to say. I can't even begin to tell you how much this means to me."

"You know the VGC has your back. Oh, and I haven't even told you the best part. Your costume." Simon opened his mouth and then paused as if suddenly thinking better of it. "You know what? I want it to be a surprise. We've come this far without telling you. I can't wait to see the look on your face. Let me text Ben and Allison and see if they need me to take any measurements. Tiffany, I guarantee you are going to freak out."

I crossed my fingers it was going to be the good kind of "freak out." I was already nervous enough about having to perform a talent (which I still didn't have) in front of a couple hundred people. Adding in some random costume was sure to make it worse, but if Simon had a solution he wanted to surprise me with, then I was going to trust him. I owed it to him. He'd done so much for me. The least I could do was let him help me. *A little faith. Have a little faith, Tiffany.*

I glanced around at everyone working and had to swallow down my emotions. The *real* planetarium fairies had shown up. In a way, it was even more miraculous than what I had been able to do with my cosmic power. We were back on track. The wheels were in motion. Now all I needed was a talent. I still had four days. That was *oodles* of time to come up with something that I didn't have to steal from someone else. I mean, I hadn't really developed any talent the first twelve years of my life, but then again, I'd never seen meteors crash into each other until one day I suddenly did. Finding the right talent was bound to happen.

CHAPTER 31

Game On

*I*t didn't happen.

I mean, a lot of stuff happened. But coming up with some brilliant talent that lived up to the reputation of Tiffany "Prison Break" Tudwell was not part of it.

The VGC were miracle workers. They worked overtime; brought in friends and family members. Every time I set foot in the planetarium there were more people. By the time Friday rolled around, every exhibit wasn't just operational, but given a complete face-lift with professionally manufactured signs, LED lights, the works. We even got the moon-walker rig to finally cooperate thanks to Riley's uncle, who happened to be a crane, lifting, and rigging contractor.

It was all nothing short of a miracle, but there was still a problem: I needed another miracle.

I sat in my kitchen on Saturday morning, aimlessly stirring my cereal, feeling exactly like I had to take a test on a book I'd forgotten to read. The exhibits were complete, yes, but I was hours away from performing at a talent show with no actual talent. I'd spent the entire week trying all the talents I'd ever taken, praying there was some leftover trace of skill I could access. I managed to break the Rubik's cube in half, juggle an orange straight out my open bedroom window, break a guitar string while trying to tune it, and literally scare the poo pellets out of Merlin when I tried to sing (he still hadn't forgiven me). What I was left with for a talent was hooking up an old Nintendo and speed running the first few levels of *Super Mario Bros.* It had to do with video games, but I didn't think it was going to impress too many people. There was also the fact that even after hours of practice this week, I could only pull it off, like, one out of every five times I tried it, so I wasn't even sure it qualified as a talent.

The thing that nagged at me even more than not having a talent, however, was knowing just how easy it would be to ride down to the mall, swing by the guitar shop or Vinni G's (heck, I'd take Build-A-Bear at this point), and put together a performance for the *ages*, but I just couldn't bring myself to do it. I was stuck between betraying my conscience and being noble, between winning and choosing to lose.

About an hour before the competition started, I finally made my way over to the planetarium. Every step felt like I had lead weights around my ankles and an extra one in the pit of my stomach. Cars already filled the small parking lot and had begun parking on the surrounding dirt. *So many people.* I gulped awkwardly. Some of them were surely here to see Tiffany "The Talent" Tudwell do her thing. How on earth could I live up to their expectations without stealing someone else's talents?

I walked through the front double doors and was met

with a scene my dad had only ever dreamed of seeing. The exhibits were swarmed with people. Tables to the left and right were set up to both collect last-minute raffle tickets and display the prizes, anything from themed baskets donated by local businesses to space toys and science kits. Kids huddled around every touchscreen panel, playing interactive games, watching video demonstrations, and even controlling the lunar rovers. An intense competition was underway between four boys at the meteor-impact exhibit to see who could create the biggest crater by firing marbles into different types of dirt. And to top it all off, a long line wrapped around the moon-walker exhibit, where a young girl squealed with joy as she bounded into the air, assisted by a complex array of bungees and springs. The only louder laugh was my dad's, who currently manned the exhibit like some carny at the county fair.

"Hey, Tiffy," my dad called out, giving big, exaggerated waves as if I was spotting him from two hundred yards away. "Whaddaya think?"

"Pretty impressive," I said, walking up to the moon-walker rig and knocking on its metal frame.

"I just can't believe we pulled it all off." My dad beamed. I couldn't remember ever seeing him look happier. With the Video Game Club pitching in, I didn't feel the need to keep the planetarium fairies' work a secret, so my dad had actually worked alongside everyone nearly the entire week. "It's truly a sight to behold. Even better than I imagined.

Can't ever thank your friends enough. Now we just gotta raise the money."

"They were already having to park on the dirt out there," I said, motioning my thumb over my shoulder. "So that's a good sign."

"Indeed it is. Hey, you better get into your costume, little lady. It's coming up on showtime."

"I know," I said, checking the time on my phone. Where *was* Simon? "I've got a guy bringing it right now. I think."

"Well, I'm sure it'll be awesome."

I sure hope you're right.

"I gotta go double-check all the A/V levels soon. I got your Nintendo all linked up. You should be good to go. Good luck, Sparkles."

"You too, Dad," I said, giving him a big hug. However much this meant to me, I knew that pulling off a flawless event was everything to my dad.

I left my dad at the moon-walker rig and decided to explore a bit more as I waited on Simon. Toward the start of the curved hallway, a large poster displayed the contestants' names and clubs. A cappella, hunting, art, LEGO robotics, drama, debate, improv, math, and magic, and at the very bottom I saw my own.

"Tiffany Tudwell. Video Game Club," I read aloud.

I had been to events like this before, even attended a couple of the Shining Star competitions in prior years, but to read my name, to be part of it, to be *performing*, was the surreal cherry on top of everything that had happened since the meteors collided. The Tudwell name didn't belong on programs and poster boards, and yet there it was.

I eventually worked my way around the hall, turned into the auditorium, and entered a different world. Swirling nebulae of every color of the rainbow filled the domed ceiling while epic instrumental music played from the speakers. At the back and to either side of the stage were tall curtains rigged up on scaffold poles, behind which the contestants could presumably get ready and await their turns. Two huge rocket-ship props stood just in front of the curtains. My dad must have gotten some last-minute help to pull all this together. The tech crew in me appreciated the handiwork.

A girl in a full-size cardboard LEGO figurine costume shuffled up one of the aisles while a boy in a white Elvis costume was tuning his guitar to the left of the stage. I made my way toward the stage and bumped into another kid who was hurrying in the opposite direction, a coiled-up microphone cable in his hand.

"Tiffany? What are you doing here?" It was Marco from tech crew. "I didn't text you this morning to volunteer."

"I'm not here for tech crew, Marco. I'm a contestant."

His face corkscrewed in confusion. "You're *what*?"

"I'm a contestant," I repeated as if about to explain the word to a small child. I'd always been able to outsmart Marco, but I'd never been able to directly stand up to him. Today was different. Today, I'd finally been given the upper hand. "Must be weird taking orders from a Tudwell, but don't worry. My dad's got pretty high standards and stuff, but as long as you do *exactly* what he says and don't screw up at all, he's a pretty reasonable dude. *Super* particular about his planetarium shows, but a reasonable dude. Thanks, Marco."

I smiled and patted him on the shoulder as I continued down to the stage, leaving him speechless in the middle of the aisle. While I never would have purposely sought that confrontation out, it was the perfect little boost of confidence I needed heading into the Shining Star. Unfortunately, that boost lasted for all of about six seconds before popping like a cheap birthday balloon. Candace strode through the doors and into the auditorium like she owned it and everyone here was her guest. Like the other contestants I'd seen, she was already wearing her costume, which consisted of a lot of professionally done makeup, gorgeous hair, and an outfit straight out of a Lady Gaga music video.

She scanned the room and locked eyes with me. She could have been a murderous, starving lion and me a fatted, injured gazelle, and she still wouldn't have looked at me with a more predatory glare. I did my best to stand my ground as she stalked down the aisle and stopped in front of me. She looked me up and down with an expression like my mere existence was an insult to her.

"I know you're representing the Video Game Club, Phantom, but I don't think dressing up like a social reject is going to impress the judges very much. You know, if you want to make it super accurate, you're gonna need to get someone to throw some gum in your hair."

My mind went blank like someone had just shut off the Wi-Fi to my thoughts. This was no Marco. This was the final boss, and however much I had hoped I'd be ready to face her, I wasn't.

"I see that Brady's been using you for clicks," Candace added with a smile that stopped short of her eyes. "He likes to prey on clueless girls like that. I bet you felt *super* special while it lasted. Anyway, *best* of luck."

I felt my face flush hot with embarrassment as the beginning sounds of multiple words croaked out from my throat. I couldn't have frozen stiffer if I was having a conversation with Medusa.

Mercifully, my phone rang, giving me an excuse to break eye contact and walk off, Candace's chittering laughter pelting me from behind.

"Hello?"

"Ahoy, Queen Astrid!"

"Simon? Where are you guys?"

"We're out front."

"Thank the stars," I said, checking the time again. "On my way."

I jogged out of the auditorium, trying not to dwell on the encounter with Candace, trying not to think about Brady or how this whole thing would come crashing down and that I'd freeze during the Q&A, my talent would flop and that—

I nearly bumped into Simon as I headed out the main planetarium doors.

"We come bearing gifts," Simon said.

"Boy am I glad you're here," I said, looking over what everyone had brought. There was a cape, what looked like some kind of plate armor, a leather bodice, a golden crowned helmet. It all seemed strangely familiar. Then I saw the staff of twisted metal with a giant blue crystal shard on top. "Stars above. You replicated my *Warcraft of Empires* outfit?"

Simon smiled. "Down to the last detail. Can you think of a better way to represent the Video Game Club than to *be* your in-game character? To *be* Queen Astrid?"

"No, I honestly can't. It's perfect." My mouth turned up in a smile that matched Simon's. I reached out and took a pair of gauntlets that looked like they were made from over-lapping sections of weathered steel, but were actually foam. "How did you do this?"

Simon shrugged. "Ben and Allison are big cosplayers. They make these kinds of outfits all the time. We all pitched in and got it done. We would have been done days ago, but we ran out of Plasti Dip halfway through the main breastplate, and I screwed up on cutting out the forms on the last sheet of EVA foam."

I put my hand on Simon's shoulder. "Simon, I don't know what Plasti Dip or EVA foam is, but *you* are a lifesaver." I turned to the group. "You guys are *all* lifesavers. I seriously can't thank you enough. I don't deserve this."

"You represent all of us," Ben said, stepping forward to hand me my staff.

"And *all of us* should look awesome," Simon said, tapping the helmet he held in his hands. "Just wait until you see what Allison can do with cosplay makeup."

Allison leaned toward me and cupped one side of her mouth as if telling a secret but whispered loud enough for everyone to hear. "All of us also want to see you take down Candace."

Was I really about to do this? Transform into Queen Astrid herself to take on Candace Palmer? *Have a little faith, Tiffany.* I set my jaw and nodded to myself. "To all of us!" I raised my staff skyward. "Game on."

CHAPTER 32

From the Ashes

*E*yes closed, I sat on an overturned five-gallon bucket; the smell of toilet-bowl cleaner and recently used paint cans filled the room. We didn't want to overrun the only women's restroom with this big a crowd, so we'd opted for the storage room to conduct my little cosplay transformation.

"Another thirty seconds and I'll be done," Allison said, blending the makeup along my cheekbones with rapid back-and-forth sweeps from her brush. We'd been at it nearly thirty minutes, but it wasn't because Allison was slow. There was simply a lot to do to turn Tiffany Tudwell into Queen Astrid: the blueish skin tone, gemstone freckles, deeply shadowed eyes, dramatic fake lashes. They even used spray-on hair color to dye my hair green. Getting into my armor had taken a fraction of the time, although I did have an army of people to dress me.

"Five minutes." My dad's voice came over the planetarium speakers. "All contestants please report to the auditorium in five minutes."

Allison made a few last swishes with her brush and then stepped back. "There. Wish I had more time, but I think that'll do."

"By Grabthar's hammer," Simon said, peering over Allison's shoulder with the look of a father seeing his daughter in a wedding dress for the first time. He pulled out his phone. "Here, strike a pose."

I used my staff to stand up and blankly stared forward, not really knowing what to do.

"Oh, come on," Simon said, slumping to the side. "You look like Queen Astrid, now you gotta *look* like Queen Astrid. You know what I'm saying?"

"Okay . . . how about this?" I planted my staff and awkwardly put my other hand on my hip.

Simon snapped a few photos and excitedly handed me his phone. "What do you think?"

"Whoa," I breathed. I couldn't believe it was me. This wasn't some simple makeover. I looked otherworldly. I switched to the camera and held it out like I was taking a selfie, inspecting myself. "Allison, you're a miracle worker. I don't know how to thank you and Ben enough for this costume."

Allison gave a modest shrug, admiring her work. "The world needs more epic battle sorceresses. Just glad I could help."

I absolutely loved it, but the longer I looked at myself, the more I got a sense that something was just a little off. "Hmm."

"I miss a spot?" Allison said, quickly looking me over.

"No, no," I said. "This is *beyond* incredible. There's just something . . . missing."

Simon gave an uneasy laugh. "Tiffany, we pored over screenshots of your character for days making sure we—"

"Simon, this is *amazing*, it's just . . ." I turned my head from side to side and reached up to my earlobe. "I'll be right back." I hastily handed Simon my staff and made for the door.

"Where are you going?" Simon called after me. "It starts in a few minutes!"

"I gotta get something!" I said over my shoulder, hurrying as fast as my costume would allow. Cape billowing behind me, I sprinted out of the planetarium, to my house, up the steps, through the door, and into my room.

"Hey, Merly," I said, gasping for breath. "It's me, don't be alarmed. Just need to get something."

I went to my dresser, withdrew my wooden jewelry box, and opened it. "There you are." I reverently picked out my phoenix earrings and, with a bit of effort, forced them into my old piercings. Fiddling with my earlobes so much over the past two years must have helped keep the holes open. I turned and stared at myself in the mirror. The green hair, the blue skin, the wild makeup, the armor of a warrior queen. I had never looked more different, more bizarre in my entire life. It was quite the departure from my makeup when I went to Brady's basketball game, but for the first time in a very long time, I recognized myself.

I looked at my reflection and cracked a half smile. "There you are."

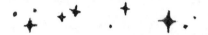

"Ladies and gentlemen. Boys and girls. My name is Chip McGee. You may recognize me from the Channel Five evening news, but I'm joining you tonight on a different assignment. I have the pleasure of being your emcee for the annual Shining Star fundraiser!"

The audience cheered while the other contestants and I waited out of sight behind the curtains. I stood straight, shoulders back, chin up, my hands clasping my staff in front of me. It was a confident pose, a *warrior's* pose. I never would have done it if not for my costume, but it would have felt wrong for Queen Astrid to slouch, fidget, or pace back and forth like the rest of the contestants—well, the rest except for Candace, of course. She stood in the shadows on the other side of the stage, eyes laser focused on nothing but me. With her perfect hair, perfect makeup, and perfect talent, she had an air of expectation about her, as if there were no other possibility than for her to get what she wanted. And why would she think any differently? She'd yet to go up against Queen Astrid, until now.

She narrowed her eyes and smirked, and I could almost hear her unuttered cackle. It was seared into my memory from every time she had bullied me, every time she had tortured me, from "Ugly Cry Girl" to "Phantom." I gripped my staff tighter, forcing down the rising urge to take Brady's advice and find a way to take her talent and humiliate her like she'd humiliated me. Heavens knew she deserved worse.

"All right," Chip said in his newscaster voice. "You want to meet our contestants? Huh?" The crowd cheered. "I can't hear you." The crowd cheered even louder. I'd seen the size of the audience, I knew exactly how many chairs fit in the planetarium, and yet every time I heard the crowd it seemed like thousands were on the other side of the curtain, not hundreds. I closed my eyes and let the nervousness wash over me. "All right, then. Let's see who we have here. In no particular order we have Mary Siggard, representing the LEGO Robotics Club. Jeremy Barrett from the Hunting Club . . ."

The real Queen Astrid would have been able to cast some kind of spell of enhanced focus or drink a courage potion, but it looked like I'd have to settle for several calming breaths. In through the nose, out through the mouth. In through the nose—

"Tiffany Tudwell from the Video Game Club."

"Huzzah! Huzzah!" The chant broke above the applause before I even made it onto the stage. I had never seen the planetarium so full. Every seat was occupied. People were sitting in the aisles and standing along the walls. Whether it was going to help me or haunt me, I had a feeling that Tiffany "The Talent" Tudwell had made an impression.

"And last but not least, Candace Palmer from the

A Cappella Club." Candace strode onto the stage waving like she'd just won Miss America.

The applause crescendoed, accented by a chorus of deafening, high-pitched squeals. Candace's squad was out in full force tonight. I was lucky that "volume of crowd cheer" wasn't one of the categories, or I'd have already lost, although I'd take my huzzahs over earsplitting shrieks any day.

"One last round of applause for our ten fabulous contestants!" The audience continued to cheer, and Chip stood there soaking it in as if they had all come just to see him introduce a bunch of twelve-year-olds. "Now that you've met your contestants, it's time to meet your three judges. We have Stephanie Downs, the first-ever winner of the Shining Star; José Lierow, author of *Astrology and Me: A Guide to Understanding Ourselves Through the Stars*; and George Grahams, professor of astrophysics at Ridgetop University. These three wonderful judges will be giving our contestants a maximum of ten points each per round and will be basing their scores on how well they feel the contestants represent their clubs and show the world why *they* are a shining star. Ten points for the video, costume, talent, and Q and A. For the raffle, ten points will be awarded to the person with the highest tickets sold and the other contestants will get their points relative to how many they sold. So, if the winner sells a hundred and second place sells seventy, then the winner gets ten points and second place gets seven points. Fifty tickets would be five points. Clear as mud? All right. Then let's move on to the first round this evening, and watch ourselves some videos. Hope you got your popcorn ready!"

A few sympathy laughs echoed from the audience. This guy's cheesiness bordered on cringe, but at least it kept me distracted. Shortly after he ushered us offstage, the lights dimmed and the first video appeared on the far end of the rounded ceiling, projected from the back of the room. It was Mary Siggard of the LEGO Robotics Club. The video started by showing how a variety of LEGO robots helped her get ready in the morning, anything from oscillating her toothbrush to spinning out three squares of toilet paper before tearing it off. It ended with a quick stop-motion animation video of LEGO characters getting into a rocket ship and taking off into space. Both the audience and judges loved it. It scored a 9.5. Apparently, Candace wasn't the only person I needed to worry about.

"Good job, Mary," I said, walking over to her and patting her on her boxy, cardboard shoulder. "That was super clever."

"Thanks," she said with an exasperated look on her face. "You have no idea how long that stop-motion part took me."

"It was really cool. I honestly don't know why you didn't get a ten," I said.

Mary looked around to make sure no one else was listening and leaned in close. "Stephanie Downs, that one judge who was the first winner."

"Yeah?"

"Candace's cousin," Mary said with the look of someone who takes pleasure in breaking news.

"What? No way."

Mary nodded her head, or at least the best she could with her cardboard helmet on. She was known to be a bit of a gossip, but if she was right about this one, my odds may have just gone from bad to worse.

With each video I saw, I got more nervous about my own. Simon had been right. The ones that stayed true to their club theme got the best scores. The a cappella, magic, hunting, music, and drama clubs scored the highest, while the math, improv, and debate clubs scored lower. No one got above a 9.5 and no one below a 5. Candace had scored a 9 on a super serious, highly stylized video that looked like a cross between a perfume commercial and a Billie Eilish music video. With my video being last, I got the sinking feeling that it was going to *be* last.

The familiar image of me holding a basketball in Brady's backyard appeared on the domed auditorium ceiling. I had seen the video probably more than anyone on the planet, and this was the first time it had ever given me a pit in my stomach.

"Hi, my name is Tiffany Tudwell," the image of me said. "I'm representing the Video Game Club at this year's Shining Star fundraiser. But gaming is the . . . gaming is the . . . gaming . . ."

I stood in horror as the video glitched over and over. The image broke apart and re-formed in digital static while the pitch of my voice modulated to a squeak, then fell to something that sounded close to Optimus Prime. I didn't dare look out at the audience, but I could just picture my dad bumping some switches or accidentally twisting some knobs on the control console. It'd be poetic for the curse to come back and have a Tudwell torpedo another Tudwell.

The screen went black and an indistinct murmur rose up from the audience just as two words flashed up on the screen.

GAMING IS . . .

"Huh?" I said out loud, despite myself.

TEAMWORK

The screen changed to a video of *Warcraft of Empires*. A party was in an intense battle with a giant three-headed ogre, and it didn't take me long to recognize that it was a screen recording from one of our raids.

"We're all gonna die!" Simon's voice came over the speakers as the video of his webcam appeared in the bottom corner of the screen. "I think we're gonna have to wipe." The rest of the team repeated similar dire comments.

"Hold on." My voice cut through the chaos. "I have an idea. Ranged weapons are actually doing some decent damage because they can reach the ogre's eyes. We need the paladins to fall back and cast every defensive spell possible on the barbarians so they can just keep sitting there and draw attention. Everyone else with a damage-boost spell needs to supercharge our rangers."

"Yeah, okay," Simon said. Others agreed, and before

long the giant ogre groaned, crashing to the earth like a felled tree. A chorus of cheers chanted "Queen Astrid" over and over. I smiled. It was one of the greatest moments of my video gaming life. Heck, it was probably one of the best moments of my life in general.

The screen went black again and more words popped up.

GAMING IS . . . FRIENDSHIP

"Anyone got a heal?" someone asked, their hit points critically low.

"I got ya," I said in return.

The clip changed.

"I'm getting overrun!" someone else shouted, their character backpedaling away from a zombie horde.

"I'm here," I said, Queen Astrid unleashing a concussive blast that knocked the zombies backward.

Several other similar clips followed in quick succession, someone expressing a need, me there to lend a hand. I couldn't imagine how much video Simon and the others must have combed through to pick out these moments. I had no idea how much highlights from a video game would impress the judges, but my chest literally ached with gratitude. It wasn't just that it gave me the best chance possible in this competition. It was that Simon had cared about me, appreciated me, seen something in me that I didn't even see myself. Maybe part of the ache was that I hadn't appreciated him back.

GAMING IS . . . LIFE

The video zoomed in on my character standing still,

holding her staff. The image morphed into a picture of me in my costume. The crowd did a little gasp at the similarity and burst into applause. How in Saturn's rings could he have done that so fast? He had taken that picture of me not thirty minutes ago.

Chip walked back onto the stage as he had done between the other videos. "I tell ya. I might have my kids play *more* video games after watching that. Am I right? Let's see what the judges say." There was a pause. I held my breath, closed my eyes. "An eight point zero! Good enough to be tied for third place with the Magic Club."

I was going to kiss Simon next time I saw him. Well, that might send him into cardiac arrest. I was at least going to give him a prolonged hug. I looked over at Candace and returned her scowl with a playful raise of my eyebrows. I was in this thing. I just somehow needed to figure out how to win a talent show with basically no talent so that my dad wouldn't lose his job, we wouldn't lose our home, and I could finally fulfill my grandma's dying request. No pressure.

CHAPTER 33

Visitors

*A*n eight point zero for the LEGO Robotics Club," Chip said, patting Mary Siggard on the back of her bulky, cardboard torso with a few hollow *thunks*. "With that score, Mary stays in first place, but we still have a few more to go. Up next in the costume round, we have Tiffany Tudwell from the Video Game Club."

I steeled myself, swallowed hard, and shuffled past Mary on my way up the stage. My costume was a bit restrictive with my crowned helmet, my staff, and the various layers of leather, foam, and cloth, but looking at Mary, I had nothing to complain about.

As other contestants had done, I walked the length of the stage floor several times, pausing at each end. The one part of the costume that I was glad Simon and company had *not* faithfully re-created was Queen Astrid's heels. I was trying to pull off a "super cool sorceress" vibe, not a "medieval town drunkard" impression. I eventually came to a stop next to Chip, where I raised my staff high and solemnly planted it on the stage with a thud.

"Whoa there," Chip said, jolting back a little bit. The audience burst into laughter. "Don't turn me into a newt! Am I right, ladies and gentlemen?" The laughter stopped.

This guy was the embodiment of cringe. "I've got to say, the attention to detail on your costume is exquisite. So, tell us about your costume. Where'd you get the inspiration? How'd you pull it all together?"

My heart hammered in my chest. Tiffany Tudwell would never be able to pull off a clever little conversation with Chip McGee in front of a crowd of hundreds. I knew myself too well to think otherwise. Luckily, I had a different strategy altogether. I hadn't come to the stage as Tiffany Tudwell. I had come as Queen Astrid. Only fitting that *she* should be the one answering the questions.

I bowed my head and paused before slowly lifting my eyes, never looking at Chip as I spoke. "The helm of champions was given to me as the sole survivor of the grand troll caverns raid. My breastplate was discovered in a treasure chest at the center of the dragon labyrinth. And the Staff of Eternity was taken from the innermost chamber of the Tombs of Endless Night. All obtained alongside my brothers and sisters of the Teton Raiders."

"Huzzah! Huzzah!" the Video Game Club chanted, followed by a hearty laugh from the audience.

"All righty, then," Chip said with a small laugh of his own. "And what about those fancy earrings. You got those from winning some kind of a wizard's duel, no doubt."

"I got these . . ." I trailed off as I absently reached up and stroked one of the phoenixes dangling from my ears as if I was rubbing a genie's lamp of old memories. "I got these from my grandma."

"Oh," Chip said, surprised. "Well, there you go. Not everything can be magical, I suppose. All right, then. Judges?"

The judges deliberated a bit longer than usual and finally held up a card. "A nine point five!"

My eyes shot open and I let out a very un-Queen-Astrid squeal. *A 9.5!*

"That's just fantastic. Thanks, Tiffany. Or should I say, Queen Astrid?" Chip gave a forced laugh and pointed off-stage, letting me know I could leave.

"Awesome job," one of the other contestants whispered as I walked back behind the curtain. A 9.5 would catapult me into a tie for first with Mary, for now. Candace was up next, and she strutted around like a runway model before ending her walk with a twirl. *Tryhard.*

"So, Candace, tell us about your costume."

"Well, Chip," she said like this was the hundredth time she'd been interviewed by the man. "In a cappella, you don't have any instruments to back you up. Your talent and ability has to stand on its own, which is exactly what all great singers have done. They're unique, they're them-selves. Madonna, David Bowie, Elton John, Lady Gaga, Bil-lie Eilish. While I look up to these incredible artists, I'm not one of them. I'm me. So, I wanted an outfit that expressed my *own* look. One that would make a statement, just like they did."

The crowd cheered loudly. Her answer didn't even mean anything. It was just well-practiced hot air said with a confident smile. I wasn't surprised when the judges came back with a 9.5 for Candace; I had just hoped to have gained some ground with my costume, especially now that the easy parts of the competition were over. I didn't even have to do anything for the video, and the costume was basically walking back and forth in front of everyone. The talents were next, and if I couldn't outdo Candace with this ridiculously awesome costume, then I didn't see how me playing a Nintendo game was going to do it.

By the time the remainder of the contestants showed off their costumes, I was tied for second place with 17.5 points. Candace was, of course, in first with 18.5. To give every-body time to prepare for their talents, the audience was treated to one of the planetarium shows, *Beyond the Milky Way*, projected onto the entire area of the domed ceiling. With nothing really to prepare, I just stood there, going over the first few Mario levels in my mind. I mean, if I actually pulled off a successful speed run, it could be pretty cool . . . maybe? Who was I kidding? I could have had an incredible talent, an *impossibly* incredible talent, but I'd chosen not to and now I'd suffer the consequences.

I'd seen the planetarium show a couple times before, but still found myself staring upward, mesmerized by the kaleidoscopic nebulae and galaxies. My dad had said to look to the stars for answers, but in a universe where there were more stars than grains of sand on Earth, the vastness of it all just reminded me of how insignificant I truly was, now more than ever. I wasn't a shining star. I was the blackness *between* the stars. I couldn't even win a local talent show after being graced with a cosmic superpower. What meaningful difference could I *ever* hope to contribute to the universe?

I stood there, wet trails streaking my blue cheeks, contemplating my place in creation as the other contestants readied set pieces or goofy props.

"Hello, dear."

I turned, quickly blotting my face with my hands, trying not to smudge my makeup. I recognized that voice.

"Eleanor?" I said. She sat in a wheelchair with Frank behind her. Stefano stood to the side, leaning on a cane. "What are you all doing here? How did you get out?"

"We don't live in federal prison, Tiffany," Frank said. "It's not *illegal* for us to leave. Sorry we're late. We're not the quickest moving crew, as you could imagine. And we did actually kind of have to escape. Not gonna lie."

"We came to see *you*, fragolina," Stefano said warmly.

"And to give you a few things," Eleanor added.

I set my staff down and gave them all hugs. "I appreciate it and all, I'm just kinda in the middle of something."

"We know, dear," Eleanor said as Frank brought around a large black duffel bag. "We brought a few items we thought you might find useful for the talent show, seeing as how you were so conflicted about stealing people's talents and all. We thought we'd offer some of ours."

Frank unzipped the bag and pulled out a pair of old black-and-white tap-dancing shoes.

"While I haven't danced in quite some time," Stefano said, raising his cane and shaking it, "these shoes should still remember a few steps."

"I'm not sure if these are going to fit, Stefano," I said, inspecting the shoes.

He hobbled forward on his cane and placed a hand on my shoulder. "Dancing is not in the shoes you wear, princepessa. It is in here." Stefano predictably pointed to his heart. "Take the talent. Your feet should know what to do next."

"You *sure* you're not going out dancing later tonight?" I asked Stefano.

He flashed a playful grin. "Relatively sure, yes."

I grabbed the shoes with both hands and searched for any trace of talent. There was nothing on the surface. If getting the talent from Brady's aunt's violin was like blowing off a layer of dust, this was like digging through dirt to find buried treasure, but after a while, I finally found it.

"Thank you, Stefano!"

I looked back to the duffel bag and almost passed out when I saw Frank pull out a full-size wood-and-metal rifle.

"You brought a *gun* into the planetarium?"

"Yeah, that part might actually be illegal," Frank said, scratching the back of his neck. "But it's not for you to shoot. A lifetime ago I used to be part of the Marine Corps Silent Drill Platoon. Lots of precise movements, rifle flipping, that sort of thing. I haven't even attached the bayonet yet, but if you're uncomfortable twirling around an M1 Garande in public, then just touch the gun and I'll hide it back in the bag. I'm sure you'll think of some way to put the talent to good use."

I hurried and touched the gun. Similar to the tap-dancing shoes, it took me a while, but I eventually found and extracted the talent.

"And last but not least," Frank said, pulling out a metal handsaw with a wooden handle.

I looked back and forth from the saw to Eleanor, confused. "Am I supposed to cut something?"

Eleanor shook her head and smiled as Frank pulled out a violin bow. "You're supposed to *play* it, dear. Life was very different when I was your age, Tiffany. The war was all around us. We had nothing. No food, no possessions, no home. We scrounged, we scrapped, we survived. The saw was my father's, found in an abandoned barn outside of London. The bow was in the bombed-out rubble of what used to be a music store. I'd seen a man play the saw at a traveling carnival years earlier, so I was determined to teach myself how to do it. In those days you were forced to make something meaningful out of tragedy. May you do the same, my dear."

"I don't even know what to say," I said, reverently taking the saw and the bow.

"Say nothing." Eleanor clasped my hand. "Now's the time for doing."

CHAPTER 34

Thirteen Steps

I stood behind the curtain, dressed as a battle sorceress, violin bow in one hand and an old saw in the other. Not exactly a position I thought I'd be in when I woke up this morning, but that's how life goes sometimes.

"All right, folks," Chip said, as *Beyond the Milky Way* finished and the lights came up. "Time for our very favorite part of the evening. The talent portion of the competition! The judges will be using three main criteria to determine their scores for this next round: entertainment value, in theme with your club, and raw talent. So, let's get right to it and see what you can do!"

Well, I could tap dance, I could play the saw, and I could twirl stuff with extreme precision. I wasn't sure how this all was going to feed into a "video-game-centric" talent, but at least I now had something to work with. Maybe I could twirl my bow and do a little dance, then end with a song. No, that would be boring. Twirl the saw? Seemed dangerous, but oddly enough it didn't *feel* dangerous. I guess Frank flipping around a rifle with a dagger attached to the end of the barrel was more dangerous than me with a handsaw.

I looked up at the stage and watched Jeremy Barrett of the Hunting Club perform a skit with a Nerf gun and his friends dressed up as a deer and a duck. It wasn't going over very well. Having talent was one thing, but knowing what to do with it in this competition was a different issue altogether.

Jeremy finally finished his skit, and Chip announced the judges' score of a 5.5. It was one of the lowest scores of the evening.

There were only two more acts until it was my turn. I needed to think. It was just like strategically using the different abilities in my party during a raid, except the abilities were all inside me, and instead of killing a three-headed ogre, I needed to impress a panel of three judges. Basically, the same situation, although I was pretty sure I'd much rather try to kill an actual three-headed ogre. I wondered if that would win over the judges. Epic music blasting as Queen Astrid squared off with a real live ogre. How awesome would that be?

"Oh, I can't wait to see this," Candace said in a low voice, looking down at the saw in my hand. "Gonna build something for us, Phantom?"

I glared at Candace, expecting to cower, to wilt, to freeze, but I'd leveled up since our last encounter. "Yeah, your friggin' coffin," I said, lifting the saw.

Candace's eyes went wide like I'd just taken off one of my gloves and slapped her across the face with it. She blinked hard several times as if trying to rekindle her shaken confidence.

"Whatever . . . Ugly Cry Girl. Hope you enjoy—"

I held up a hand to interrupt her. "Let me guess, *Candace*, you got some snarky comment about how you think my costume's dorky, or how I smell, or how my hair looks, or how big my nose is, or whatever. Well, guess what? I'm poor. I don't own anything. My mom left when I was five. I live in a trailer—right over there, actually. I have to cook my own dinner unless my dad remembers to microwave a hot dog, and most of my friends are in their nineties. If you want to pick on me to feel better about your perfect little life, then go ahead, but I don't envy you and I don't want to be you. For someone with such a beautiful talent that can affect so many people, you certainly are cruel. But I guess that's kinda the definition of a super villain, isn't it."

If Candace was surprised by my comment about the coffin, she was dumbfounded by this rant. Her mouth worked up and down for something to say, but what *could* she say? I'd just admitted all the aspects of myself that she could use to make fun of me.

"You're gonna lose the Shining Star," she finally blurted.

I dismissed her with a wave of my gauntleted hand. "You wouldn't know a shining star if you accidentally swallowed one and farted sunlight for a day."

At that, Candace scoffed and walked to the far side of the curtain.

I took a deep breath and blew it out. I'd finally done it. I hadn't backed down. I'd said what was on my mind, and I'd stood up to Candace Palmer. I felt electric, like I'd just beaten the biggest, most epic raid of my life.

"Hey, Tiffany, you need this?" I turned to see a giant LEGO person holding out my staff. It was Mary Siggard.

"Oh my gosh, yes. Thank you," I said, taking the staff. I had set it down to give Eleanor, Frank, and Stefano a hug.

"You and Candace really have it out for each other, huh?" Mary asked.

"You could say that."

Mary glanced back at Candace and leaned close to me. "Is it about Brady?"

"What? No," I said. "Why would you think that?"

Mary's boxy costume briefly shrugged up. "I've lived next to Brady my whole life and I could die a happy girl if he so much as remembered my name, let alone made a video with me like he did with you. The part I find odd is why Candace would care at all who Brady spent his time with after what she did to him."

I furrowed my eyebrows beneath my crowned helmet. "After she did what to him?" I didn't know why I even cared at this point, but it was something I had always been curious about.

"You don't know?" Mary's eyes lit up.

"He didn't talk to me very much about the past."

"Well," Mary said, settling into a gossipy tone. "You obviously know they used to go out, right? It was last year, before Brady had to spend a semester at Thunderbird. He and Candace used to cause a lot of trouble together. Dry-ice bombs in people's mailboxes, shoplifting, that kind of stuff. Well, they got caught and Brady took the blame for everything, guessing that Candace would think he was some kind of noble knight in shining armor."

"And I'm guessing she didn't."

Mary gave a sarcastic laugh. "That's an understatement. Not only did she just *let* him take the fall, she totally threw him under the bus. Wiped her hands of him. She blamed all her bad behavior on his influence so she wouldn't get in trouble with her parents, and got away without so much as a slap on the wrist. Meanwhile Brady had to go to court and spend a semester at Thunderbird, and he lost his spot on the basketball team, which, knowing how intense his dad can be, was probably the worst part. I'm not saying Brady didn't deserve what he got—he did some bad stuff—but Candace definitely *didn't* get what she deserved."

"Interesting," I said, finally taking my staff from Mary. This didn't absolve Brady from tricking me and using me, but it definitely helped me understand why he'd done it.

"Whoa, that's pretty awesome," Mary said, pointing to me. "You getting warmed up for your talent?"

"Huh?" I said, not even noticing that I was twirling my staff behind my back like Darth Maul with his double-bladed lightsaber. I looked up at the stage. It was the last act before I needed to perform. I'd gotten distracted with Mary. I never figured out how I was going to combine my talents. Then, like a shooting star materializing in the blackness of night, an idea flashed in my mind. I had maybe a minute to coordinate all the pieces. "Sorry, Mary, I need to do something real quick." I yanked my phone out of my leather satchel and ripped one of my gloves off with my teeth so I could fire off texts to Simon and my dad, explaining my idea.

"C'mon, c'mon, c'mon," I whispered, waiting for them to reply.

You got it, my dad replied.

Serious? Simon texted back.

"An eight point five for Kyler Dugan from the Math Club," Chip said. I was out of time. "Let's give him a round of applause."

YES, I'm serious. I texted as fast as I could, casting glances up to the stage. *Can you do it?*

I stared at my phone, willing it to send me the reply I wanted, the reply I *needed*. Three flashing dots popped up on my screen letting me know he was typing his reply. "C'mon, Simon!"

His text came through. *I've waited for this moment my entire life. Game on.*

I blew out a huge breath and didn't notice how much my hands were shaking until I fumbled putting my phone back in my satchel and slipping my glove back on.

"Next up in the Shining Star's talent showcase is the Video Game Club's very own Tiffany Tudwell."

"Let the world see your Shining Star," I whispered under my breath, and took the most deliberate thirteen steps of my life.

In a room full of hundreds of people, I could only hear the slight creak of the stage and my own heart drumming in my ears.

I was finally here, bathed in the spotlight at center stage.

The light might as well have been coming from the sun itself, warming a body kept far too long in the cold of darkness. I could see Candace out of the corner of my eye, off in the shadows of the curtains, but I ignored her. It was now my turn, my *opportunity* to perform. It had been only thirteen steps, but taking those steps had been a journey of a thousand miles.

I set my staff down and readied my saw in one hand and bow in the other. I looked around for a place to sit and finally settled for hanging my legs off the front of the stage. I clamped the saw handle between my thighs and grabbed the end of the blade with my left hand, pushing it down and flexing it inward to create an S shape. I took the bow in my right hand and placed it on the non-serrated back edge of the saw. After another deep breath, I looked up, locked eyes with my dad and Simon (who now stood together at the control console), and nodded.

With the crowd holding its breath, I ran the bow down the back of the saw. A ghostly, warbling tone echoed from the blade, changing pitch as I bent the saw up and down and ran the bow along different spots. I wasn't playing any particular song. I was conveying a mood, one of sorrow and sacrifice, one of yearning and struggle and, eventually, victory. It was Eleanor's story as much as it was mine. I could sense the desperation behind the talent, the hopelessness out of which it was born. It was more than just the ability to create music in a unique way; it was a statement to the world that one could take the ruin they were handed and return it to beauty. I was grateful that Eleanor had given me this lost talent to share with everyone, but I was even more grateful that she had shared a bit of herself and her history with me.

I fought back tears as I rang out the final note and waited for its echoes to be swallowed up by the planetarium's near perfect silence. I gently set down the bow and saw and returned to center stage to pick up my staff. I walked to the edge of the stage and gave my staff a few experimental twirls before returning to a fixed and readied position. Freshly recorded by my dad, the song I had just played came over the speakers, accompanied by Simon's overdramatic narrator's voice.

"There is a question as to whether heroes are made or born," Simon began as I broke into a freestyle routine of graceful footwork and precise jabs, spins, and twirls of my sorceress's staff. I had no idea how Frank and Stefano's talents would meld together or how it looked from the audience, but I felt like an absolute warrior ninja. "Whether they are called to adventure or call on others to join them. For Queen Astrid, battle sorceress of Triberia, conqueror of Lygore's champions, defender of the Pass at Parsinnon, chief strategist of the Teton Raiders party, the answer is simply . . . yes. Born to this world to lead, forged stronger by the trials of her quests, called by a higher purpose, and a banner around which others rally. Queen Astrid is the ultimate hero. A hero measured more by her scars than by her medals and trophies, although she has many, more by what she has overcome to reach her treasures, than by the treasures themselves. Behold! Queen Astrid, made flesh!"

I finished with a flurry of quick, spinning steps while twirling my staff above my head like a helicopter blade. With one final swiping motion, I froze as still as a statue while the last note of my singing saw faded away. The crowd paused, then exploded into applause.

I knew the cheering was for me, but I also knew that it couldn't *possibly* be for me. Tiffany Tudwell did not receive applause. She did not perform in front of crowds, stand in spotlights, and compete in competitions. But today, I was more than just Tiffany Tudwell. I was Eleanor and Frank and Stefano and Simon and the whole rest of the Video Game Club. And I had never felt better.

I dabbed the sweat dripping down from under my helmet and didn't bother repressing the smile stretched across my face. I looked up at my dad and Simon and mouthed the words "thank you" as Chip appeared at my side.

"Well, wasn't that something else," Chip said, clapping his hands. "I thought that saw was one of your fantasy weapons, am I right, folks?"

I raised an eyebrow despite myself and I heard only a single forced laugh from the crowd.

"And the judges give Tiffany a . . . nine point zero! Just fantastic. Great job, Tiffany."

Although they cheered the score, a distinct murmur bubbled up from the audience, punctuated by a few people calling out for a 10.0. A 9.0 was a great score, but I did have the feeling I'd been cheated out of a perfect score. I also knew it wouldn't be enough to gain ground on Candace. She was already a point ahead of me and we'd yet to do the Q&A, which would be my weakest event by a mile. I joined the other contestants offstage and was greeted with a series of high fives, open mouths, and pats on the back, from everyone but Candace, of course. She stood apart from the group, bejeweled microphone in hand, a sneer curling her shiny red lips.

Wait. Her bejeweled microphone. She had brought her *own* microphone. One that she was sure to have sung into a thousand times with the full force of her talent. All I would need to do was reach out and touch the microphone, and not only would she *finally* get what she deserved, but I'd be in prime position to win the competition. Brady's words from earlier came to mind. *If we don't do this, then there's no one, Tiffany.* Candace turned her back from me, getting ready to walk onstage. I inched toward her until the microphone was within reach. I could touch it without her even noticing. She was completely at my mercy.

I reached out but paused. No. I wouldn't use my power to punish Candace. I wouldn't use my upper hand to slap her. That was a Candace move. I wanted to use my power to amplify other's talents and connect with them. Plus, if she got up there and couldn't sing, that would be her excuse. I wanted to beat her after she'd given her best, not her worst.

A little faith, I thought as I put my hands at my side and watched Candace confidently stride to center stage.

CHAPTER 35

The Moon

Candace smoothly pulled back her glittering microphone as she belted the final note of her pop song. Despite how much I despised her as a person, there was no denying she was a rock star. I knew that better than anyone. I'd had her talent for an evening, after all.

The judges came back with a 9.5, putting her a point and a half in front of me with only the Q&A and raffle totals to go, and there was nothing my cosmic ability could do for me in either of those rounds. I was on my own.

Chip invited all the contestants up to the stage.

"All righty, folks. We've seen what our contestants can do, now it's time to see how well they think on their feet. Since we're running a bit behind on time, they'll each be answering one question that I'll randomly select from a batch of questions submitted earlier by the judges. The first question is for . . ." I held my breath as Chip reached his hand into a bowl and pulled out a slip of paper. "Jeremy Barrett from the Hunting Club. Jeremy, your question is . . ." He reached into another bowl. "How has being a member of your club changed your life and how has it positively impacted the community as a whole?"

"Um." Jeremy chewed at the side of his cheek and looked

like he was about as comfortable as a deer that knew it was sitting in a hunter's crosshairs. "I've always gone hunting with my dad. It's always been real fun and stuff. He's taught me a lot about, like, nature and the outdoors and stuff and how to, like, respect it and all that. We've been on a couple of hunts to cull coyotes 'cause they were killing people's dogs and cats and stuff, so I guess that's, like, good for the community because then people's pets aren't getting, like, mauled to death by the coyotes. And it's not a good death. Them coyotes are mean."

Chip held the microphone in front of Jeremy for a few more seconds to see if he wanted to say anything else. It wasn't the most polished answer I'd ever heard, but it was still ten times better than what I'd tried to come up with in my head.

"Thank you, Jeremy," Chip said with a broad smile. "I do remember hearing about those coyotes. Thank you for your service. Judges? A . . . seven point zero. Well done, Jeremy."

My stomach dropped, probably harder than Jeremy's did. I'd need to do significantly better than that to hang with Candace, especially since I was pretty sure her cousin had already fed her all the questions beforehand. I braced myself every time Chip pulled out a name. The Magic Club, Math Club, Art Club, and so on. Every time, I tried to come up with what I would say, and every time, my brain could barely cobble together a complete sentence, let alone something that was profound or impressive. The kids from Debate, Improv, and Drama had the best responses and earned 8.0, 9.0, and 8.5 respectively, but they'd still be several points behind Candace overall as long as she didn't completely choke.

"Only two more left," Chip announced as he stuck his hand yet again into the bowl. "Candace Palmer of the A Cappella Club. Your question is . . . with all the other great contestants on the stage, why should the judges pick you as this year's Shining Star?"

Candace tilted her head like she was thinking, but to me it looked like an actor playing a part. I was sure she'd seen this question before. "Thank you for the opportunity to answer that question, Chip. I truly believe that all the contestants here are deserving to be this year's Shining Star." She looked up and down the row of contestants while conveniently skipping over me with her eyes. "But, unfortunately, in the end, there does have to be only one winner. A shining star is something that all others look up to and many people follow. A star inspires us because of its beauty and its consistency. I've tried every day of my life to embody these qualities of a shining star. If the judges feel like someone else has proven a better representative than me, then I truly think they should be this year's Shining Star. Thank you."

The audience clapped and cheered, while the only thing I wanted to do was throw up, preferably all over Candace's designer shoes. What a load of garbage. She didn't hesitate, she didn't stutter, she didn't stop to think about what to say next. It was so obviously practiced that Frank could have figured it out with his hearing aids off. When the score came back it appeared that the judges *didn't* think that someone else was more deserving of this year's Shining Star. A 9.5.

An hour or so ago it was game on, now it was game over.

"And that leaves us with Tiffany Tudwell from the Video Game Club. Your question is: What does it mean to you for someone 'to be a shining star'?"

Chip held the microphone a foot in front of my face. There was nothing in my brain. I was standing in my house with no pants on looking at Brady through the screen door. "Well, um. Thanks for that question, Chip." The microphone cut out on the last two words. Chip pulled it back and tapped on the top a few times, a thump only coming over the speakers once.

"Looks like it's dead," he called out, holding up the microphone.

Divine intervention. I had a few more seconds to think, or maybe *all* the microphones would be dead. Wouldn't that be great? *Welp, can't answer the question, better just give her an awesome score and wave her through to the raffle. Crap, I should be thinking of my answer.*

Before I knew it, another microphone was held out in front of my face, but it wasn't Chip who held it.

"Here, Sparkles," my dad said softly. "This one should work better for you."

I pulled out of my stupor and hesitantly took the microphone from my dad. I stared at it. It was an older model, dented on top with scratches along its black paint. On the side of the handle was a word attached with a label-maker sticker: Tudwell. I looked up at my dad, who smiled and gave me a knowing nod.

I briefly closed my eyes and probed my dad's personal

microphone for any talent. It was everywhere. I didn't have to *find* it, I couldn't *avoid* it. If the talent in Eleanor's handsaw had tasted of sorrow, desperation, and hope, this was of passion, wonder, and solace. In that moment, I understood my dad, I *empathized* with him. I felt how he loved connecting with people through his planetarium shows and sharing his passions with them, how he *needed* this connection after my mom left. He wasn't wasting his life away at the planetarium. He was rebuilding it. He was giving it meaning. I had known these things, but never understood them, never felt them, until now. It took everything in my soul not to be completely overcome by the moment.

I absorbed the talent and stood up straight. It was no longer a matter of answering the question, it was a matter of narrowing down which answer I wanted to give. I didn't bother handing the microphone to Chip and immediately felt all the muscles in my body relax as I paced the stage. "You know, Chip, Candace wasn't wrong when she talked about the consistency of stars. For us, the stars are unwavering, a nightly guidepost as we humans hurl our way through the cosmos. We have *always* looked to the stars for answers. For direction during long and perilous voyages, for structure when developing our calendars to allow for farming and food cultivation. In a similar way, I have also always looked to the stars, but not by glancing up. The shining stars, the bright lights in the darkness, the guideposts, the structure, the help, have been the *people* in my life. I'm not sure I always realized it, but I do now. My friends, young and old. My dad.

My grandma. *They're* my shining stars. I'm just the moon, only visible because of their reflected light. Thank you."

As I lowered the microphone, I knew that whatever happened with the rest of the competition, my curse was over. I would still have problems, things still wouldn't go my way, but the curse of feeling alone and unwanted and a laughingstock was no more.

It seemed like the whole audience didn't even dare to breathe as I handed the microphone over to Chip, who, for once, appeared speechless.

"Uh, thank you, Tiffany. That was great. Let's see what the judges say." The three judges leaned their heads together and deliberated for the longest time yet. While I wanted a good score, I *needed* a good score, I was at peace with whatever happened.

"A perfect ten!" Chip said, as the judges held up the number for the first time in the competition. "Just fantastic."

I couldn't believe it. On my worst and most dreaded category. A perfect score. It was an impossibility and yet it had happened. I could still win.

I didn't even bother looking over at Candace. I could feel the lasers from her eyeballs boring a hole in the side of my head. She was now only one point ahead of me. It was all down to the raffle tickets. I'd need to beat her by at least one and a half points to win outright. If I sold the most, I'd get a 10. Everyone else's score would be based on how much they sold compared to me. So if I wanted to beat her, she'd have to have less than 85 percent of my total.

I pulled out my phone and texted Simon, asking how many tickets the VGC had managed to sell.

> We gave it our all, my queen. 160 was the final count.

Holy Stardust. The VGC had come through huge. It wasn't the astronomical 375 my dad had figured we'd need, but I knew Candace would manage to sell above-average quantities as well. I'd just have to trust that together as a group of contestants our raffle ticket sales numbers would work out.

I typed in 85 percent of 160. It was 136. I typed a few more numbers in. I wasn't sure how they rounded up the point totals but it looked like if Candace got anything above 152, then she'd win. If she got anything less than 136, then I'd win. Anything in between would be some sort of tie. There was nothing I could do now but wait.

"All right, folks," Chip announced. "We've come to the final part of the evening: the raffle-ticket count! Here, contestants receive a final score based on how many raffle tickets they've sold. If you've purchased any raffle tickets, then make sure to hang on to your numbers. We'll be doing the drawing for prizes immediately after the program. And remember, if you bought a raffle ticket from the winning contestant, then your name will be put in five times for every ticket! Hope you all backed the right horse. Are you ready to find out who will be crowned this year's Shining Star?"

CHAPTER 36

The Shining Star

I shifted from one foot to the other, my knuckles turning white as I clenched my staff. While I finally felt free of my curse, I also now understood with perfect clarity after taking my dad's talent just how much he depended on the planetarium. I'd fallen short of the 375, but if the other contestants pulled their weight, if they came up big, we could still do this thing. We just had to work together.

"And in tenth place, Dylan Macdonald of the Debate Club with seven tickets."

Crud.

"*Seven* tickets?" someone who sounded a lot like Simon blurted from the crowd in disbelief. Dylan went bright red and the whole audience burst into laughter.

"Now, now," Chip said, waggling a finger. "All proceeds go toward funding great planetarium shows like the one we saw earlier. Every bit counts."

Apparently some bits more than others, Chip.

The other totals were read out and their numbers slowly climbed up, but they weren't groundbreaking. Nineteen, twenty-seven, forty-two, fifty-nine. It was adding up but not to a record-breaking sum. As the numbers came in, I came to the horrible realization that the only way to reach the number we needed to save the planetarium was actually for Candace to blow me out of the water. I wouldn't win, I wouldn't give Mimi her place in the stars, but if Candace were to pull off some enormous number, then at least the money would be raised. She, yet again, wouldn't learn her lesson, but it looked like I could either win this thing and lose the planetarium or lose the Shining Star and maybe keep the planetarium. If the cost of saving the planetarium was swallowing my pride, then so be it.

"And now we're down to three!" Chip said. The other contestants had been dismissed from the stage as their numbers were read. Me, Mary Siggard, and Candace. "In third place is Mary Siggard from the LEGO Robotics Club with a staggering ninety-six tickets! Very close to our all-time high!"

Mary waved to the audience and waddled off the stage.

"And wouldn't you know," Chip said, scanning me and Candace. "The final two are also currently in first and second place. This competition is coming down to the wire."

I went over the numbers again and again in my head. To win outright, I'd need Candace to get less than 136. For her to win outright, she'd need more than 152, but if she was going to beat me, I wanted her to beat me big to raise as much money as possible. Otherwise, it'd just be adding insult to injury.

"And in second place"—Chip did a little drumroll noise with his tongue—"is Candace Palmer with a whopping one hundred and fifty-five tickets, which is by far the most of any contestant in Shining Star history!"

Candace forced a smile, not knowing if this meant she'd actually lost. I forced a smile because I knew she'd actually won, and it was the worst possible outcome. Mimi would not get her place in the stars. The new star would be Candace's to name. The thought made me queasy. What did Candace know and appreciate about the stars? Having her stake her claim among the cosmos felt as right as someone building a McDonald's in the Vatican. To rub it in further, I knew the money wasn't going to be enough to get my dad the time he needed. I'd worked so hard on the exhibits, *we'd* worked so hard on the exhibits, but in the end, we'd have to pull the plug on this place. One month, six months, I didn't know. I just knew I'd come up short.

"And if Candace broke the Shining Star record for raffle tickets, I bet we're all curious to see what Tiffany was able to do. Well, brace yourselves, folks, because Tiffany from the Video Game Club was able to sell an *astronomical . . .*"

One hundred and sixty tickets, I finished Chip's sentence in my mind.

"Four hundred and forty-six tickets!"

I breathed out a disappointing sigh . . . *Wait, what?*

"Looks like Professor Braithwait is going to have to break out the ol' checkbook, because with that absolutely impossible sum of tickets, Tiffany Tudwell of the Video Game Club has officially won the Shining Star competition!"

The audience erupted in cheers and applause as Candace

stormed off the stage. I stood numbly, grasping my staff to keep from toppling over in shock. What had happened? How was this possible? What was going on? The other contestants appeared at my side, shaking me, jumping up and down. A sick feeling twisted my stomach. They must have miscounted the tickets. At any moment Chip's annoyingly fake voice would cut through the clamor and inform everyone that *Candace* was the real winner. The awkwardness would be unbearable. It would be the curse's greatest moment. I should have seen it coming. Losing wasn't the worst thing. Thinking you'd won was the worst thing.

I scanned the crowd, anticipating some anxious lady to hurriedly sprint down to the stage with the corrected totals in hand. And then I saw him. Standing at the very back of the room, arms folded, with a broad smile. Brady Northrup. We locked eyes and he pulled out his phone and pointed to it. A few seconds later I felt a buzz in my satchel, then another, and another. I took out my phone and checked my messages as I was mobbed by my fellow contestants. Three links to YouTube videos, all from Brady's channel, all with some title about "helping to save the planetarium." One more message came through from Brady.

Had a few tickets come in last minute. Hope you don't mind. Don't worry. It's all legit. I'd like to talk.

"Tiffy?" My dad was there, his strong hands on my shoulders. "Tiffy, sweetie, you did it! You beautiful, beautiful girl, you saved us!"

I burst into tears and fell into my dad's chest, nearly collapsing from the relief. All the stress, all the worry, all the anxiety, the disappointment, the fear, the uncertainty, it all burned away in that one moment. I sobbed into his shoulder, not caring what I looked like or what I did to my makeup. I eventually wiped my eyes and looked around the room. Eleanor, Frank, Stefano, Simon, Brady.

I took a deep, shuddering breath and stared at the galaxy of stars projected on the ceiling. "I had a lot of help, Dad."

"Congratulations, young lady." Professor Braithwait adjusted his circle-rimmed glasses as he bent down to shake my hand. The man might as well have been astronomy Santa Claus with his bald head and bushy white beard. "It looks like I'll be making quite a sizable donation."

"Sorry about that," I said with an uneasy smile. A good portion of the crowd had either left or gone to the foyer to hear Chip read off the raffle prizes, but there were still a few dozen who had hung around to see this interaction.

"No need to worry." He laughed. "It merely indicates a renewed interest in astronomy for this town. And that is something I will gladly support."

I breathed a small sigh of relief. There was a part of me that honestly thought the professor would be upset. "I can't thank you enough."

"The thanks are all mine to give, young lady. My love of science and the stars started right here, believe it or not, many years ago. It broke my heart to see the planetarium fall into disrepair. Your father's efforts in recent years have been a godsend. Any idea what you'll name the star?"

"Lillian," I said without hesitation.

"A friend of yours?"

I nodded. "Someone who's already up there. I just wanted to give her a place to call home."

"Well, it looks like this went to the right person, then. Congratulations, my dear." The professor patted me on the shoulder and turned to leave.

I hopped off the stage and walked up the aisle to where the Video Game Club was waiting.

"Huzzah, Queen Astrid! Huzzah, Queen Astrid!" The club thrust their fists in the air and cheered as I approached.

Simon stepped forward. "The queen, after having vanquished the mighty foe, has returned victorious—"

"We did it!" I threw my arms out and crushed Simon in a hug. "I can't imagine any of your older brothers or sisters performing better than you did, and on, like, fifteen seconds' notice. Thank you, thank you, thank you."

I felt Simon go slack, then heavy, then *really* heavy. "A little help," I croaked. A few other members of the party rushed over and helped me lower Simon's unconscious body to the floor.

One of the kids bent down and examined him. "Is he okay?"

"I think he . . . fainted," another one said. "How hard did you hug him?"

I shrugged. "Not *that* hard." I couldn't believe it. He honestly fainted.

Simon gasped and bolted upright. "The goblins stole my backpack! Wait . . . wha, what's going on? How'd I get down here?"

I laughed and held out my hand to help him to his feet. "Are you okay?"

"Yes, I'm fine." Simon took my hand and stood up. "Only mostly dead."

"Phew," I said. "There's a shortage of perfect friends in the world. It would be a pity to damage this one."

Simon's eyes went wide and for a moment I thought he was going to faint again. "Tiffany!"

I smiled, but played ignorant. "What?"

"*The Princess Bride.* You quoted *The Princess Bride*!"

"I'll be honest, I just looked up the quote, but we should watch it together sometime," I replied.

"How about the next VGC meeting?" Allison said.

Simon's face lit up like he'd just stumbled on the meaning of life. "We could have a VGC victory party!"

"Count me in," I said, spying Frank, Eleanor, and Stefano at the far side of the room. "Hey, can I catch up with everyone a little later? I've got some old friends I need to see before they have to take off."

"As you wish," Simon said, placing his hand on his heart and bowing slightly. "Huzzah!"

The group echoed Simon, chanting the word over and over until I thrust my staff skyward and joined the refrain. "Huzzah! Huzzah!"

The VGC continued cheering as they marched out of the auditorium. I smiled and shook my head as I made my way over to where Frank, Stefano, and Eleanor were waiting.

"Brava, fragolina!" Stefano said, embracing me and kissing me on both cheeks. "You were meant for the stage."

I performed a quick little tap-dancing jig and threw my hands out wide. "I learned from the best."

"You would have made a fine addition to the drill platoon, Tiffany," Frank said, giving me a quick salute.

I put on the most serious face I could muster and saluted him back. "Not sure they accept battle sorceresses in the marines, Frank, but maybe one day."

"You were marvelous, my dear," Eleanor said.

I walked around to the front of her wheelchair and took both of her hands in mine. "Thank you so much for sharing that part of your life with me. It was beautiful, Eleanor."

"Thank you for letting me experience it one last time." Eleanor gave my hands two quick squeezes. "Something I thought would be impossible to experience again."

"Just needed to have a little faith," I said.

"Yes, dear." Eleanor smiled warmly. "Just a little faith."

As the last of the crowd wished me congratulations, the steady thrum of vacuum cleaners let us all know it was time to head home. I wasn't going to argue. The surge of performance adrenaline had been replaced with an exhaustion that seemed to soak through to my bone marrow. But it was a satisfying exhaustion, one that I savored as I made the short walk back to my house, strolling under a cloudless late-evening sky.

I strode up my front steps, making sure to skip the middle one, and walked into my house. It was still the same cramped, messy, embarrassing hovel, but I'd never been so glad to call it my home. I had saved it. There was a pride in that even if it was the house equivalent of owning a starving, mangey rescue dog. I collapsed on the couch in the front room, too tired to even take off a single layer of my Queen Astrid costume.

"Knock, knock," I heard someone say from the front door.

I sprang off the couch, despite my fatigue, and found myself yet again staring at Brady Northrup through my screen door.

"You know," Brady said, looking me over from head to toe. "One of these days, I'm going to show up here and you'll be in, like, a normal pair of pants and a T-shirt."

I tilted my head. "Challenge accepted."

"You seen the latest video?" Brady said, holding up his phone. "Looks like you and Candace are finally trending together. Can't wait to see the memes from this one."

I braced myself as I peered through the screen door at a slow-motion video of when Chip read the final ticket count. I watched my expression slowly morph into wide-eyed shock while Candace's beautiful, confident face twisted into disgusted rage. Someone edited steam shooting out her ears.

I laughed, as much from relief as from the absurdity of seeing Queen Astrid and a dolled-up Candace pulling those faces next to each other. "I'll take it."

Brady put his phone away and stuffed his hands in his pockets. "I've been trying to get ahold of you, you know?"

"And I've been trying harder to avoid you."

"I picked up on that." Brady glanced briefly at his feet. "And what about now?"

"I guess it depends." I shrugged. "What should somebody do when they owe someone both a punch to the face and a kiss on the cheek?"

"Well," Brady said, rubbing his chin. "If you're referring to *us* then I'd say I'd take both, but I'm not sure I'd survive the punch. Ten bucks says you have some old boxing champion's glove lying around here just for this moment."

That actually wasn't a bad idea. Never knew when you'd suddenly need the ability to knock someone's lights out.

The rhythmic chirping of crickets filled the silence between us before I finally spoke. "Look, Brady. I still don't even know if this whole thing between you and me grew into a real friendship or if it was always just so you could get back at Candace, use me for views, and cheat your way back to a starting spot on the basketball team."

Brady pursed his lips and looked like he was swishing his response around in his mouth to see if he liked how it tasted. "I would say it started with all those things, turned into a bit of an unexpected wake-up call, and now I'm hoping it can grow into a real friendship."

I studied Brady's face. It had always been impossible for me to detect when he was telling the truth or when he was lying, but something *did* seem different. I hoped it was a bit of sincerity leaking through.

"I know why you did it, Brady. I know how Candace hurt you. I know how much basketball means to your dad. I've *felt* how much it means to *you*, and while it helps me not be mad anymore, it doesn't change that what you did was wrong."

Brady stuck his hands in his pockets and nodded. "I know."

We stood there, staring at each other from opposite sides of an old, weathered screen door, Brady bathed in a yellow porch light.

"Just wanted to say, I'm sorry, Tiffany." He stood there a moment longer before turning to leave.

I froze, chewing on my bottom lip, watching him disappear into the dark.

"Brady." I pushed open the screen door, hopped down the front steps, and threw my arms around him just as he turned around. "Thank you."

He paused, as if unsure how to respond, before finally returning the hug. "I'm not gonna find cake in my pocket, am I?"

"It's always a possibility." I laughed softly. "Please be real, Brady. Please be true to your word."

He gave me a faint squeeze. "I got your back, Tudwell."

Just don't stick a knife in it, please. There was a life lesson in there somewhere. I wanted so badly to trust him. I needed good friends in my life, as many of them as I could find.

As I hugged Brady, I looked over his shoulder. Just above the curved horizon of the planetarium dome, a pair of shooting stars crisscrossed in the night sky.

CHAPTER 37

Lucky Charm

On our small IKEA kitchen table, on top of a stack of unopened mail and astronomy magazines, sat a pockmarked, metallic rock the size of a cantaloupe.

I downed a glass of water and wiped the sweat from my forehead with a paper towel. "What do you think it's worth?"

My dad stood back, staring at it like he expected it to suddenly crack open and a baby dragon to climb out. "To a collector or to the planetarium?"

I knew what my dad was asking. This was the find of a lifetime. There was no way he was going to sell this to some faceless collector. This chunk of rock would put our little planetarium on the map. I'm sure the wheels were already spinning in my dad's head for how he could clear out space to properly showcase the meteorite.

He'd all but given up on looking for fragments, but I'd made it a point to ask my dad to go out every Saturday since winning the Shining Star over a month ago. I actually had no expectation of ever finding anything; I just wanted to spend more time with him. It gave us the chance to talk, to plan how we were going to build up the planetarium over the next few years, and how we could use my cosmic ability to help. Yes, my dad knew. Frank had told him during the Shining Star, and while my dad didn't exactly know what was going on, he trusted Frank enough to mess with Chip's microphone so he could get me his.

"I still can't believe you found this thing, Tiffy," my dad said, squatting down to look at the meteorite more closely. "You're a human dowsing rod, kiddo. Just look at this thing. I've seen plenty of meteorites before, but they're usually just hunks of iron or stone. This seems to have all the colors of the rainbow. It's incredible. Your grandma would be proud."

"I certainly hope so," I whispered, more to myself than to my dad, as I instinctively reached up and fiddled with my crescent-moon earrings. I still wasn't sure Mimi had anything to do with the curse, but I was positive she had given me the means to break free of it.

"I'm going to go get the nice camera and document this thing," my dad said, straightening. As he passed me, he patted my shoulder. "My lucky charm."

I laughed, despite myself. *That* was something I'd never been called before.

Acknowledgments

There are always a lot of people to acknowledge at the end of a novel, but the first and last thanks forever belong to my wife, Jill. She believes in me, she listens to me, she supports me, she puts up with me, she loves me. It's been a pretty good formula.

Thanks to my three kids, Abby, Owen, and Sienna. Their brilliance, personality, and humor are the best source of inspiration for my stories and joy in my life. Special thanks to my youngest, Sienna, for her love of *The Talent Thief*. The only night she didn't ask for "just one more chapter" was when we got to the end. When I asked why she didn't want me to read the final chapter, she looked up at me like the answer was obvious.

"Don't you want to savor it, Dad?"

I do, but more so just the moment with you, kiddo. *That* is why I write.

Sienna *will*, however, be forever disappointed that Tiffany didn't give Simon a big smooch. You can't have everything in life, I guess.

As always, a huge thanks to my writers group, The Principal's Office. Allison Hymas and Ben Hewett again provided insightful feedback and suggestions along the way that made this book what it is. You guys are the best.

Thanks to my editor, Holly West, for believing I had

another cool idea in me after *The Double Life of Danny Day*. Her edits and direction helped me find the true spirit of *The Talent Thief*. Thanks also to the scores of other editors that provided feedback: Avia Perez, Janine Barlow, and Hana Tzou.

Thanks to Simini Blocker for lending her artistic talents to bring Tiffany to life and come up with a truly awesome cover.

My entire life, my imagination has been stuck in overdrive. While that does fuel my creativity, it's also kind of a curse. I'm tortured a bit by all the things I wish I could do, I wish I could become. It was a lot of fun to watch Tiffany take shape and to really explore the possibilities of what a talent-stealing power could do for an awkward preteen. I hope you enjoyed this story. Whether you did or didn't, the good news is the same: I've got tons more *other* ideas I can't wait to share with you. Until then, be kind to one another. This world's going through a lot lately. Be a Simon for some Tiffany out there.

Thank you for reading this Feiwel & Friends book. The friends who made *The Talent Thief* possible are:

Jean Feiwel, Publisher

Liz Szabla, Associate Publisher

Rich Deas, Senior Creative Director

Holly West, Senior Editor

Anna Roberto, Senior Editor

Kat Brzozowski, Senior Editor

Dawn Ryan, Executive Managing Editor

Kim Waymer, Senior Production Manager

Emily Settle, Editor

Rachel Diebel, Editor

Foyinsi Adegbonmire, Associate Editor

Brittany Groves, Assistant Editor

Mallory Grigg, Senior Art Director

Avia Perez, Senior Production Editor

Follow us on Facebook or visit us online at mackids.com. Our books are friends for life.